THE LOOSE ENDS SAGA

Paul Levinson

Connected Editions

For Tina

CONTENTS

INTRODUCTION

I began writing "Loose Ends" in the mid-1970s, as a novel first entitled *Cross the Cartesian Rainbow*, then *Deuce of a Time* and then *Differents in Time*. It attracted some interest but ultimately no publisher via any of those titles, but in the mid-1990s I refashioned the first part of the story into a novella, "Loose Ends," which was published in *Analog Magazine* in 1997. "Loose Ends" was nominated for the Hugo, Nebula, and Sturgeon Awards, and was translated and reprinted in the Italian anthology *Strani Universi* in 1998. Meanwhile, the sequels "Little Differences" and "Late Lessons" were published as novelettes in *Analog* in 1998 and 1999. Connected Editions published all three stories as ebooks on Kindle, and the newly written concluding novella in the saga, "Last Calls," in 2015. The four stories appear here in one volume for the first time.

LOOSE ENDS

First published as a novella in Analog, May 1997. Nominated for the Hugo, Nebula, and Sturgeon Awards for Best Novella of 1997.

Jeff felt a certain hardness under his backside, like he had fallen asleep on a plush chair and come awake on a park bench somewhere.

He opened his eyes and stared at his destiny: a large and messy lounge of some sort, outlines indistinct in what must have been the reflected light of evening street lamps. There was no doubt about it. The broken-down couch in the corner, worn wooden study tables to the right, books and papers and misshapen armchairs strewn around like some old rummage sale -- this was a far cry indeed from the cool flowing continuum of the control room. The Thorne had worked after all.

Jeff strained to keep his adrenaline in check. Not even a cleaning person in the unlit room. Good. It was late at night, maybe even a weekend. No one to bump into. He pulled a low intensity fireflighter from his pocket. In the weak approximation of daylight, the lounge looked even more 20th century. Remarkable! On the floor near his feet, he noticed a ratty looking issue of *Look* magazine. The August 23, 1963 date on the cover caused another rush in his veins, but told him not enough of what he needed to know. The magazine could have been lying around for years by the looks of this room.

He had to know the exact date of his arrival. It would tell him which of the eight plans to implement. Clutching his deliberately nondescript suitcase, he walked quickly to the door. He noticed a torn *Time* magazine dated October-something, 1963, and frowned.

Jeff delicately opened the door and patted the shirt of his janitor's outfit. He was an academic with strong ties to the working class -- his great-great-grandparents had slaved in sweatshops -- and he welcomed the prospect of testing out his jargon, costume, and identity on the local populace. Unfortunately -- or fortunately -- no victims were in sight. He walked out, carefully closed the door behind, and strode in search of an exit.

"Sher-er-ry, Sherry baby. She-er-ry..."

For some moments now, Jeff thought he had been hearing a faint falsetto whining. He walked down the last flight of stairs, out into the street, and recognized the shrieks as "Sherry" -- an early rock hit by the Four Seasons. More inconclusive evidence, not particularly heartening. He'd done a special lecture on the Seasons and the Beachboys just last year, and knew for a fact this song came from the summer of 1962.

The air felt chilled, like maybe early October. A '59 or '60 Fairlane 500, from which the Seasons' song seemed to be emanating, was no more help in establishing an exact date than the song.

The street beyond the Fairlane looked clearer and uglier than he'd expected -- a bright messy watercolor spilling onto itself. He wondered what his expectations about this place were really based on. Probably more on Andrews' "Village Square" hit of last year than the hours of 1980s film and photographs he had reviewed till his eyes had burned with fatigue.

He spotted a blonde girl in what used to be called dungarees walking towards him. "Uh, pardon me, Miss," he said as nonchalantly as he could, "do you know the time ... and the date please?"

She gave him a strange look and glanced at her watch. "A quarter to twelve," she said, without slowing a step.

Well thanks a lot, Jeff thought. "Excuse me, Miss, I'm sorry to bother you, but if could you tell me the date as well..." He found himself shouting after her. She just kept walking. He shook his head and walked the other way.

The chill was beginning to eat at him as he made his way towards West Fourth Street and Washington Square Park. There the usual complement of derelicts and weirdos -- some things never change, he smiled -- were keeping the late-night vigil. No point in trying to get a straight answer about the date from that crew. He sighed, then noticed the quaint old phone booth on the corner. He picked up the receiver and pumped in eight quarters in rapid sequence to make sure he would get a connection. "Hello, Operator, could you tell me what today's date is?"

"The date, sir? I'm sorry, but we're only supposed to give out numbers."

"Well, is there a number I can call to find out the date?" A faint odor of urine permeated the booth.

"Checking, sir. No, I have a number for the time, but I don't see one for the date."

"Well, then, do you think you could be a human being instead of, uh, a com-puter, and tell me the date anyway?"

"I'm sorry, sir, but we're only supposed to give out numbers."

"And have you no function in the universe or reason for existence other than giving out phone numbers?"

"I have no function, sir."

Jeff slammed the phone down and shook his head. I'd make a great diplomat, he thought. At this rate, I--

"Having trouble with the phone, Jack?" Jeff turned to find himself addressed by -- was it a slacker or a hippie? – about 25 years of age. "The phone company's been hangin' *every*one up lately, man."

"Yeah," Jeff smiled, "it's getting worse and worse. Look, I wonder if you might be able to help me. I'm disoriented, I've got to know what the date is." Jeff leaned out of the booth, deaf to the quarters that clanged in the coin return.

"I can dig it, man, really."

"Good, then, can you tell me what the date is?" He inhaled

4

deeply of the less tainted air outside the booth. Compared to what he had just been breathing in, it smelled like perfume.

"Well, like, that's a difficult question, man. I mean it's November 21st now, but it'll be November 22nd in a few minutes. And of course for the cats over in England it's already been November 22nd for a few hours, and--"

"Ok, good," Jeff said. "And the year?"

"The year?"

"Right, the year -- as in 19..."

"Oh, well that's the same everywhere, man. 1963."

"What?"

"I know it, man, time flies faster and faster these days..."

Jeff walked dazedly down the street, fighting to think through flashes that spat at his brain. What the hell was this? He was supposed to have emerged some time in the Fall -- the end of November was cutting it a little close, but ok, that still gave him at least some weeks to get to NASA, Morton Thiokol, whomever. He knew the Thorne wasn't perfectly precise. How could it be -- generating the kind of savagely powerful local field needed to keep the Artificial Worm Hole open long enough to operate across time. So it couldn't be that exact. But 23 years? What could he do to prevent the Challenger explosion back here in 1963?

He shook his head and it cleared a little. He had no choice now but to return to the lounge, activate the mechanism for return to 2084, and try the damn thing again. He retraced his steps to the Student Building. But his legs moved slower and slower, as if they opposed the decision to return. Finally he stopped.

He stared at the Student Building across the street. He focused on its gargoyled facade and played with a quarter in his pocket. He pivoted suddenly and walked quickly again in the direction of the Park. A hundred and twenty-one years was a long time to have traveled into the past just to rush right back. He could take a few more minutes to think this over.

***

He wandered towards Sixth Avenue, then inside a coffee shop. He sat down and read the sticky plastic menu without comprehension. The cracks in the red leatherette upholstery jabbed his thighs.

"Had a rough day, huh honey? What'll it be?" The dyed blonde waitress was right out of a turn-of-the-cen video. Upset as he was, Jeff the cultural historian liked this.

"Just a tea with milk, please." By any conceivable logic, he ought to return as soon as possible to 2084, so he could try this again, and with any luck arrive at least a few months before January 28, 1986. To do that, he had to go back now to the lounge in the NYU Student Building from which he'd emerged, the exact same place, that was the way the Thorne worked.

But something in Jeff rebelled against this logic -- something in his nature which said, look, you've gotten this far, it's not good, but you may never get this far again, so you better take what you can of this chance to save the space program...

But how?

He'd have to improvise.

He thought about the endless, careful plans his team had made for him to avoid getting caught up in some paradox – keep the loop clean, don't do anything in the past that might undermine the very foundation of this project. Steer clear of everyone's great-grandparents... Jeez, how the hell was he supposed to do that back here, 23 years earlier than he'd planned to arrive, when he had no idea where everyone he was supposed to avoid even was?

Jeff rubbed his head. Every second that he stayed here was a knife at the throat of his future. He was off the screen, way out of equation-range -- a single word to a wrong person, some land-mine of the past, could set in motion a chain of events that erased his colleagues, maybe even him, from existence. True, he had no close family, no one that he really loved deeply anymore -- well, maybe still Rena, in a way -- but he certainly hadn't undertaken this job to kill his friends, make himself a martyr to a reconstituted future that might never know he'd existed in the first place.

On the other hand, how really likely was it that he'd run into such a landmine? Painstaking tests had shown that the effects of most interjections in the past were sooner or later washed out in the myriad of everything else that remained the same. And how could anyone from his vantage point truly know what was intended all along? Maybe he'd always been supposed to arrive here back in 1963 -- maybe he was ordained to help the space program, or humanity, in some way other than stopping the Challenger. Maybe that's why the Challenger blew up after all, because there was no way he could influence events this far back to stop the explosion that took the heart and soul out of the space program, had set up the 21st century to be little more than an age of commentary looking back on the bygone Golden Age of Space Travel, an age that barely had gotten off the ground. His head spun. He could feel the sweet buzzing vortex of paradox whispering in his brain, drawing him in... No, I have free will, I'll do what I damn well choose, I don't have time for paradox now, I only have time to act.

He looked at the clock on the wall. Twelve minutes after twelve. Too much lead time for the Challenger -- the shuttle had barely been conceived of in 1963. He supposed he could live the next 23 years in normal time here, and devise a new plan to thwart the explosion. Thiokol Chemical Corporation had been awarded the NASA contract to build the shuttle's solid rocket boosters on November 20, 1973 -- just about 10 years from where he was now -- so if he could hang on for a decade, he might even be able to begin doing some good then. Leroy Day had been picked to head planning for the shuttle in 1969, a few years nearer.

But this didn't seem appealing. Ten years, even five, was a long time to stay out of trouble. And he couldn't even be sure that the Artificial Worm Hole would remain operational that long. The most their tests had confirmed was safe return after 18 months in the past.

He of course knew exactly what else he might try to do on

this date. He knew its obvious significance. He didn't have to be a cultural historian by training to know it. Jeez, he'd arrived at the edge of the oldest cliché in the science fiction encyclopedia. Everyone and their great-aunt Martha had written a story about it.

What was the likelihood that some error in the team's calculations, some unexpected flux in the AWH, had landed him here on this of all dates? Maybe it wasn't an accident that he'd somehow been dropped at the doorstep of what *Time* a century after the event had dubbed one of the top five murders of the millennium.

But if so, what was the deeper purpose of his presence here?

Surely not to stop the events in Dallas tomorrow – there really wasn't enough time. He was in New York City, after midnight, on November 22, 1963. Way too soon for Challenger. All but too late for JFK.

All but too late ... But what else could he could do back here, then? What else had he perhaps been *meant* all along to do here and now?

He shook his head.

Did they even have air service to Dallas this late at night? He had no idea. What kinds of planes? Propellers? No, probably jets already.

Dallas was a thriving city even back in the 1960s, and at the very least he would probably be able to get a businessman's flight early in the morning. But would that leave him enough hours? What was the point of flying all the way to Dallas just in time to hear that the President had been shot?

But what was his alternative if he didn't use the AWH to return to his starting point? Sit around like a jackass and wait for Walter Cronkite's tear-choked voice to announce the assassination on TV?

Blondie arrived with his tea. Fortunately it was lukewarm, and Jeff was able to drink it down in two gulps. He pulled a crumpled bill out of his wallet and left it on the table. Some bank clerk in the next few weeks would be stunned to see a 1981-

issue ten-dollar bill with Donald T. Regan's signature, but he had no other money, and had to take a chance that such a minor anonymous anachronism wouldn't disturb the time-line. Loops could be perfectly clean only in theory. The bill would likely be dismissed as a clumsy counterfeit or a joke. Or who knows, maybe it would be lost before it even got to a bank teller.

He walked out onto Sixth Avenue and surveyed his options yet one more time. The city was harsh, the air stank, he didn't belong here. The sensible thing to do was return to 2084. And yet...

He flagged down a passing cab. "Kennedy, uh ... Idlewild Airport. On the double, Chief." As the cab pulled away, Jeff recalled George Bernard Shaw's line that the reasonable man adapts to his surroundings, the unreasonable man attempts to change his surroundings to suit himself, and all progress depends upon the unreasonable man.

There had to be something more to this than Dallas, but at this point Dallas seemed the only way to get to it.

Inside the coffee shop, the waitress stuffed the bill in her bosom pocket and laughed. "I tell ya," she said to the fat man stuck behind the cash register like a melon, "these actor types are all the same. They never remember to wait for their change. I'm gonna keep this for good luck."

***

"Tunnel or Bridge?" the cabbie grunted through chewing gum.

Jeff wasn't completely sure what he was talking about. "Do what you think best, Mac. Just get me to the airport as fast as you can." He shifted his weight on the springy seat and looked through the dirt-caked window ...

"Just got off the late shift, right? My brother-in-law does the midnight-to-eight shift for Helmsley. You gotta do what you gotta do to make a living these days, right? What's the use of talking."

"Yeah, the inflation's impossible," Jeff agreed. Can't go wrong in any century griping about inflation. And he made a note to himself to get out of the janitor's outfit as soon as he got to the airport.

"Yeah," the cabbie growled, "ain't it the truth."

Jeff felt in his pocket for his reassuring puterwafer but got no comfort from it. He knew he was fully on his own now, plans pertaining to 23 years in the future all but worthless. In a worst-case scenario, if all he could catch was an early morning flight, he'd have maybe an hour or two to get to the Book Depository Building in Dealey Plaza after his plane arrived in Dallas. If he could somehow get to the Building by 11, he'd stake out the upper floors and try to intercept the gunman ... or gunmen ... or gunwomen. He wondered whether he'd find Lee Harvey Oswald up there by those windows. Historians would give their right arms to know. A hundred-and-twenty years of theorizing had left them no closer to knowing who had killed Kennedy than the unsatisfying "lone nut" explanation of the Warren Commission.

One thing Jeff did know: the assassination of JFK probably did more to ultimately harm the prospects of humans in space than even the horrible Challenger disaster. His team even had briefly considered sending him back here to 1963 in the first place, but rejected it on the grounds that too much was still unknown about the assassination for them to mount an effective plan to stop it. So here Jeff was without a plan, anyway ... rushing like a moth to a flame that he had little chance of extinguishing, but was too attractive to resist.

"Any special terminal, Mac?" The grunt drew Jeff back to the real world, though this ride seemed scarcely more real than his musings. He looked at his watch and whistled. This old gasser had gotten him to the airport in under an hour. "American Airlines, Chief, and thanks." Jeff set his watch to the time on the foolish-looking clock pasted on the cabbie's dashboard. It was now 1:07 in the morning of November 22.

He paid in dirty dollar bills printed 20 years in the future and sprinted into the terminal, a garish but not uncharming combination of wine red carpet and shiny chrome trimming. It reminded Jeff of early technicolor movies. He ducked into the men's room, unpacked clothes from his suitcase, and shortly emerged a stylish 80s businessman. He expected this wouldn't cause too much of a problem -- if his clothes looked a little odd, people would likely chalk that up to his dressing European. There was more difference in hemispheric styles in this century.

He approached what appeared to be a mock-wood ticket desk. The pert red-headed kewpie-doll behind the counter added to his feeling that he was in an ancient film. "Am I in time for the late-night flight to Dallas?" he asked with his friendliest smile.

"Oh, I'm very sorry, sir, but our last flight to Dallas left at 12:30. Our next one leaves at 8:00 this morning, and I believe that Delta has a flight that leaves at 6:20. Shall I make a reservation for you?"

Damn. "Could you tell me what time the Delta flight arrives in Dallas?"

She pulled out a paper directory and checked. "Nine fifty-seven Dallas time, sir. Shall I make the reservation?"

"Yes, please do," Jeff said, "and could you point me in the direction of the airport hotel?" Jeff paid in cash -- he had a bunch of credit cards too, but they were all way out of date, in the wrong way, to make things even worse. She counted the money and Jeff held his breath. The bills were small denomination, suitably soiled, from the 1970s. She didn't notice anything askew.

Jeff thanked the redhead walked slowly to the end of the terminal. It would be ridiculously close in Dallas -- even if the plane landed on time, he'd barely have an hour to get to the Book Depository and stop the killing.

***

The bed in the International was unexpectedly comfortable, though the room like the airport terminal had some faintly artificial smell. Jeff fell soundly asleep, and dreamed he was in a classroom giving his "Earth Was Never Room Enough" talk while Dion's "Abraham, Martin, and John" played in the background. Rena sat in the front with her legs seductively crossed, but her face looked a lot like Sandra Dee's. He could hear someone talking just outside the classroom, going on and on and utterly ignoring his lecture. It was James C. Fletcher, NASA administrator who had had the most to do with the shuttle program. Jeff was screaming at his students to pay attention when the phone rang.

He fumbled with the ungainly receiver and dropped it. Then he smacked himself in the mouth with it. "Hello," he finally managed, rubbing his eyes and looking in vain for the viewer.

"Good morning, Dr. Harris! Five thirty wake-up call!" a female sing-song voice chimed merrily.

"Thanks." Jeff replaced the receiver with great effort and sat up. He rubbed his sore lips and fought off the impulse to go back to sleep for just another 15 minutes. He could sleep for 15 days the way he felt, but he dragged his body out of bed and quickly dressed. Last night's businessman with maybe a blue knit tie to go with the grey wool suit would do fine.

The coffee house was a zoo. He didn't have much appetite, but forced himself to eat the soggy eggs for strength. Looking around, he realized again that there was a lot he didn't like about this place. Historians like their history from the safety and convenience of the future -- the past on a platter with all the comforts of home. Not like this.

"Excuse me, sir." The waitress startled Jeff as she leaned over with the check. "That's an interesting bracelet you've got on there. My husband's a jeweler, and I don't think I've ever seen anything like it."

"Uh, thank you." Jeff glanced down at his watch, scooped up the check, and quickly left the table. "My, uh, kid's studying electronics," he said half over his shoulder, "and it's something he designed for me." Great. He'd been wearing this flector for six years now, and with all the departure commotion yesterday he'd forgotten to take it off. Hustling to Delta Departures, he removed the silver sliver from its embed on his wrist and placed it in a side compartment of the suitcase. Then he took out the clunky Timex analog someone had given him, and stopped a moment to set it and strap it on his wrist. He shook his

THE LOOSE ENDS SAGA

head in self-disgust. First the future bills he was handing out everywhere like candy, and now this. The money he had no choice about, but the flector was sheer stupidity on his part.

He sighed. It didn't really matter. If by some wild luck he could stop the JFK assassination in Dallas, nothing that he did now would make much difference. If not, well...

The Delta was a sardine can, and Jeff sat white knuckled in a window seat waiting for takeoff. Finally it began making taxiing noises, the comforting rumblings of some great beast's innards, and Jeff leaned back and tried to relax. The stewardess had a tight skirt on, pitching her derriere right at him, a better view than the window.

Well, so far his rating of 1963 was food and decor not too good, women a distinct possibility. This seemed in line with that refrain from the classic Woody Guthrie song about the social fallout of relativity: Can't go North, can't go South, or up, or down, anymore. But I can still go in and out, Mr. Einstein, I can still go in and out...

It remained to be seen whether he could get in and out of the Book Depository in time.

***

The 707 pierced like a needle through the remnants of haze over Dallas. Jeff peered through his peephole at the airport below as the captain announced they'd be landing momentarily.

He had so little time. Everything depended on his getting to the Book Depository as quickly as possible. He'd shove through lines, jump over turnstiles, knock people down if need be. No gesture of asinine civility could be allowed to slow his exit.

The screech of aircraft hitting the ground hiked his pulse. He felt the seconds ticking, each in phase with his pounding blood. He braced for the performance. He could see nothing but taxi at the end of the tunnel, the taxi that would bring him face-to-face with God-knew-what at the Book Depository.

The plane shuddered still. Its doors grumbled open. Debarking passengers spilled like mindless ooze into the terminal. But one of their number was more minded than he'd ever been in his life: single-minded in his determination to dive into that cab. Get out of my way, you goddamn fools. I don't have time to say I'm sorry.

Jeff swam in powerful strokes through the current, halfway through the terminal, now three-quarters through and almost out. Every shred of his being, every ounce of his purpose, was focused on closing this last little gap to the exit. He was almost believing that maybe he would stop the assassination after all, maybe this was the way indeed that he was destined to save the space program. He saw JFK's face before him, superimposed on the Challenger, superimposed on the flames, superimposed on innumerable winking stars--

Which was why he never saw the towering cart of luggage that fell upon him less than three feet from the glass doors, and knocked him unconscious.

***

He opened his eyes to a throbbing headache and blurry white of what must have been a hospital room. Fumes of formaldehyde hung in his nostrils and made him gag. "I see you're awake, Dr. Harris," a lazy Texas accent jarred him. "You ran into a rack of luggage at the airport and sustained a moderate concussion, but you're going to be just fine."

Jeff leaned up on an elbow to get a look at the nurse. "Where am I?"

"Dallas General Hospital. We'll need to run a few tests on you, and if everything's all right you'll probably be able to leave in the morning."

"I..." Jeff fell back on the pillow and tried to breathe slowly. He felt cold and clammy and slightly in shock. He took several deep breaths, and tried to focus more clearly on the nurse. Her eyes looked red and puffy. Outside his room he heard what sounded like a radio or holocenter blaring in the corridor -- a tumult of loud talking and wailing. "What's going on out there?"

Nurse K. Arthur burst into tears, and Jeff got a sudden feeling in the pit of his stomach that he knew exactly what the ruckus was about.

"They killed the President," she sobbed. "I really shouldn't disturb you with this. They rushed him to Parkland Memorial, but he was too far gone." She heaved with tears. "He was so young, so beautiful. Why would anyone want to *do* something like that?"

Jeff reached out to comfort her. "Ow!" Pain sliced through his back like a stiletto.

"Here, let me help you." Arthur leaned over and gently eased Jeff back into bed. "You probably wrenched a muscle or two." She puffed up the pillow and smiled. "There. I'll tell the doctor you're up and I'm sure he'll look in on you a little later." Her smiled suddenly wavered and tears welled up again in her eyes. "They wounded Vice President Johnson and killed Governor Connally. They say it was one of those Communists. What's going to happen to the country now?"

"I don't know," Jeff barely answered, too tired to tell her that although her information was wrong, her sense of impending catastrophe was all too on-target. The Vietnam War, riots in the cities, more assassinations, Kent State, all of that now lay squarely up ahead in history.

He slept fitfully the rest of the day, pestered and punctured by a procession of interns and orderlies bent on waking him up, taking his temperature, and telling him he needed more sleep. He asked for a TV or radio at least five times and got nothing. The phone by his bed was broken. He couldn't tell whether the morgue-like atmosphere was standard or a consequence of the assassination. The assassination -- every time he thought of it, he felt like retching. A leaden, queasy thickness of despair hung over everything.

He fell asleep at last into something deeper that let him dream. He watched a team of 19th century surgeons, long hair and whiskers and bitter-sweet alcohol smell in the room, work over what must have been a very important patient. Straining his head closer, he could see that the patient was a fish, cut open and spread apart down the middle. The Chief Surgeon produced a mallet and began pounding the fish, while others cut off pieces and put them in little bags. "Oh, I'm only joking, old boy," the Surgeon turned to Jeff and said in a crisp British accent, "this is dinner, of course!"

Jeff sat up sharply in bed, awakened by yet another nurse come to stick something in him. "What do you want now?" he rasped, wincing from the pain that came as he propped himself up.

"Just some intravenous for the evening, Dr. Harris. It'll help you sleep." She wheeled some torture-like contraption over to him. She was a big-boned, handsome, light brown woman, about 35, who spoke with a lilting accent.

He shook his head to clear some of the cobwebs. "I already ate your lousy supper. Why do I need intravenous?"

"Pity the nurse who has a doctor for a patient," she said in the mildly scolding tone of voice that seemed a part of every nurse's repertoire whatever the century. "Now why don't you just lie back like a good boy and let me get this working." A strong arm pushed Jeff back gently but firmly, and she began applying alcohol to his skin.

Once again the door flung open, this time admitting two burly black men carrying an impossibly fat TV set.

"I tell you what, Nurse, ah, Daniels." Jeff freed himself from her grip. "I'll take this intravenous only if it's prescribed and administered by an intern or resident. So you want me on that, you call in a doctor, fair enough?" This should buy him a little time to think this through. There was something he didn't like about this nurse, not to mention that he wasn't particularly partial to the prospect of being festooned with intravenous needles and tubing, 1960s style, carrying who knew what kind of viruses and sub-vees they didn't even know about back here, and he might not have been inoculated against.

Daniels looked at the two men hooking up the TV set and then back at Jeff. "No meat off my behind, honey," she said, and abruptly wheeled the equipment out the door.

Good -- she'd apparently decided it wasn't worth making a scene in front of the techies. "Thank you, gentlemen," Jeff told them as they finished up. "See? It's not true what they say about the media always causing problems. Sometimes a TV screen can be very helpful."

They looked at him like he was crazy, and left.

Jeff pivoted gingerly in the bed, placing his feet on the floor in slow, exaggerated motions. Pushing himself up shakily from his seated position, he found he could stand. He walked unsteadily to a chair by the window, and sat himself down with the utmost caution. The pain he expected in his back was now mercifully slight. He reached for the suitcase lodged neatly against the window and fished inside for his clothing. Thank God the case hadn't been lost at the airport. And a good thing, too, that it had been programmed to open only in response to his and no one else's sweat-signature. Otherwise he'd have had some explaining to do about some of the contents.

He had to get out of here right away. He had to get back to New York, back to the student lounge. He reached deeper inside the suitcase. The rough fiber of the janitor's uniform finally chafed his fingertips. He doubted that an NYU janitor looked anything like the hospital variety, but this was still his best choice. He dressed very carefully, praying that his body would hold up long enough for him to walk out of this horror-movie of a hospital -- and this horror-show of a world.

Suitcase under his arm, he tiptoed to the door and opened it a crack. His room seemed to be in the middle of a long, orange-pink tiled corridor that stretched in either direction with no one in sight. Peering out a bit more, he could see what looked like a nurse's station down to his right. He hesitated. His mind felt swollen and paranoid. He had no confidence in his judgments. He didn't feel good about just walking out, but he felt much worse about staying. He opened the door and strode as casually as he could to the left.

He slowly became aware of voices ahead of him. He took a few more steps, then stopped and listened. They were definitely moving closer. He looked down the corridor the other way. Too long a distance to risk a return to his room. He glanced quickly around at the rooms within reach and tried the door of the nearest one.

Locked!

He tried another one.

Same result!

His hands grew moist and his head light and the voices louder. He felt nauseated, as if he was about to vomit and pass out. He breathed deeply, steadied himself, and tried another door.

It opened! He leaned against the inside of the door, thankful and quaking, until the entourage passed. From what he could hear, they seemed to be just a team of porters.

Relaxing a bit, he groped for the light switch to see upon whose room he had intruded. This was an extremely stupid move, he realized just as his hand flicked the switch, for the patient might well begin screaming. Fortunately the room seemed to be some sort of storage facility.

He looked around and stopped on a lumpy something stretched out in a far corner. Again his heart started pounding, for he suddenly was sure he was looking at a dead body. He forced himself to walk over and focus. The lumpy something was a long bag of stained linen.

He carefully left the room and resumed his journey down the corridor, this time with a bit more assertion in his gait. He turned randomly down several connecting passages, passed several orderlies and nurses and made a point of not avoiding their gazes. He eventually wound up at what looked like a service elevator. Its doors were open. He walked in and pressed Lobby and hoped for the best.

The elevator wobbled its way down, Jeff envisioning himself a dead man dangling from a slowly descending rope. The doors finally re-opened on a poorly lit hallway that said Ground Floor. He walked a few feet, and was glad to see the hospital lobby. He wondered why the act of leaving a hospital always felt like escape from a high-security prison, not that he actually had had any experience with that.

He hailed a cab and said take me to the airport. The cabbie talked Kennedy, but Jeff was too tired to give more than grunts in response.

He sank into bed in the motel room, utterly drained. He closed his eyes and looked again at the lumpy bag in the hospital laundry room. It was a woman's body, face down, wearing only a 20th-century bra and shiny beige panties that clung snugly to her rear. She looked familiar. He turned her over and found eyes staring blankly up at his. He tried to scream, but his throat was stuck. The eyes were Rena's.

He sat up in bed, broken out in a cold sweat, and shuddered for a long time ...

I guess I'm not as cut out for time travel as once I thought, he thought. But how could anyone know that beforehand? You had to actually live through these loops, bristling with serrated edges, to know the toll they took.

***

Twelve hours later, he was on a plane for New York. Staring out of the window as the engines revved up, Jeff realized he was losing a golden opportunity to stop the killing of Lee Harvey Oswald. He looked at his watch. That would happen tomorrow. He toyed with the idea of making a last-minute dash from the plane and calling the Dallas police. He'd have plenty of time and ... No! For once he'd do the cautious thing and return to New York and then 2084. No chance the police would take his call seriously anyway -- just another crank come out of the now volcanic assassination woodwork.

Of course, a crank who knew about Oswald's murder would be someone Jeff would want to meet. Wasn't there some story that the Dallas police were indeed warned by someone about the shooting of Oswald? Was that someone Jeff? Or someone else on trespass from the future?

He fidgeted with his seatbelt. Maybe the attempt on his life in the hospital last night -- if that nurse with the intravenous was indeed trying to kill him -- was intended precisely to stop him from interfering with Ruby's murder of Oswald. No, that sort of reasoning would get him nowhere. It was paranoid nonsense. Yet he was here on this plane, leaving the scene of the crime of the century, when there were plenty of things he still might do.

The plane's lift-off ended his reverie. Jeff tried to direct his thinking to what awaited him -- going back to 2084 through the Thorne, then into it again, one more time to another time, through a new AWH to 1985, the time he should have arrived in the first place, to stop the explosion of the Challenger. He stared steel-eyed out the window. No one could help JFK -- that should had been obvious all along. You can't change history on that major a level. But the Challenger -- that was more mechanical, presumably an accident of technology, not of sick human intention, more amenable to the time traveler's ministration.

At least, that was what he kept telling himself. But it gave him little real comfort. Obviously, traveling back to 1985 wasn't as easy as he and his team had thought -- if it was, why was he here at this moment? There were things about time travel he and his people didn't understand.

He laughed bitterly. The last thing he wanted to be was a "Fourth Magi" -- that additional wise man from the East who had gotten a late start in his journey to give the infant Jesus a gift. The potentate then spent the next thirty years in a vain search for Jesus, always arriving in places a few hours after Jesus had left. When he finally caught up it was too late -- Christ was already on the cross. Just as Jeff had been with JFK. Would he be that way with the Challenger, too? Arriving just in time to see that horrendous explosion that took so much else with it? Impotent witness wasn't the role Jeff wanted.

***

He landed at Idlewild in the early evening. The sadness in the air was thicker than the pollution. Soon it would harden into the cynicism and outrage that had disrupted the sixties and deformed a good deal more of the years and decades that came after.

It's not my fault, Jeff kept telling himself. My job was to stop the Challenger tragedy -- I never really had a chance to stop what happened in Dallas. I wasn't properly prepared. It was crazy even to try.

He took a cab back to the Village, the same trip he had taken 48 hours ago, in reverse. Everything was different. It was Saturday night, and throngs of people were out, but the sounds and colors were drained of vitality -- as if someone had pulled the plug on the watercolor, and all of its light had leaked away.

His cab pulled up to the Student Building. Three green-and-black police cars huddled like ugly roaches near the entrance. Students were milling about, five or six officers were conferring on the side, and the night air crackled with the sound of police bulletins and the glare of pulsing lights.

"What's going on here, Officer?" Jeff demanded, more sharply than he had intended.

"Who the hell are you?"

Jeff fumbled for his faculty ID, crafted to look like a 1985 edition, and hoped it would get by the beefy, florid-faced policeman. "Sorry, Officer. I teach at the College of Liberal Arts and Science here."

The cop eyed the ID, Jeff, and softened. "You're a teacher from another division?"

"Right," Jeff said, not really knowing what that meant.

The cop nodded. "The student lounge was broken into two hours ago and severely vandalized. These kids got no respect for property. Hey Professor, you ok?"

Jeff felt his knees buckle. He reached out to the police car for support. "Officer, I've got to get up there right away. I ... there are some important papers that I must get a look at." He was pleading.

"Out of the question." A big arm restrained Jeff, already in motion towards the building. "The place is a mess. Glass and garbage all over. Someone torched that whole floor -- probably some kid didn't like his grades. Believe me, Professor, it's not safe."

Jeff pulled free of the blue arm. For a second he considered making a run to the building. But he knew it was hopeless. He hadn't a clue about what was really going on, what had happened in the lounge and why. But he knew with cloying certainty that his life was now seriously derailed.

Maybe the AWH had imploded, maybe some kid had torched the place as the cop had said, but whatever had happened, there was no way that soft shimmering light would be there now for him -- surely no way he could code it for use and enter it even if it was there now, without a dozen witnesses looking on. A few dozen dollar-bills out of time he could take a chance on leaving back here; walking into the AWH with 1960s people as an audience, maybe some of them even trying to follow, was insane. He couldn't risk what that would do to reality -- might do to his very existence.

So he turned and walked shakily down the street. The cop might have said something but he couldn't hear it. The off-key amusement park quality of the Village congealed now into a proper smarmy nightmare. Jeff staggered a bit further, then grabbed on to a corner lamp pole. Then he leaned over and did what he had wanted to do for nearly two days: he threw up what seemed like every ounce of substance in his stomach.

He looked at the mess he had made on street, and wondered what part of that food might have come from 2084. It would be a long, long time if ever, he knew, before he was likely to see any of that again.

***

A Beatles' song was playing somewhere in the distance. A DJ was talking. No historical occasion, no hushed build-up. Just the Beatles...

Jeff opened his eyes. He looked out of his window at the street below. Mid-April sunshine coated the sidewalk like clarified butter.

"... traffic light in most places but still heavy on the Kosciusko Bridge," the radio continued. "HOA halfway through the third shift with you on WABC. Good morning!"

Jeff hoisted himself out of the easy chair. His clothes felt stale and rumpled -- he had spent the night in them – and he needed a shave. He stripped, showered, shaved, and approached the pile of clothes that served as his wardrobe closet. Today would be a special day. He put on a blue button-down shirt, dark brown corduroy slacks, and pulled his Navy blue knit tie into a loose fitting double-Windsor, the only kind of knot he knew how to make. He slung a corduroy jacket over his shoulder and ambled down the three flights of stairs.

Jeff played with his scrambled eggs at the Yorkville Restaurant and considered his situation for a thousandth time. He pushed three pieces of egg to one side. His arrival 23 years earlier than planned, the luggage accident in Dallas, the destruction of the student lounge -- were these all related, or three pieces of random, rotten luck?

He couldn't accept his being a Robinson Crusoe in the past. He understood his predicament, his utter stranding in the 1960s, logically enough. And yet some part of him had been waiting here these past five months, hoping that one of his team would one day miraculously appear to rescue him. He'd imagined Rena in this role, but how could she? The hole to 1963 had been sealed with the implosion or trashing or whatever had taken out the NYU lounge. He'd been back up there several times, when no one was around, but the room had been totally reconstructed, with no sign of the AWH.

The team had no way of knowing he was even here -- presumably all they would know is that he hadn't succeeded in stopping the Challenger disaster. If they sent anyone else back, it would likely be to 1985, where he was supposed to have gone, not here. And who knows if Rena or whoever would succeed any better than he. Maybe Steven Hawking was right in his chronology protection conjecture -- maybe the universe protects itself from alterations via time travel -- removes unwelcome Thornes from its side -- whether by misdirecting travelers, blowing up AWHs, both, or more.

So he was probably stranded. But maybe not totally without options. He had to gingerly probe the contours of time travel --

see just what small things it might allow, and then perhaps he'd try a few larger things. What he had in mind for today was the first modest step in this direction.

Jeff paid for his breakfast and walked out into the cool morning sunlight. His money problems were finally over -- he had a job with a decent salary. Some parts of the team's exhaustive planning had worked out after all, had survived his immersion in a time 23 years earlier than expected. The team's massive search of historical records had uncovered fourteen Harrises who had done graduate work at universities in the mid-20th century. One, named Geoffrey, had earned a Ph.D. in social psychology from the University of Edinburgh in 1958. Jeff and Geoffrey's names and academic disciplines were close enough that Jeff with a mixture of Geoff's credentials and Jeff's own knowledge of the field would have been able to demonstrate a convincing identity in 1985-86 -- the team's reason for coming up with this. But the preparation turned out to also be enough for Jeff to land a job back here as an Adjunct Professor at the third school whose ad he'd answered, his act sufficiently polished, hinting at just enough knowledge of new trends in the field to kindle admiration without suspicion. It was a last-minute Spring teaching appointment, to fill in for a regular Professor unexpectedly on leave, that required only cursory credentialing. But it was a foot in the door of academe, and it paid real money.

He squinted at the sun and inhaled deeply. The polluted air still bothered him, and he sometimes felt as if little pieces of black soot were burning holes in his chest. He wheezed slightly. But the day felt promising, even beautiful, and he caught the crosstown bus to the IRT subway on West 86th Street. This would take him to the "Intro to Sociology" class that he taught at City College on 137th Street in Harlem.

***

Further up the subway line, near a place called Pelham Parkway in the Bronx, Mrs. Sarah Harris also made her way to work. The day was beautiful to her too, and she also wheezed a bit -- from asthma -- as she walked down the block to

Saperman's Bakery where she worked behind the counter. Her mind was filled today, as it was on many days, with images of the Ukrainian countryside around Kiev, and with pictures of her father. She could see him as clearly as if he were standing right in front of her, even though she had last seen him more than 60 years ago and a continent away. Her brown eyes, still keen and always wise, glistened a drop, not from soot but sentiment. Those eyes were almost identical to Jeff's. She was his great-great-grandmother.

***

At City College, in a place presciently named Harris Hall, Jeff labored, to make a concluding point about media theorist Marshall McLuhan. "So you see, it's not what we watch on television that's important, it's the fact that we're watching television -- rather than reading a book or listening to the radio -- that McLuhan says really counts. This is what he means by 'the medium is the message.'"

Jeff looked at the students, most of whom were scribbling his words without the slightest comprehension. The three girls from Queens who smiled at him certainly had no idea what he was talking about. Neither did the foreign kid, his mouth continuously hanging open, who at least made no attempt to disguise his puzzlement. But a few in the class did seem to have some tiny understanding of what Jeff was saying. The girl in the back with the soft grey eyes seemed to be in touch with him. Anyway, Jeff liked the way she looked at him.

"Ok, that's about it for today. Read the pertinent sections of *Gutenberg Galaxy*, and I'll see whether I can get you some advance copies of *Understanding Media*." Jeff grabbed his corduroy coat and strode out the door, smiling at the girl with the soft grey eyes.

He hurried to the subway at 137th Street. He looked at his watch -- the flector model, for Jeff no longer cared about keeping such minor aspects of his cover. In fact, he hoped future artifacts like this might attract someone's benevolent attention, maybe someone else from the future, who could help him. He'd have gladly kept spending his 1980s money too for the same reason, had he not been afraid that sooner or later some Good Samaritan would have him arrested for counterfeiting.

It was 11:56 -- more than enough time.

But the subway took longer than expected, and it was 12:35 when Jeff ran down the long flights of stairs at the Pelham Parkway station in the Bronx. Saperman's was only a few minutes away by foot, so Jeff wasn't too worried. Still, he half-walked, half-ran.

He was sweating when he reached the bakery. He realized this was more from anxiety than exertion. His great-great-grandmother had died in 1992, at the age of 97. His grandfather, whom Jeff had spent some of the most satisfying times of his childhood with, had been just 6 when Sarah Harris had died, but Grandpa carried memories of her warmth and voice and summers they had spent together in their cottage on Cape Cod Bay. Jeff felt he knew Sarah through this.

But he stopped, suddenly not sure he could do this. What would he say to this woman? How would she react? A smell of apple strudel permeated his thoughts -- Grandpa's strudel, an old family recipe Grandpa had loved to bake -- and this gave Jeff courage. He walked in.

"Hello," he said in the direction of the three matronly women who stood behind the counter and looked up at him as a clanking bell on the inside of the door announced his presence. Not a single one of them looked anything like his great-great-grandmother. "Can I help you?" one of them said in a soothing Jewish accent that he'd heard only in the movies.

"Uhm, yes ..." he began, not quite sure what to say. "Does a Mrs. Sarah Harris work here?"

Just then he heard a rustle from the back. His great-great-grandmother walked out from behind a curtain, carrying some sort of cake in an open box.

"Sarah, a *boichik* to see you," one of the women said with a laugh.

Jeff felt like shouting with joy. He suppressed this, along

with the urge to jump over the counter and hug her. She looked great -- like her best picture, from someone named Sol's bar-mitzvah, come to life.

Sarah was smiling, a wonderful smile he had seen in his father and some of his aunts and uncles and his grandfather. "You look like I know you," she said. "You're one of Louie's grandsons?"

"Right, Louie," Jeff answered quickly. His mind sped through family history. Louie was Sarah's older brother. The two had come to New York City with a middle brother -- Hymie -- around 1900. Sarah was a little girl then, about five years old, and Louie was like a father to her. Her real father and nine other brothers and sisters she would never see again. Louie -- Uncle Louie, Jeff's grandfather had always called him -- had moved to the West Coast after World War II. He had fathered a big family himself, and Jeff recalled that these in turn had given Louie dozens of grandchildren who from time to time showed up at weddings and bar mitzvahs on the East Coast. Good. Jeff for now would be one of them.

Sarah took off her apron and moved out from behind the counter. "I'm taking the rest of the afternoon off," she announced to the matrons. "You tell Murray I'll make up the time this weekend, ok?"

"No, no, please, Mrs. Harris," Jeff raised his hand and smiled. He didn't think he could take more than a few minutes with his great-great-grandmother in this first meeting. "I've got just a little over an hour before an appointment downtown, and I don't want you to lose time from your job. How about we go for a cup of tea at the Dairy Restaurant by Lydig Avenue? It's kosher, right?" He had checked out this whole neighborhood a week ago.

Sarah laughed heartily. "It seems you know me and this neighborhood very well. OK, let's go to Lydig. Tell Murray I'm back in an hour," she said over her shoulder to the counter.

"So it seems you know my name but I don't know yours," Sarah said as the two walked the half a block around the corner to Lydig Avenue.

"I'm Jeff. Jeffrey Rosenberg." Jeff was 99% positive that Rosenberg was Sarah's maiden name.

Sarah's eyes widened in pleasure. "Yosef was the name of my father. Wonderful of Shlomo to name you after him. We have only one son, and we named him after my husband's -- Yitzhak's -- mother. So you're Shlomo's boy, then?" Now Sarah's eyes furrowed in some confusion. "Or are you Harry's?"

Jeff smiled and thought frantically as they entered the restaurant. He ushered Sarah to a table, and once seated, ordered two cups of tea -- with lemon for Sarah, milk for him -- from the elderly waiter who looked like he had about five minutes left to live.

He figured that Sarah prided herself on perfect recall of every relationship in her extended family. Right now she was probably realizing that as far as she knew, Shlomo had no son named Jeffrey, and neither did Harry. Jeff breathed in sharply. Time to talk about the impossible.

"I'm not really Louie's grandson," he said slowly.

In another time and place -- in fact, in most times and places, including this one -- such an admission would have been cause for alarm for Sarah. But her powerful intuition told her this was not a stranger to be feared -- not a stranger at all.

"You're much closer to me than Louie's grandchildren," Sarah finally said. Her eyes looked loving, not challenging, Jeff thought.

"You've traveled very far in your lifetime, Sarah," Jeff said softly. "Do think it might be possible to travel across years, across time, just like you've traveled across great distances?"

Sarah chuckled. "You mean like angels? Or maybe like the *meshugenas* on the *Twilight Zone*?" She pronounced the "w" like a "v," so the show sounded like "Tvilight Zone."

Jeff couldn't help laughing. He would have sworn that the only TV this woman would have ever watched other than the news was the Lawrence Welk Show. "Yes, something like that." Jeff felt much better after laughing. He put his teacup down. "Sarah, I'm going to tell you something now. You're a very intelligent woman, and what I'm going to tell you will seem totally crazy to you. But please hear me out. It will take just a minute. And then I'm going to ask you to do a very important favor for me. You don't have to agree now, but please promise me that you'll think about it."

"It's about what Hitler did in Europe?" she asked with a cry in her voice. Her hand shook, and she spilled some of her tea, though the cup was only half full. Jeff suddenly felt very guilty. His great-great-grandmother looked so much younger than he had pictured her, seen her in her pictures, that she had seemed at first not so old to him. Now she looked every one of her sixty years, and Jeff felt terrible that he was stirring up these demons about the holocaust and who knows what else. But he had to finish what he had started here.

"No, it's not about Hitler." He paused. "I'm your great-great-grandson, Jeffrey Harris."

A small shriek came from Sarah, and the blood left her cheeks.

"Sarah, it's ok," Jeff took her hand. "I have to leave now. But I need you to do something for me that is very very important -- my life may depend upon it. In 25 years, you'll get to know my grandfather, when he was just a little boy and you'll be much older." Jeff realized there were tears in his eyes. "And you'll be a wonderful Grandma to him, believe me. But I want you to promise that you'll tell him -- your little grandson -- about this meeting. I'm not asking you to believe me now. You can tell your grandson that you had this meeting with a crazy man who claimed to be your great-great-grandson years ago. But everything depends on your telling him something -- something about me, about this -- 25 years from now."

Sarah's head shook -- not saying no, but from tremors. Her eyes were a confused mixture of anger, uncertainty, and love. Now she did slowly shake her head no. "I don't know you," she whispered.

"I know. But I'm part of you -- I'm your DNA, your blood." Jeff stood up, then leaned over and kissed her. "I love you, Sarah, I always will. Go by your instincts in this." He put a five-dollar bill on the table, and hurried out the door.

Now the April breeze caught the back of his head and moved him along. He walked in a daze, not really knowing where he was going, to the Pelham Parkway station. He paid his fare, walked through the wooden turnstile -- nearly getting a splinter in his thigh -- and sat down on the rotting green bench to wait for the train.

And then he remembered. His grandfather swinging with him on the hammock. Talking about a summer he'd spent years ago when *his* grandma was still alive, on Cape Cod. He was four, maybe five years old, so it was 1990 or 1991. His parents and little sister had gone out to Cooke's for supper. He'd had a bad cold, and had to stay in the cottage. Grandma Sarah stayed with him. It had started raining -- very hard -- an August Cape Cod storm that seemed to drench the beach and every living thing. And she told him about the strange man who had come to her long ago in Saperman's, the bakery where she used to work...

Jeff was shaking. Thank you, Sarah -- you came through for me. He felt like running back and hugging her, but didn't dare, lest this somehow throw a curve into what had just happened here.

He was sure this memory of what his grandfather had told him about what *his* grandmother had told *him* hadn't existed before. It proved that he was real in this convoluted past -- that he could do things here which could indeed change the future, even if the change were as slight as a grandmother's words in a Cape Cod storm some 60 years before he'd been born. But those words, his memory of his grandfather's conveyance of them, meant everything. Sarah Harris had given Jeff his first real hope. If he could change the future through her, he could figure out a way to somehow contact his team, and get back to where he belonged.

He was crying. For he also realized that in a deep, indescribable way he missed Sarah Harris even more than his world of 2084, and he knew there was no way he ever could have both.

***

"I think he's very attractive," Carla Caplan of Flushing said. "You know, not in the Marlon Brando or Paul Newman way, but in a cuddly way. Like a teddy bear." She stroked her left thumbnail with an emery board.

"Oh, I don't know," Amy Jacobson replied. "His accent is a little strange. And anyway, he never pays any attention to us. The only girl he ever looks at is the girl in back of the class."

Carla moved her hand along the nylon stocking on her leg. "That's not true, Amy. I've seen him look at us lots of times."

"The two of you are ridiculous." Sandy Greenfarb shook her curly brown hair. "Besides, teachers don't date students in this pathetic school. City College is too old-fashioned for that."

"Who said anything about dating?" Carla replied. "And you're wrong, anyway. Didn't you hear about Atwick in the Bio Department? They say he got a girl pregnant. Put some Spanish Fly in her drink."

Sandy blushed. "That's absurd. And anyway, Professor Harris is nothing like Professor Atwick. He's much more refined -- more of a gentleman."

"How would *you* know?" Amy jumped back in.

"No one knows much about Professor Harris. He just started teaching here this term," Carla said.

"He's not married. That's all Carla needs to know." Amy laughed.

"Shh," Sandy said as Jeff walked into the room.

"Late as usual," Amy whispered.

"Well, I've read through most of your papers." Jeff slouched into the chair on wheels and stretched his feet out under the desk. "And I'm sorry to say that they were more gruesome than I expected."

A murmur of irritation rippled through the class.

"Now to begin with..." Jeff began, as one student, even later than he, hurried through the door. It was the girl with the soft grey eyes, who bit her lower lip in an apologetic smile and slipped into a rear seat as inconspicuously as possible.

"Miss, uh..." Jeff inquired, returning the smile.

"Laura Chapin."

"Yes, uh, Miss Chapin, I was just telling the class that most of these papers on the McLuhanesque interpretation of the Beatles missed the point entirely. But there were a few exceptions. And yours was among the most refreshing."

Amy shot an I-told-you-so glance to Carla.

Laura's eyes dilated with delight. "Thank you."

Jeff finished the class five minutes early and headed quickly out the door.

"Professor Harris," Laura called after him.

He stopped a few feet down the hall and turned to face her. Jeff realized she looked taller and older than he had thought, her brown hair jostling invitingly around her shoulders. "I wanted to thank you for what you said about my paper," she said, slightly out of breath.

"You earned it. You have a fine mind."

She smiled without looking too embarrassed. "I was wondering if we might be able to talk sometime -- in your office -- I, um, have some questions I'd like to go over with you about grad school."

Jeff looked at his watch and gestured Laura to walk with him towards the stairs. "Look, I'd ask you to join me for lunch right now, but I've a departmental meeting to attend. Why don't we have lunch together next Monday?"

Now Laura's face flushed a bit. "I ... that would be very nice, but I've got labs starting at noon that run to four o'clock. Do you think it might be possible for us to meet in your office at 4:30 on Monday?"

Jeff stopped and looked steadily at Laura for a moment. Those eyes were alluring. "Monday at 4:30 it is, then," he said crisply, and strode away.

***

"I almost didn't keep our appointment today," Jeff said, sipping the third glass of red wine he and Laura had partaken since they'd adjourned their meeting from his office.

"Oh? And what possibly could have kept you?" The wine had lowered Laura's voice to a quiet, warm contralto. The cafe, five minutes on the subway from his office, had the smell of fine spirits and food.

"I didn't want the aggravation," Jeff said.

Laura considered his deadpan face, then burst out laughing. "Well thank you very much."

"What would you say if I told you that I could predict the future?" Jeff asked off-handedly, taking another sip of his wine.

"You mean in a socially forecasting way?"

"I mean in every way."

"Well, Professor Harris, you told us in one of your lectures that for very good reasons no one can ever really know the future. So I would say either you were lying ... or speaking metaphorically."

"Good," Jeff nodded, "but let's say I stubbornly insisted that I did know the future, and that this in no way contradicts what I said in my lecture about no one ever being able to know the future. What would you say then?"

"I'd say you were kidding me or crazy." Laura thought for a bit. "I don't think the future exists yet -- it doesn't exist until it's actually created, in the present -- so there's no way you or anyone could really know it in the way that we know we're here in this little bistro on Broadway, for instance."

"Fair enough." Jeff waved to the waiter for another refill of wine, which was quickly supplied. "You're sharp. But let's say I were to tell you that Lyndon Johnson will beat Barry Goldwater by a landslide this November?"

Laura shook her head. "No. Not good enough. Everyone expects Goldwater to get the nomination, and there's no way that Johnson won't win big with all the Kennedy sympathy vote. You'd have to do better than that."

Jeff smiled and rubbed his lips with his fingers. The Beatles' "Thank You, Girl" played languorously in the background. "Ok, how's this: Let's say I tell you that in about a year and a half from now, the Beatles will have a hit record called 'Help' from a movie by the same name?"

Laura laughed. "You've got imagination, professor, I'll say that for you. But I still don't think I'd be convinced. How do I know that you're not a personal friend of George Martin's with some inside information about the Beatles' plans?" Laura frowned for a moment then snapped her fingers. "No, I've got it! You tell me what number on *Billboard*'s Hot 100 a *non*-Beatle record -- one that won't almost certainly make Number One -- will be in 1966, and I'll believe that you know the future!"

Laura extended her hands in a triumphant gesture, pitching over a nearly full glass of red wine onto her shirt in the process. Jeff jumped up, napkin in hand, and began patting Laura's soaked sleeve dry. He progressed from her sleeve to her cheek, and suddenly was less than an inch from Laura's upturned face. Her eyes were rosy with wine, her mouth was parted. He touched his lips to hers, gently at first, then found himself in a sweet realm of warmth...

He finally pulled away. "Well," he managed, gasping a bit for breath, "no one can ever say that I don't give my students personal attention."

"I'd be glad to write you a letter of recommendation," she said, smiling. "Now you see why I didn't want to have lunch with you."

"You found this aggravating?"

"Quite the opposite," Laura replied.

Still standing over her, Jeff touched her hair with his finger. "I've got a lot I need to tell you," he said softly. "By the way, no one but someone in the music industry would know the exact number on the charts of a record even now, so your test of my knowledge of the future is too demanding."

***

They walked hand in hand a few evenings later along groves overlooking the Hudson River. Across they could see the Palisades of New Jersey, carved whole out of stone as if by some supreme civilization, and near them the palette of Wave Hill

Park in the late Spring. Wave Hill -- home of Mark Twain, of Toscanini, and an Easter parade of notables across a century. In the late 1800s, William Henry Appleton had lived here, amidst his publication in America of Darwin and Spencer. JFK had lived in a house across the street in the 1930s. Recently a British ambassador had donated most of this to the people of New York.

Jeff knew it wouldn't especially help his larger predicament to get involved with Laura, to tell her what he was really about. On the other hand, what harm could it do -- set in motion a jagged time-loop which would yank him out of existence? Not likely. And his need to talk had been compelling -- as he'd told her -- as had the smell of her neck. And here he was, still around, and feeling fine.

He breathed in slowly. Fragrances real and recalled bathed his brain. "You know, when I was a kid, my grandfather used to tell me about summers he spent on Cape Cod when he was a kid himself. At night, sometimes two or three in the morning, he'd walk along the beach and gradually leave his cottage in the distance. Sometimes he'd turn around and, still seeing the light of the cottage, would walk further until it was completely gone. Then he'd close his eyes and think, there's no difference between what I see with my eyes open and my eyes closed. He'd sit in the salty water, a foot or two deep, and feel the cool fluid pulse of the cosmos throbbing through his clothes. Then he'd get up and walk back, a little cold but not shivering, until he made contact with that spot of light that was his cottage. He was never sure until it happened that he would see that light again. But when he did, he'd walk with the satisfaction of knowing that after having gone out to the very limits and beyond of his usual reality, he was about to enter it again. I never really fully understood what my grandfather was saying to me -- until now."

Laura looked at him, stroked his face with the center of her palm. "You're serious about this, aren't you?"

"Serious about what?"

"The time travel," Laura said.

Jeff said nothing.

"I'll be with you anyway," Laura said. "I don't have to believe it's real. I can pretend to believe it's real, play along that you're from the future, like you say you are. I'm not sure there's all that much difference between really believing and pretending to believe anyway, if you pretend sincerely enough."

"You've got quite a philosophy there," Jeff said.

Laura took his hand, put it to her lips.

"And you're not worried that I really *am* crazy – maybe dangerous?" Jeff asked.

"Oh, you're dangerous all right," she said, grazing her teeth over his index finger. "And as to your story -- my feeling is that whatever the truth of it, you're a good man. I feel sure about that."

Jeff sighed. "You remember what I said the first day of class about no one really knowing for sure that anything is real -- we could well be dreaming all of this, and might even dream that someone pinched us and tried to awaken us and nothing happened -- but that we'd all go insane unless we took at least some leap of faith, and assumed on nothing better than faith that the world is real and we were really here?"

"I was late for that lecture, wasn't I?"

"No, I'm quite sure you were there," Jeff said. "Look, I'm trying to say that--"

"I know what you're saying." Now she looked at him very intently. "You want me to take that leap of faith with you and your story. You want me to assume that what you're saying is true, even though I have no evidence for it and it flies in the face of reason. You want me to say, look, I know this is crazy, but I'm going to give you the benefit of the doubt, entertain your insanity, see where it leads us. In other words, pretense isn't good enough for you -- you want to make this really hard for me." She turned away.

"Something like that, right," Jeff said.

"What is it about me that's always attracted to lunatics," she murmured. And she turned around and kissed him full and long on the lips.

***

"Two Papaya." Jeff held up two fingers to the man at the Papaya King on 3rd Avenue and 86th Street. "One to drink here and a quart to go." There was nothing like this drink in his time. Whatever the hell it was -- whatever its special mixture of pulp and sugars -- it was delicious.

He walked down 86th Street, package in hand, towards his place by the East River. His place ... he was feeling more and more comfortable in this place, and that made him feel uncomfortable, out of place. There were things he missed from his world -- faces on the phone, words on the screen, poles of the planet as easily accessible as the north and south parts of this borough -- but he missed them less and less. Especially when he was with Laura.

Still... He picked up a copy of the *Daily News*. Lyndon Johnson was on the cover, saying he was going ahead full force on the space program, and on the inside was a picture of Gus Grissom. Jeff had thought about doing something to prevent the fire that would kill Grissom, White, and Chafee in their Apollo 1 capsule on January 27, 1967. But that was still more than a year and a half away, and he couldn't be sure what impact that might have on the Moon landing, which was still the lonely high watermark of human penetration of space. No, he didn't dare mess with that -- better to bide his time, and wait the 19 further years, almost to the day, for a chance to avert the Challenger catastrophe, and the fatal blow it had delivered, in retrospect, to the space program.

But Jeff didn't suffer abiding time very well. What was the point of time travel, anyway, if not to short-circuit ordinary time, make new things happen? It seemed the last thing that should be required of the time traveler was patience. Jeff knew now, ever since his experience with Sarah, that he could change the future -- which meant that his existence here could make a difference. But he had to get some word back to his team in 2084. How? He'd even tried taking a page from Asimov -- what was that novel, *The End of Eternity*? -- and had placed small, discrete, but clearly informative ads in a variety of significant journals and newspapers like *The New York Times*. But nothing had happened. He had no idea if any of the ads had even come to the attention of the team -- 1964 was after all well before the age of online information, and an ad in a newspaper this old might well have slipped by the mass scanning in the new millennium.

He opened the door to his apartment quietly, so as not to wake Laura. She'd been sleeping over a lot, and Jeff figured she'd be moving in with him soon. He wasn't sure how his colleagues at City College would take this -- the 1960s were one of the decades of sexual liberation, but Jeff wasn't enough of an expert on that aspect of popular culture to know just how far that went.

He tiptoed into the bedroom. He liked looking at Laura when she was sleeping. Her eyes were open just a crack, and he could see the bottoms of her soft grey eyes tracing some sort of REM-dream diagram. He hoped it was of him. He looked at her body, her breasts, one nipple partly exposed. He could do a lot worse than spending the next 23 years with her.

He walked carefully back into the kitchen, put the papaya juice into the refrigerator -- he loved it, a living antique, right out of the Smith-Sonyian -- and took out some eggs. Was cholesterol verboten in this decade? He'd been meaning to ask Laura. It certainly wasn't in his. He started a pot of water boiling for the eggs, and sat down at the table to read the paper...

"Jesus!" he shouted.

"What's the matter?" Laura shuffled out of the bedroom, rubbing her eyes.

Jeff shook his head in shock and disbelief.

"What's the matter, honey?" Laura walked over, put a concerned hand on his shoulder.

Jeff pointed to the paper.

"What? What is it?" Laura asked.

Jeff jabbed at a picture. "I know her," he rasped. "She was a member of my team. Rena Sarrett."

***

Laura leaned over, and read aloud the article associated with the photograph. "... run down by a bus on Central Park South last week.... died the next day ... her co-workers say she was hired by Gaulin's, an insurance firm, about six months ago ... attempts to locate Miss Sarrett's relatives have all proven unsuccessful ... police would appreciate anyone with information contacting them..."

"She was part of your project?" Laura asked.

"Yeah," Jeff said, his voice choked with emotion.

Laura had the presence of mind to turn off the water, which was now furiously boiling. "And you and she were lovers?"

"What?"

"I'm sorry," Laura said.

"Yeah, we were lovers. Once. A long time ago -- actually, in a time which doesn't even goddamn exist yet. Does that matter?"

"Did you love her?" Laura asked.

"Yes," Jeff said, tears in his eyes. "But not as much as I love you."

Laura put her arms around his neck and her face against his chest. "That's all that matters to me. I love you too."

Jeff tenderly kissed her head.

"What does this mean?" Laura asked. "I mean, your friend getting killed..."

"It means they sent her back too -- maybe to find me here, who knows, maybe they got one of my messages after all," Jeff said. "Or maybe they were trying to send her back to 1985, to do the same job I was supposed to do, but for some reason she got sucked back here to the 1960s too. I don't know."

"What are you -- we -- going to do now?" Laura asked.

"I don't know," Jeff said.

***

"I don't really want to go to this party," Jeff said, trudging reluctantly after Laura up a steep street in Washington Heights.

"Come on," Laura turned around and pulled his hand. "It's been over a month since you found out about Rena, and all you've been doing is brooding -- it's time you got out and saw some people. It's summer already."

"Not brooding -- thinking," Jeff said. "I was knocked unconscious in Dallas, Rena was killed by a bus, both in places we shouldn't have been. There's got to be some comprehensible pattern in this."

"I know," Laura said, more softly. "It's almost as if there's something in the nature of things that doesn't want people to time travel -- and punishes them when they do."

"You know I dreamed about Rena dead, shortly after I got out of the Dallas hospital," Jeff said, recalling this for the first time. "I wonder if that has any connection to any of this."

"Well, remember you told me Kip Thorpe—"

"Thorne," Jeff corrected.

"Right," Laura said. "Kip Thorne and his people hypothesized that people flipped into alternate universes when they changed history through time travel -- that that's how the loops opened by the Thorne stayed clean -- so maybe, somehow, because you're here in the past, you've caused an alternate universe to come into being, and in that universe you'd already lived past knowing about Rena's death, because that universe is progressing at a different pace, and somehow your dream connected you to this alternate version of your self..."

Jeff smiled. It was at times like this that he could understand how he had come to feel so close to Laura. "You don't think I'm such a lunatic anymore, huh?"

Laura snuggled against him. "You're definitely a lunatic -- no doubt about that -- but maybe not about time travel."

Jeff squeezed her hand.

"Well, here we are at Joannie's building," Laura said. "Don't worry, I'm sure there'll be other professors there. Just think of this as another great safari into 1960s culture."

***

"What can I fix you, Professor?"

"A scotch and water would be fine." Richard Atwick adjusted his thin-rimmed glasses and quietly eyed the hosed legs and sleek red dress of his benefactor. "Why thank you, Carla," he said, taking the drink from her hand, "and I must say you're looking as lovely tonight as always."

He gulped half his drink down in one swallow and, sloshing the rest around in the glass, began walking through the six rooms of Joannie Pernelli's parents' apartment. The place was packed with partiers in varying states of dress, intimacy, and inebriation.

"Professor Harris." Atwick strode over and extended his hand to Jeff. "I've seen you around Campus, but I don't think we've ever formally met. I'm Richard Atwick of Biology." He suddenly put his hand to his ear as the Beatles' "It Won't Be Long" blared forth without warning.

"Nice to meet you," Jeff said loudly over the twanging guitars. "Do you know Laura Chapin?"

"I don't think so, but I'm glad to now." Atwick said. "Are you doing graduate work?"

"Thanks for the compliment." Laura smiled sweetly. "But I'm afraid I'm still undergrad. And if you two gentlemen have no objections, I think I'll go off and mingle now with some of my own kind."

"Nice." Atwick watched her walk off and nodded at Jeff approvingly. "And what are you having to drink, Professor?"

"Please, call me Jeff." Jeff tried not to respond to the nod. "I guess I'll have some white wine if there's any around."

"Well, let's just go and find some, shall we?" Atwick tugged on Jeff's arm and started towards the bottles on the far side of the room. "You know, I'm delighted that you'll be joining us again this Fall in the Sociology Department. Sociology -- that's a discipline of the future! It's good we're building up our faculty in that area."

"Well, I'm happy to be here at City College. It's certainly one of the best schools in the country."

"Well, we like to think so." Atwick beamed. "Ah, here's some sort of Soave. Will that do? Good." Atwick began pouring. "Now I've heard your specialty is mass culture. And you did your graduate work at..." Atwick handed Jeff a brimming paper cup.

Jeff sipped a little and spilled a little on his shirt. "University of Edinburgh. And my specialty's really mass media -- you know, the work of Marshall McLuhan -- rather than mass culture." Jeff got a pang as he thought again about how he had successfully re-cycled the cover the team had provided – any thought of the team brought along painful images of Rena...

"Edinburgh, yes," Atwick was talking. "Splendid mountain in the middle of the city. You worked under Phillip MacKenzie?"

"Mackenzie? Nope, don't think I did," Jeff said, wondering what he would say next if pressed. His credentials would after all not stand up to anyone who knew the real Geoff Harris, or even very long to anyone who knew someone who knew Geoff...

The sound quieted down a bit, and it occurred to Jeff that Atwick had a familiar British accent, maybe like a surgeon he half-remembered hearing once in a hospital...

"Of course, it's a large university--" Atwick began.

"Professor Harris, it's good to see you outside of the classroom!" Carla joined the men. Jeff was delighted for the intrusion.

"You know, I'm really *mad* at you for that C+." She batted her eyelids flirtatiously at Jeff.

"Well, Carla, if Professor Harris had graded you for good looks, I'm sure you would have received an A+. Am I right Jeff?"

"Absolutely," Jeff said -- thinking that, if his grasp of history was right, in a few decades that kind of bantering could bring both Atwick and him up on sexual harassment charges. He shuddered. Insane days they were, at the end of the 20th century. He'd be doing the world a big favor if the only thing he did back here was change *that*...

"Aw, I can't stay mad at you guys, you're too charming," Carla mewed. "Do you believe in dancing with students, Professor Harris? Professor Atwick has already honored me with one of his cha-chas."

Atwick bowed. "The honor was all mine."

"Well, I'd be pleased to dance with you Carla," Jeff laughed, "but I'm afraid these new dances are too much for me."

Carla smiled and subtly shifted her body so that her curves

were even more prominent. "I was thinking of something nice and slow."

"Well, in that case, I'd be a madman to refuse." Jeff winked at Atwick and extended his arm to Carla. He looked in vain for Laura as Carla escorted him to a room in which "The Best of Johnny Mathis" was playing incessantly.

An hour and who knows how many red dresses later, Laura came up behind Jeff. "Hi," she whispered in his ear and kissed it. "Find out anything interesting?"

"Actually, yeah," Jeff said, and handed Laura a glass of wine. "Amazing how many people seem to know the future when you're primed to hear that in their conversation. One kid told me that he thinks the Beachboys will go on to become second only to the Beatles in musical importance. Now how could he know that on the basis of 'Surfin Safari' and a couple of other uncreative songs in 1964?"

"Tall, blond, sun-tanned boy, Mark?" Laura asked.

"Yeah, I think so."

"Well, he looks like one of the Beachboys, so maybe he's just self-impressed," Laura laughed, and spilled her wine. "Oops."

"You've got no luck with wine, have you?" Jeff was laughing too now. He had to admit he was having a good time. "Here, take mine, I just poured it, I'll go get another."

"I think I've had *fantastic* luck with wine at least one time," Laura said.

Jeff went to fetch another bottle in an adjacent room. The music there was louder than anywhere else. Jeff cringed a bit under the sound assault, then realized he was hearing something else mixed in with the music ... a piercing wail coming from the next room. He dropped the bottle and ran in the room and found Laura shrieking on the floor.

"Laura, what's the matter?" He lifted her face and looked intently into her eyes. They were grossly dilated. Her shrieks suddenly turned into hysterical laughter.

"Professor Harris, is she sick or something?" Sandy, who Jeff realized had been standing over them, was nearly in tears herself.

"I don't know, Sandy. Look, could you please call me a cab?"

Jeff helped Laura to her feet. She was yelling something at the top of her lungs but Jeff couldn't make out what she was saying. She passed out in his arms in the elevator. He carried her into the back seat of the cab that arrived a few minutes later. "Get me to the closest hospital emergency room," he told the driver, who looked like he'd seen it all.

He carefully put her head on his lap and wiped big beads of sweat from the bridge of her nose. Her eyes were tightly shut and she drooled slightly from the corner of her mouth. He gently wiped that also. She was moaning and half-singing some Beatles song.

He had read of the effects of sixties' psychedelic drugs on people -- assuming that's what this was, though it seemed a little early in the 1960s for that. He could see this was a very bad reaction, likely from something more nasty than LSD. Who the hell had given it to her?

In his day and age, treating it by simple suffusion would be child's play. But here more than a century earlier, with no nano-syndics at all -- jeez, he hoped these "doctors" were up to this. What would they use to cleanse her chemistry? He sighed, and stroked her face. There was no point in torturing himself. That wouldn't stop her from dying. He had no choice but to put Laura in whatever primitive doctor's hands this cabbie placed her.

But why did this happen?

Another damn mishap?

He had a searing insight for an instant. Yes, of course ... Then he lost it.

He looked down at Laura's lips, and trembled.

***

Jeff had always found strength in the rivers of New York. He had spent hours as a child wandering along the banks of the Bronx River -- more a stream, really, than a river – admiring its waterfalls, sticking his toes in its pools, following its path through the Botanic and Zoological Gardens. Years later, he would sit on the terrace of Rena's high-rise on 125th Street, watching the powerful Hudson roll through the ninth decade of the stagnant 21st century. Good in medicine, agriculture, the intra-physics that the Thorne embodied, but not much else. Good in looking inward, backward, not outward. He walked now around Carl Schurz Park, looking down on the East River and its reflection of this 1960s city, hoping to find something he could use to recover his balance.

Laura was ok, resting in his apartment, well out of danger. That wasn't the problem.

"Close," the doctor had said. "Good thing you rushed her over here. Combo of booze and that kind of drug is dangerous. Good thing it responded to--"

Better get used to it doc -- you'll see a lot more of it before this decade is over.

Thank God Laura was ok.

But Jeff wasn't.

He had slept maybe an hour after bringing her home from the hospital, undressing her, tucking her safely in their bed. He'd had nightmares -- older and younger versions of his great-great-grandmother coming in and out of his life, changing it with each appearance, editing the narrative that was him so many times that he had no bearings. Only alterations -- of alterations.

Jeff had always valued the sanctity and clarity of his mind. That's why he'd steered clear of the psychedelic drugs of *his* century -- better to improve external reality than just your perception of it. But he figured the contamination now of his past and future was far more toxic to the psyche than the worst drugs. Coleridge, de Quincey, Huxley, Leary, Goonatilake -- you're all pikers compared to me.

But why was he feeling the brunt of this now?

Something Laura had said or done -- not her almost OD'ing, but something that had happened then, though he didn't know what -- had unhinged him--

"Hi honey." A soft, cool hand touched his as he leaned against the stone embankment. He turned to Laura. She still looked pale.

"You shouldn't be out yet. How are you feeling?"

She held up her palms in an I-don't-know gesture. "I think pretty much better. I was losing my mind in the house, and you were gone a long time. I was worried."

Jeff pulled her close. "Oh, Laura, Laura," he said softly, sadly. "What's going on?"

They parted and held hands, looking down at the lights that slid upon the inky water below. "I don't know," she said. "Do you?"

"I think so," Jeff said quietly.

"Tell me," Laura said.

"I think you know."

"No." Laura's face furrowed in confusion.

Jeff dropped her hand and turned to face her. "You look very nice in those shorts."

Laura patted the light red shorts she was wearing on this humid summer evening and looked even more confused. "What do my shorts have to do with anything?"

"For God's sake, stop playing games with me, Laura!" A nearby elderly woman with blue-tinted hair glared at Jeff. He glared back and lowered his voice. "Try being honest with me for a change."

She turned and looked out over the water. "I think I have been honest. I've told you how much I love you." Her voice was husky.

"I don't suppose you remember much of what you did when the DMT first hit you?" Jeff continued impassively.

"No, I don't remember much of anything. The whole experience was horrible. You know that." She started crying.

"So you have no idea what song you were singing when I took you home in the cab?"

She shook her head. "I can't believe I was singing in that state-"

"Well would it surprise you to know that you were singing

a few lines of the Beatles' 'Yes It Is' over and over again? 'Please don't wear red tonight...'"

"And you place some sort of significance on that?"

"I've been driving myself crazy, wandering around here for hours, trying to figure out what's been bothering me ever since I heard you singing those lines. I didn't even know until I saw you and your red shorts a few seconds ago that that song was the problem. But now I'm starting to understand. You still want to claim you have no idea what I'm talking about?"

"I haven't the foggiest notion." For the first time, annoyance was in Laura's voice. She had stopped crying.

"I think you do. Do you know what today's date is? June 29, 1964. Now the Beatles so far have released two albums in America, *Meet the Beatles* and *The Beatles' Second Album*. Actually, they also have a third album on VeeJay Records with some early songs. There's also an album with songs from their *Hard Day's Night* movie and a few new songs, *Something New*, which will be released here in a couple of weeks. You see I know all of this because I taught history of rock music for five years when I first got my Ph.D."

"I know all about your past and future," Laura said tartly.

"Good," Jeff grabbed her arm and raised his voice again. "And do you also know that 'Yes It Is' is on none of those albums? None of them! And in fact it won't be heard in America until an album called *Beatles VI* is released sometime late next year?

Laura pulled away and laughed sarcastically. "And that's what all this is about? That when I was stoned out of my mind on some Brazilian drug maybe intended for you I sang some song that won't be released in the U.S. for another few months? There are a thousand explanations for that. I might know some English guy who heard Lennon and McCartney perform that song in a personal appearance. You yourself might have sung the song in your sleep. What's the big deal?" Her voice was rasping, and she started to cough.

"Your life's at stake," Jeff said. "That's the big deal. Don't you get it?"

Laura just looked at him, eyes wide and brimming with tears. She started to walk away.

"Listen to me, goddamn it!" Jeff caught up to her, spun her around, and put his hands heavily on her shoulders. "Rena died, I think I was almost killed. You were almost killed. These are serious forces we're playing around with here."

She turned her head away, as if from the intensity of his reasoning.

"Tell me the truth!" he demanded.

"I love you," Laura said.

"We need more now," Jeff insisted.

Laura exhaled, squeezed close to Jeff, then pulled away. "It's getting windy out here," she said and shivered. "Let's go back to the apartment and I'll try to tell you as much as I can."

***

The kettle whistled. Jeff carefully poured the water into the porcelain teapot, let it warm a bit, then added two servings of Darjeeling tea and the extra one for the pot.

Laura was on the couch, arms around her knees and legs tucked under, talking. "We knew there was danger right after the arrival, but we didn't think it continued years after."

"None of our little expeditions before mine ran into any trouble at all," Jeff said. "As far as I know, I was the first not to return -- the first whose AWH self-destructed, or was destroyed by something else, after my time jump."

"None of those little events before yours were intended to profoundly alter history," Laura said. "Your Challenger attempt was the first big-scale operation."

Jeff shivered, then touched the teapot for warmth. The number of lives lost in the Challenger explosion -- if only he hadn't been funneled back here to the 1960s... "Suppose you start at the beginning," he said, "though it still bothers me to talk of beginnings that in one sense haven't even happened yet."

"The gist is this," Laura said. "My team was – will be -- situated about 15 years after yours in the future. We knew about your team. Knew about you, Rena, her getting killed here. When your team uncovered her death in a cache of old microfiche, they stopped the project. Sealed all the files. *My* team found out about it and decided, secretly and illegally, to re-open it. My job was to--"

"Don't tell me -- to stop the killing of JFK."

"No," Laura said.

"But you're here in the 1960s," Jeff said.

"My job was to keep an eye on you -- assuming I could find you," Laura said.

Jeff's mouth hung open. "They sent you back here to find *me*?"

"Actually, not back here -- to 1985," Laura said.

"But--"

"Right," Laura said. "But I wound up back here, just like you, and just like Rena. My team didn't understand that at first. Neither did I. But I think it's clear what's going on now. The Thorne operates by creating basins of subatomic attraction, at both ends of the artificial wormhole. But if you create enough artificial basins, all in one place, that in effect must begin to operate like one hugely powerful natural basin, attracting all out-of-time units in its temporal vicinity. Like a well worn ditch attracting rivulets of water."

"Three AWHs were intended to go back to 1985..." Jeff mused.

"Yes," Laura said, "and they all ended up here more than 20 years earlier. Think about it. Your team perfected time travel, tried to bury it, my team dug it up -- you can't as a society, a species, unlearn a kind of knowledge. There must be thousands of time travel operations throughout the future. And the likely place for many of them to focus is JFK – first assassination on film, on tape, copied onto digiscan, holoscan, mirrorims, and who knows what new media. It's the cultural icon of assassination, the beacon against which all others are measured."

"The glittering prize for time travelers," Jeff said, bringing Laura her tea.

"Yes," Laura said, gratefully sipping.

"And pulling any other time travelers back here who happened to be floating around nearby in the time-flux," Jeff said.

Laura nodded. "Look at this very year. 1964. The Beatles, Bob Dylan, Marshall McLuhan -- the sexual revolution, Civil Rights, feminism, the ecology movement all get big boosts in the next few years. Why all of that packed into this one decade? Couldn't be coincidence. The answer is that the 1960s were infected -- and inspired -- by time travelers. Despite all of our attempts at curbing possible cultural contamination from the future, it can't be done. You've seen that. Some of it leaks out -- and causes massive cultural upheavals."

"John Lennon was a time traveler?" Jeff asked.

"I don't know, maybe," Laura said. "Maybe that's why he was murdered. At very least I'd say he was touched by time travel."

Jeff's head was reeling. Someone else who didn't deserve to die, whose death he'd like to prevent if he could. Surprise Chapman in that Dakota alley, break his goddamn gun-hand... Was Jeff bound to spend his whole life now as a shackled witness to history? "How'd you find me?"

"Wasn't too hard," Laura said. "Once I got back here, and realized I was stranded, I figured I might as well see if you had landed back here too. We knew you were a teacher. You had to live, earn money somewhere. So I went around to every school in the area, saying I wanted to be a Sociology major, and asking for information about the faculty. This was my plan for 1985, so I had some good credentials ready, and made them just right with a little alteration. And when I talked to your Chair at City College, I knew I hit pay dirt -- he showed me your syllabus, and its emphasis on McLuhan. McLuhan's been well known in Canada for over a decade, but not down here as yet."

"Why didn't you tell me who you were?" Jeff asked.

"I didn't want to spook you -- have you run away on me, where I couldn't find you again."

"Good you succeeded at least at one thing," Jeff smiled tiredly.

"Yeah."

"With all the people who came back to save Kennedy, not a single one succeeded at that, did they?" Jeff asked.

"No," Laura, "at least not as far as we know in our universe of knowledge." She shook her head. "I really do think that there's something about history that resists attempts to change it."

"Hawking's Chronology Protection Conjecture?" Jeff said. "Thorne and his colleagues claimed to have refuted that, though I admit the math was a bit beyond me."

"Refuted in theory -- with the assumption of clean loops with no causality interference -- but loops are much dirtier in practice, especially with big events affecting so many people like assassinations," Laura said. "Attempts to change those either fail completely, or maybe just change the events a little bit -- or cosmos forbid, maybe even ironically set up the events to happen in the first place."

"Not to mention that they're hazardous to the health of the time travelers," Jeff added.

"You really think we're in danger?" Laura asked.

"Obviously. My guess is the universe sort of cleans up after itself -- does what it can to make sure there aren't too many loose ends, joints out of time, around at any one time. From that perspective, we're irritants to the universe – our very being here disturbs it. But that doesn't mean we'll definitely be killed. Maybe we're just, I don't know, more accident prone, more likely in a statistical sense to meet harm than others. If we're really careful, maybe we'll live. After all, you and I are still alive and kicking."

Laura pulled him down next to her on the couch.

Jeff's mind flipped back to the images of the Challenger. "It's so frustrating. To be back here, and not be able to even do anything about it. I mean, we have almost 20 years to plan some sort of intervention -- maybe we can do something, something small that won't rock the boat too much, but just enough to deflect the disaster, or the worst of it." He saw the faces again. "Over a hundred kids were killed when the Challenger crashed into that schoolhouse near Miami. The kids dead, the astronauts dead, those images and flames burning into everyone's brains all over America and the world -- no wonder it stopped the space program dead in its tracks. No President or Congress could support it after an accident like that – even dictators couldn't force it on their people--"

"What did you say?" Laura looked at him.

"What? About the Challenger?"

"What do kids in a schoolhouse have to do with that?" Laura asked.

Jeff looked puzzled.

"The Challenger explosion was a terrible thing for the country, and the space program, yes," Laura said. "It was horrible -- everyone saw those seven astronauts walking to their death, waving to the cameras, right on television. But it blew up just a minute or so after launch -- nowhere near Miami or a school filled with children."

Jeff gasped. "And the space program continued in your timeline?"

"Oh yes," Laura said. "I mean, it's got its problems. Serious ones. But we've got settlements on Mars and the asteroid belt and--"

And for the first time since he had stood in front of the NYU Student Building with police lights mocking him in the night, Jeff had more than a whisper of hope.

"Maybe the difference between your version of reality and the one I remember," he said, "is us."

LITTLE DIFFERENCES

Sequel to "Loose Ends". First published as a novelette in Analog, June 1998.

Dion was singing "Abraham, Martin, and John" on the radio. Jeff was making breakfast.

When Dion got to the part about Bobby, Jeff took the egg he was about to crack and threw it against the wall. Then he did the same with another. Then he took the whole box and smashed it on the floor, then stomped on it for good measure.

He was still mopping up the mess and crying when Laura walked in a few minutes later.

"Honey! What's wrong?"

Jeff shook his head, said nothing. They'd been over this before. He had to steel himself against this kind of thing. He'd never make it to 1986 if he broke down every time he heard a song about an assassination he could have stopped. But there was something about that last verse–

Laura pulled him up into her arms, kissed his neck, drew his arms around her.

"I still have egg on my hands–"

"It's ok, baby," she said. "Shhh, it's ok." She kissed him again.

"It's just that last verse." Jeff said. "I don't think 'Abraham, Martin, and John' was originally written that way – with the verse about Bobby. They just tacked it on, after he was killed. That's why his name's not in the title. It's bad enough I was here when JFK and now Martin Luther King were murdered, and I did nothing–"

"You tried with JFK," she said. She stroked his head. "It wasn't your fault."

"I tried and I failed," Jeff said. "And now Bobby. If his name wasn't in the song at first, maybe he wasn't supposed to die. Maybe I, we, were supposed to save him. And I did nada – nothing!"

"We've got to stay focused on the Challenger," Laura said.

"I know," Jeff replied.

"That's the key to all of this," she continued. "If we don't stop it from crashing into that schoolhouse in Florida and killing all of those kids..."

Jeff knew she was right. Nothing else mattered compared to changing that reality from his timeline to Laura's, from a world in which the space program died a final death to one in which just the astronauts died in the Challenger, and the space program limped along until it could take wing again in the middle of following century – the century of Jeff's birth. Still...

"It's just – this has been one lousy year, event-wise," Jeff said. He looked at the calendar on the refrigerator. It was on its last page – December, 1968. He'd be glad to pull it down and throw it in the trash with the rest of the year.

"Well, at least we'll have Apollo 8 circling the moon this Christmas, and Armstrong and Aldrin on the moon next year," Laura said.

"Yeah," Jeff said, "and Richard M. Nixon in office. He'll throttle the Apollo program barely out of its cradle, and then give the

Shuttle such poor funding that it's amazing it didn't blow up long before 1986."

"We'll just have to do something about that, then, won't we," Laura said.

Jeff hugged her, egg on his hands and all, and thought, yeah, and maybe we can still do more than that too.

***

"God, these hamburgers are gonna kill me, but I love 'em." Sam McKenna smiled across the table at Jeff, and made a motion to wipe some of the grease off of his chin.

"Part of the charm of the South Campus Cafeteria," Jeff said. "Lousy food, cold spilled coffee on your table, a good shot of getting boiling-hot coffee on your hands. But, hey, there's always a chance of picking up a juicy tidbit of conversation about another professor, maybe even about yourself, from unknowing students at a nearby table."

Sam chuckled and eyed the table next to them. "Not likely," he said, "they seem to be talking about dead Greek philosophers. I don't think any of them have tenure here."

"Well, at least we know they didn't die of South Campus hamburgers," Jeff said. "They probably aren't as bad for you as you think, anyway. There are dozens of cholesterols–"

"I don't want to hear about cholesterol," Sam said and waved Jeff off. "Let's get back to what we were talking about – the space program."

Just as well, Jeff thought. Now that he was finally in line for a tenured position himself in the Sociology Department, there was no point jeopardizing it by talking about things, even nutrition, from a future only he could know. It was enough that he was discussing the space program with Sam – the sharpest professor in the Political Science Department, and someone Jeff had become quite close to in the past year.

"I think you're way off in your concerns," Sam continued. "Politicians are crazy about space – everyone loves it. Hell, LBJ sent framed photos of the earthrise – the shot taken by Apollo 8 – to heads of state around the world, including Ho Chi Minh!"

"Johnson's out of office next week," Jeff said.

"You think Nixon's going to risk hurting the space program with the Vietnam War on his head? Scuttle the only bright thing he's got going for the American image these days?"

I know he is, Jeff thought. Not that the Democrats weren't responsible too. He'd studied Mondale's 1969 speech to Congress, to be delivered just a few months after Apollo 11. Jeff had gone over it and the entire Congressional record leading to the Challenger very carefully before he'd left – that was, what, almost six years ago now in his lifetime, before he'd come here from 2084 in the Thorne? Seemed like more than a lifetime. But he could hear the screen with Mondale's words as if they were right in front of him now. The Senator from Minnesota had been talking about the NASA proposal to go to Mars in the 1980s. *I believe it would be unconscionable*, Mondale had said in that deadening twang of his, *to embark on a project of such staggering cost when many of our citizens are malnourished, when our rivers and lakes are polluted and when our cities and rural areas are dying.* Right – but the only thing that had wound up dying had been the human exploration of space, and a possible home beyond this Earth. Yet Mondale, for all of his talk, was just a Senator then. It was Nixon as President who had delivered the crushing blow.

All that Jeff trusted himself to say to Sam was, "I think Nixon's going to surprise you about what he'll do – for the American image in Vietnam as well as in space."

"Oh, I have no illusions at all about Nixon and Vietnam," Sam said. "He says he has a plan to end the War – I'll believe it when I see it. We'll be lucky if we're out of there by the time the next Presidential election rolls around. But on space ... look, tell you what. A friend of mine at Georgetown told me Nixon already has plans to set up a taskforce, as soon as he assumes office, to map out the path for the space program post-Apollo. Surely that shows a commitment to space?"

"You're missing the point, Sam: *post*-Apollo. Why not continue it? Why not get some manned missions going to Mars?"

"So maybe he's just looking for a new name," Sam replied, "so he can distance the program from Kennedy, because missions to Mars deserve their own Greek god. Look, I'm going down to Washington for an association conference next month. Why don't you tag along? I could introduce you to my friend."

The conversation at the other table was heating up.

"The Greeks haven't done anything in two thousand years," one of the kids was saying. "Even politically, you people are the weakest country in Western Europe today."

"Papadopoulos can change that," someone with a Greek

accent replied. "He's a great man – for Greece and the world."

The first student guffawed. "Papadopoulos is a jackass – another dictator with delusions of grandeur."

Another voice with a Greek accent spoke up. "The Spiro Agnew – *he's* the greatest Greek in the world today!"

A strange feeling went through Jeff – one he'd been trying to suppress, ignore, for the past few months. But it was getting harder to give it no for an answer.

The new Vice President was known in the future for his advocacy of the space program – his almost lone-voice advocacy in the Nixon Administration. Agnew would be Chair of Nixon's Space Task Group. The one that would propose NASA missions to Mars for the 1980s. The proposals that Mondale would ridicule and Nixon would kick aside in favor of the unconscionably underfunded Space Shuttle.

But what if Agnew were in a position not only to propose, but start implementing NASA's schedule for Mars?

"I'd love to," Jeff said to Sam. "Let me just check with the board of directors at home to make sure we don't have any conflicting plans."

***

I'm just rapping with my friends, Ron...

How many times had Jeff heard Nixon say that, or something similar, in the mirror imagisms he'd seen as a kid – "the mirrorim: more pixels per byte, the retina's delight" – Nixon in stark vivid detail in new productions and copies of holoscans and videos and movies made decades or more earlier. After JFK, Nixon had been the twentieth-century president held in greatest fascination by the mid-twenty-first century. And with good reason.

I'm just rapping with my friends, Ron... Nixon to his Press Secretary, Ron Ziegler, who had come upon the President talking to a small group of anti-war protestors at the Lincoln Memorial, in the early hours of the National Day of Protest in Washington, five days after the slaughter of four students at Kent State. Except the kids at the Lincoln Memorial were neither his friends, nor was Nixon "rapping". He was barely communicating with them at all – babbling, instead, about college football scores, oblivious to their anguish.

Nixon, with little or no Secret Service protection at that Lincoln Memorial before Ziegler had arrived – accounts differed, but all agreed he had impulsively left or snuck out of the White House, bent, perhaps, on explaining himself to whatever protestors he might encounter, or maybe just wanting to spend a few minutes with Lincoln, but certainly without his usual Secret Service complement.

About as vulnerable as a president could be.

But that was still more than a year away...

"Jeff Harris?"

Jeff turned, and extended his hand. "Good to see you again, George."

George G. Landry had bushy black eyebrows and a big moustache that looked out of place to Jeff, even pasted on, but at the same time appropriate, even familiar. Then again, that's the way just about everyone had looked to Jeff since the day he'd arrived in 1963, more than 20 years earlier than his team had intended to send him, to stop the Challenger from exploding. Nothing about this world seemed in its proper place, yet it all seemed so well known – like Jeff himself, he reflected, any time he looked in the mirror. An historian's dream come to true to life – except he was the history now.

"Quite a president," George said, and looked up at Lincoln. "Don't make them like that anymore, do they."

"With the rosy vision of hindsight they all look pretty good," Jeff said.

"Well, not all," George said. "I doubt our incumbent will come out of this presidency smelling like a rose. You would agree, am I right?"

"Who are you?" Jeff hadn't intended to be so blunt with Sam's friend, who had had some very interesting things to say to them about the Space Program at lunch today. Sam had a plane to catch back to New York right after the meeting. George had asked Jeff if they'd like to resume their discussion at the Lincoln Memorial, since the April evening promised to be balmy. Jeff was delighted to agree. This was the third time Sam and he had been in Washington with George in the past few months, and Jeff was eager to find out more. But all that he knew about George and his moustache at this point is that they toiled in some murky, unnamed division of the President's "staff".

George breathed in deeply. "I can still smell the tear gas," he said, "from the October 1967 march on the Pentagon. Armies of the night. They were just kids, for crissakes. Exercising their constitutional right to assembly. Country's going to hell. And it's going to get worse."

Jeff thought about asking who he was again, but decided not to push it. Let him keep dropping these intimations of the future.

"I'm no one – at least as far as history is concerned," George said. "No rosy wisdom of hindsight in which to see me. I'm off the screen – you gotta be seen in the first place to be seen in rosy hindsight, isn't that right?"

Jeff said nothing.

"You hate this war?" George asked.

"Yeah," Jeff replied. "The bitterness it's created in this country, the fusing of Vietnam and military and space in the public mind, has poisoned the space program. I'm sure of it."

"And you're right. But you gotta hate the war itself. Do you?"

"Well, it's wrong," Jeff said. "It's unconstitutional–"

George grabbed Jeff's shoulder. "There are things in this life more important than laws and even constitutions," he said in a harsh, urgent whisper. "You better think on that, my friend, before you do what you plan to do."

Jeff stared at him, started to speak–

George interrupted again. "The Vice President is much better than Nixon on space – you were right in what you said this afternoon. But is he any better on the War? You think Agnew will get us the hell out of there any faster than Nixon?" George's voice had risen to something more painful on the ears than a whisper.

"We were just talking hypothetically," Jeff equivocated.

"I'm not going to belabor the point," George said. "And I have a dinner engagement." He made a show of looking at his watch. "So, with regrets, I'm going to have to terminate this interview. But you need to decide: Which is more important to you: Vietnam or space? And, if both are important, you'll need to think of a better way." George half smiled, nodded, then turned with a flourish and strode away.

Jeff was alone in the Lincoln Memorial. Thirteen more months to May 9, 1970, when Nixon would be here, almost alone.

Jeff breathed in the blossom air. Maybe he could smell some of the tear gas, too. He wasn't sure.

"Space!" He shouted up to Lincoln, his fist clenched, his voice ringing. "We've got to get free of this planet!"

Laura was right – that was the only damned freedom that really counted in the long run. Why couldn't this world see that?

***

Jeff was on the computer again, hands massaging the console like he was driving a car, kneading Rena's back, making love to her face with his thumbs and his palms and his lips. He strained to see what was on the screen, but he couldn't quite make it out. Words ... that didn't spell anything... They never did, this far away.

Something soft snuggled up behind him. He could feel taut nipples pressing against his neck, breasts warm upon his back. He turned. Rena ... No, Laura...

She kissed him softly on the eyelid. "Time to get up," she said. "It's way too early for man or beast, but you'll miss the bus if you don't get up now."

"Ok," Jeff said. He kissed Laura full on the lips, then leaned back, and ran his hand through her hair. "I guess I was dreaming."

Laura put her head on his chest. "Comes with the territory."

"I'm still in the future when I dream," Jeff said. "I've been cut off from it almost totally since I've been here, yet it's still in my dreams. Like a man who still feels his feet after his legs have been amputated."

"Lots of people maimed in the Vietnam War – lots of people killed," Laura said. "I don't blame you for wanting to demonstrate in Washington. I'd just feel better if I came along–"

"No," Jeff said. "I want you here."

"Then who's going to make sure you don't do something foolish? If you get yourself arrested, and the police start asking questions, looking into who you really are, where's that going to leave us?"

"That's exactly why I want you to stay back here," Jeff said. "I won't do anything crazy. I just want to ride down with the demonstrators in one of the buses, get a feeling for who they are – I can't just hang around here waiting another decade for the 1980s to come along. But if something should happen to me, it's crucial that you be out of it, safe back here in New York. You're the only one, other than me, who has any inkling of what's really going on."

Laura laughed, without joy. "We're worse than the blind leading the blind."

I'm just rapping with my friends, Ron...

"True," Jeff said, and hoisted himself out of bed. All too true. But maybe something still could be done to change that. Up until the past months, he had been thinking of his role, and Laura's, solely in terms of how they could change specific events known to have happened – JFK's and the other assassinations, the Challenger explosion. But Jeff was tired of just reacting, of trying to dis-invent the tragedies that psychos, idiots, and god knows what else had made.

Today, he would try something more direct. He had no idea how many chances he would get to influence events back here, but directly doing something, rather than attempting to prevent something, seemed a surer way of getting what he wanted.

***

The bathrooms on the Jersey Turnpike and the inside of

the bus all blended into one for Jeff. He looked at the blonde napping next to him, felt the gun in his pocket, and shivered. Easy enough to get a gun in Harlem in 1970, even for a white man. This was the world his ancestors were making for this girl. Drugs in the bloodstream, death on the street, people crowded with despair on a dirty planet with nowhere to go but down. The kids deserved more. The Earth deserved better. Could Jeff, with an act of violence which was anathema to all he had been until now – with a gun which was itself part of the illness he was trying to cure – make it all not happen? The girl opened her eyes for a moment and smiled at him... Yeah, he really believed he could.

Are ya lis'nin' Nixon? Mercifully, there was no tear gas in Washington today. Just an echo of Pete Seeger's voice, questioning Nixon in song as it wafted across the lawns, a refrain from an earlier demonstration, emanating now from a kid with a banjo. History had been right about all those earlier protest marches – Nixon hadn't listened, the politicians never did. But what did it even mean to think that history was right, when the thinker was about to change it? Jeff was determined to make this demonstration, of May 9, 1970, a little different.

He walked for hours, taking in the shifting, gathering crowds, until the light began draining from the sky. Would that the soldiers could be so easily coaxed to leave Vietnam! Would that Nixon could be made to see that he was slamming the door on the sky, bleeding it dry, with every budget cut he inflicted on the space program.

"Hey, you were sitting next to me on the bus, right?"

Jeff turned to see the blond girl, who was holding a boy's hand, a good looking guy with skin the color of coffee.

"Yes," Jeff said, and smiled at them.

"I think it's gonna go pretty good tomorrow," she said. "Reports on the radio say the crowds are huge already."

Jeff nodded.

"They're handing out cokes and pretzels over there." She pointed to a knot of people, far away.

"I'm ok," Jeff said. "You two go get something to eat. I'm going to spend a little more time here."

"Ok," she said. "You take care. Hey, I don't even know your name. You said you were a professor right? Who knows, maybe I'll take a class with you someday."

"Arthur Bremer," Jeff replied. The name just popped out of his mouth. He hadn't given it any thought – but he didn't feel good about saying Jeff Harris. Bremer seemed an appropriate name to use under these circumstances. He, or maybe someone else using his name, would take a shot at George Corley Wallace in just a few years, after having allegedly stalked Nixon.

Jeff walked faster, then slower, back and forth, edging closer to the Lincoln Memorial. Nixon was still many hours away – if the historical re-enactments were right, he wouldn't show until 4 AM – but Jeff wanted to be in position. He cursed his inability, as he had so many times, to consult any records of his history – *his* history, the future from the perspective of here, the one he used to have at his fingertips and his voice command when he lived and worked in the second half of the 21st century. He had to assume that Nixon could appear any time now. It was already dark. He'd watch for the black limousine pulling up to the steps of the Memorial.

Jeff thought again about his life, his former life, as an historian in a world that didn't exist yet – a world he had come back to change. He'd had no idea when he'd stepped into the Thorne in 2084 that he'd ever wind up at this time and this place. Just as he had no idea he'd be sucked back into 1963–

To be knocked unconscious at the airport in Dallas when he was minutes away from perhaps saving JFK. Who – what – the hell had done that to him? Didn't matter, Laura said – whoever, whatever, just rotten luck – it was an act of the universe – a universe with a stubborn streak, determined in some profound way to keep its timeline unmolested by time travelers.

But who could tell the difference between what was, and what was supposed to be?

Jeff looked around him. The Memorial steps were almost

empty. Good. Fewer witnesses.

Whatever happened, he had to do better here than he had with John F. Kennedy.

He thought back to the Kennedy-Nixon debates of 1960, also immortalized in any screen that could show anything audio-visual. Kennedy looking so cool, Nixon sweating, shifty-eyed like Mephistopheles, you wouldn't buy a used car from this guy. But neither man could have had an inkling then of the transcendent roles history had consigned for them – or the role, in Nixon's case, that Jeff had planned for him and history right now.

Jeff kept walking, around and around. Eventually he pulled out a sandwich he had acquired some time in the afternoon, a long time ago, and wolfed it down. His eyes scanned the people, the trees. For the first time since he'd been here, the trees were in the clear majority. He saw a woman walking alone. She looked like Rena. Why did so many women look like Rena to him? He had loved her and left her in 2084. And she had come looking for him in the past. And she had died in 1964.

The sky was much darker now. He looked at his watch – it was 3:25 in the morning. Nixon would be here very soon. Jeff felt his gun. It turned his stomach.

A car pulled up. A man got out. Then another.

God, it looked like Richard Nixon.

Jeff squinted – why hadn't he thought to bring binoculars?

Who was the other man? Manolo, Nixon's valet. Had to be. No Secret Service anywhere.

The two men were slowly walking up the steps.

Jeff touched his gun. He could run over to them right now. He could fire. And do what? Shoot Nixon in the back?

He felt his hand sweating on the weapon. He wondered if the wetness could ruin the firing mechanism. His breaths cut like little knives–

"Sweetheart..."

He jumped, nearly pulled out his gun and fired.

"Please." Laura put her hands on his arm. "You can't do this."

Her voice was quiet, strong, and desperate.

"I have to," Jeff said.

"No," Laura pleaded. "You're not a murderer. You're better than that. Don't let, whatever it is we're in, don't let it do that to you."

"You're wrong," Jeff insisted. "I'm the one who's doing this thing – nothing's doing anything to me!" He kept his eyes on Nixon and Manolo. They were up the steps now, inside the Memorial, under Lincoln's shadow. Jeff tried to move a little closer–

Laura was blocking his way. "You can't just kill someone – even Nixon!"

"No? Would you stop me if I had a chance to kill Hitler as a child?"

"I don't know," Laura said in quavering voice. "But Nixon's not Hitler–"

"Four students were shot dead at Kent State because of him!" Jeff said in a low growl. "He calls them 'bums'. They're just kids – they take my classes, I rode down on the bus with them. That's good enough reason for me." And Jeff was close to tears too.

"You don't know that Agnew will be any better," Laura said.

"You sound like ... ah, that's who told you about this. That's who told you I'd be here. What'd he do? Phone you? George G. Landry?"

"Doesn't matter," Laura said. "What matters is I'm not going to let you kill anybody."

Jeff shook his head and looked at the Monument. A bunch of kids were in there with Nixon already.

I'm just rapping with my friends, Ron...

"So who says I'm going to kill the son of a bitch?" Jeff rasped. "Maybe I'll just disable him so he'll have to resign. Agnew supports the Mars proposal – hell, he's Chair of the Task Force that presented it."

"You don't shoot well enough to know how to wound him," Laura said. "You're liable to kill somebody else."

"She's right, Jeff," another female voice said from behind him.

"Didn't you pay any attention at *all* in the training we received?"

"Rena–"

***

A thousand questions screamed in Jeff's skull. Rena was killed in 1964 – he'd held the damn *Daily News* with her face and the article right in his hands – how could she be here now? Was the newspaper wrong? Had Rena somehow come here first? But why? And how? Laura and he had figured out the irresistible magnet that 1963 was to time travelers ... or thought they'd figured it out.

The only thing Jeff was sure about was that this wasn't a dream, and he so glad to see Rena ... that, and his time somehow had passed to shoot Nixon. It was a subtle thing, but Jeff knew it was over.

Jeff looked at Lincoln. The entourage was still there, but Jeff felt sapped, almost drugged, his brain too overloaded with questions about Rena, with joy at seeing her again, to even pull out his gun, let alone shoot anyone.

He was a very different person, a detached part of him realized, than he had been just a few seconds ago.

Which was the more real?

Rena tugged on his arm. "Forget him, Jeff. You were meant for better things."

Laura took his other arm.

"I've got the car nearby." Jeff thought he heard Rena say. "The pickup on these 20th-century models is incredible."

The car seat felt comfortable indeed after this long day. Jeff's head felt muzzy. Rena drove, Laura gave him some tea.

He had so many questions. Had Rena come here in a Thorne? That opened up all sorts of possibilities. His Thorne had disappeared in that vandalized student lounge. Laura's had vanished a few days after her arrival, sucked back at the behest of who knew what force or command into its Artificial Worm Hole, she had told him.

Like the nothingness his brain felt it was being sucked into right now... His eyelids put up a desperate rear-guard action to stay in touch with what was happening. But they were hot pasty lead.

The last thing he heard before he gave in to sleep was Eddie and the Cruisers singing "Season in Hell" on the radio.

***

Jeff woke up the next morning, mind clearer than it had been in years.

Laura was in the kitchen making breakfast in their New York apartment.

"You drugged me last night," Jeff said.

Laura looked at him, nodded.

"Twice," Jeff said. "Once when you first grabbed my arm near the Lincoln Memorial." Jeff touched his arm with his fingertip. "I can still feel a little puncture mark here – what was it, some sort of contact needle? And then in the tea you gave me in the car. Tea's supposed to keep you awake, not put you to sleep."

Laura said nothing.

"How the hell am I supposed to trust you at all now?" Jeff barked.

Laura stared very hard at him. "You can trust me to drug you and do anything else to stop you from murdering someone – even Richard Nixon. You can count on my not letting you become the very people you despise. You risked your life and even your Challenger plans once to stop Lee Harvey Oswald. You've been miserable about not trying to stop Sirhan Sirhan. Yesterday you were this close, *this* close, from becoming one of those monsters yourself!"

Jeff looked away. "Where's Rena?" He wheeled around, saw the bathroom was open and no one was in it. He could see that the foyer and living room were empty too.

Laura took a shaky breath. "She's gone."

"What? You let her go–"

"It was what she wanted, insisted on doing," Laura said. "The Thorne only has room for one. Who else could have been the one to get in that? Your going back would cause much more of a disruption at this point – remember, in my reality, my future, in which the Challenger doesn't crash into the schoolhouse, you never returned to 2084. And as for me ... I just couldn't ... I mean, I didn't want to go and just leave you here."

Go and leave me nice and cuddly with Rena you mean, *that's* what you didn't want, a voice in Jeff said. But he said nothing aloud. Laura's reasoning was not wrong. "Why did she have to leave so soon? We could at least have talked this over."

"She wanted to get to 2084 as soon as possible," Laura said. "She was back here looking for you – one of the ads you placed in the papers a few years ago made it through to the future after all. So she knew your address. When she showed up yesterday, I knew who she was. I told her about your being in Washington, and she realized immediately what you might be up to. I guess I knew it, too, but didn't want to admit it. But as soon as Rena said it, we got on a plane, and I caught a cab to the Lincoln Memorial, and she got the car–"

"Ok, ok, I know that already," Jeff said. "Why'd you let her leave, today?" He slammed his fist on the table.

"That's what she wanted. I couldn't stop her," Laura said. "She thinks she's going to 2084, and then to 1986, to stop the Challenger." Laura put down what she was doing. "For all we know, maybe she is. What was I to tell her – don't go, don't ever get into a damn Thorne again, because, if you do, it'll bring you back to 1964, where you'll be run down by a goddamn city bus? Is that what I should have told her? Would she have listened?" Laura was sobbing.

Jeff found himself consoling her. "I guess we can't know that for sure."

"We don't know a damn thing for sure," Laura said. "Maybe we were wrong about the 1963 magnet."

"I don't think so," Jeff said. He closed his eyes, tried to picture himself standing near the Lincoln Memorial yesterday, Laura and Rena rushing to him from two different directions, bent on stopping him from doing what he was surely about to do.

"You two were like antibodies plunging towards me yesterday, set upon me by the Universe's immune system to protect the status quo. You were pulled out of New York, Rena out of the time flux. That's part of what's going on in November 1963, too – why the terminus there for time travel is so deep, so well worn. So many people going back to try to prevent the assassination of JFK. But even more, I'd bet, a lot more, being pulled into there to make sure the assassination takes place."

"That's horrible," Laura said. "Why must the status quo be JFK's death?"

Jeff shook his head. "I don't know."

"What's the status quo that the Universe is trying to protect for the Challenger?" Laura asked.

"That's a very good question," Jeff said. "It's like there's a deeper reality, a core realm of events, that nothing can change, that all forces at the Universe's disposal stand ready to protect. And all that we seem able to do is maybe push around the film a little on the surface of the pond."

"Rena had a plan," Laura said.

***

Right, but one of the twisted advantages of time travel, Jeff had learned the hard way, is that you found out right away when your plan failed – you saw its ruins staring you in the face, in the world unfolding just as you did not want it to.

Rena's plan was logical enough: Her Thorne had brought her to 1970, which led her to believe that whatever the power of the 1963 basin of attraction that had sucked Jeff back in his Thorne and its local artificial worm hole to the eve of the JFK assassination, it could not be all powerful. True enough, apparently. So Rena thought she could take her Thorne back to 2084, and tell the team what had happened. Get them to build two fleets of Thornes. Even if that took five years, a decade, it wouldn't matter to Jeff and Laura, because from their vantage point, when one of the two fleets arrived, no time would have passed. And that fleet, by virtue of its sheer numbers, should create enough attraction in 1970 to offset at least somewhat the immense power of the 1963 basin. Jeff and Laura could then each take a Thorne back to 2084, where they could live happily ever after (Jeff could hear the slight sarcasm in Rena's voice as he imagined her saying this to Laura). Meanwhile, the other fleet of Thornes would aim for 1986 – where, again, the fleet's number of time travelers would presumably offset the pull of 1963 – and the time travelers could then do in 1986 whatever was necessary to stop the Challenger explosion.

But obviously something in that reasoning was wrong. Rena hadn't been aware of Jeff's "antibody" theory for why her Thorne had come back to 1970 – she'd drawn mistaken conclusions about the strength of the 1963 basin. It was not omnipotent, true – but it took some sort of extreme crisis, like the endangering of an historically significant President like Nixon, with all kinds of horrific events still ahead, to counteract the basin's weight, to attract whatever was necessary for the job, including a time traveler such as Rena, pulled out of a spin to 1963 for a stopover in 1970. And when the job was accomplished – Jeff's rendezvous with Nixon scotched – the stopover was no longer necessary. So when Rena stepped back into the Thorne she went not where she wanted, to 2084, but to where she was originally being drawn, to 1963.

To her death.

"You see, I knew that Rena wasn't coming back, that no fleet of Thornes would ever appear, the minute you told me about her plan," Jeff said to Laura, time and again. Because Rena and the Thornes would have been there already that very morning had they ever been going to appear. The days, months, years that followed were just a redundant chorus of confirmation.

And the space program continued in its invisible decay, its fixation on the deathtrap shuttle, the road to the Challenger paved with good and not so good intentions.

"Our problem," Laura said one morning in the early Spring of 1972, "is that we have no way of telling, at this point, just when the fork occurs in our two different realities – yours in which the Challenger not only explodes but takes out a whole schoolhouse of children in Miami, mine in which it explodes just after takeoff and kills only the astronauts. Presumably the space program survives in my reality because no other people were killed in my Challenger explosion – the closest it came was a solid rocket booster, still carrying propellant, headed straight towards New Smyrna Beach after the blow-up. But the Air Force detonated the booster's destruct package by radio signal at 100,000 feet."

"Right," Jeff said.

"But you and I are both here in 1972, and this reality seems the same so far for both of us," Laura said. "It's exactly, at this point, as each of us grew up in the 21st century knowing it. So the question is, how do we know if this is my reality or yours? The answer to that affects what, if anything, we do to make sure this stays my reality, or leads to it."

"I still think the third choice of changing the political structure altogether so that Mars not the shuttle spearheads the space program is the best bet for the future," Jeff said. "But that's obvious – if apparently not possible."

"Not so obvious," Laura said. "If we try for that future, we risk losing my future, in which the shuttle is still center stage, but with just the limited explosion and consequences – and the beginning of some serious Mars exploration at last in the mid-21st century."

"I guess," Jeff admitted, grudgingly. "Not to mention that we already missed our best opportunity for getting the Mars program in motion, which would have been getting Nixon out of office, one way or another. 'I have decided today that the United States should proceed at once with the development of an entirely new type of space transportation system,'" Jeff did his impersonation of Nixon's announcement to reporters at San Clemente on January 5, adding in the shifty eyes, shaking jowls, and Nixon's patented hands-raised-above-his-head-in-a-victory-gesture for good measure. "He said he was especially pleased about the shuttle because it would make space work 'safe and routine'!"

Laura poured Jeff some tea.

"If we're stuck with the shuttle," Jeff said, "then we need to get word to NASA about the O-ring problem. But even that's a lot more complicated than it seems – the O-rings were the culprit, as far as we know, in both your and my history. But who knows, maybe there was something more at fault in yours or in mine. And there's the question of just when should we contact NASA. The plans I brought with me from the future are almost useless until 1984. If I approach someone at NASA now, and say, hey, don't give Thiokol the booster contract, you're on your way to building a Russian-roulette killing machine that will break the heart of America, I'll likely be laughed off as a crank if I'm not arrested as a terrorist."

"There were plenty of flaws in addition to the O-rings," Laura said. "The very first shuttle flight – Columbia's – lost some of its heat tiles. One of the fuel cells failed in the second flight. The astronauts' spacesuits were defective in the fifth flight – even though the contractors gave them their seal of approval. Fortunately, the crew abandoned their spacewalk because of upset stomachs – had they used the suits, they would have exploded. The engineers were dead-tired for a later flight and missed that a sensor from a fuel hose had broken off and was lodged against a valve. That little oversight, discovered by accident, could have caused the engine to blow up. The list goes on and on."

Jeff shook his head. "The wisdom of hindsight again – except we goddamn have it and still haven't a clue what to do."

"Well, maybe we should start with something a bit easier – like whom at NASA or wherever should we contact," Laura said.

"Is that really easier?" Jeff asked.

"I don't know," Laura said.

Jeff sighed. "The only one I can think of seems to have disappeared. I'll ask Sam about him again. I still think George Landry may somehow be a key to this."

***

No need to be afraid... One of the things Jeff had really loved about spending the 1960s at City College in New York was the scraggily group of kids singing Beatles songs in the Alcove behind the North Campus cafeteria. All that La Jolla, California seemed to have was this one guy, leaning up against the pastel grey building that housed the Western Coordinating Sciences Institute on Silverado, singing his song. But his falsetto gave Jeff the chills.

Jeff carefully slid a five-dollar bill under the guitar case. No sense letting it blow away in the warm ocean breeze.

"Thanks mate," the singer said.

The security guard inside looked at Jeff, then at the picture of Jeff he somehow already had a copy of on his desk, and motioned Jeff to the flight of stairs in the far left corner. The building only had two stories, and there was nothing but the pantomime guard on the ground floor, so Jeff assumed that the second floor would have what he was looking for.

It did, and more.

"Been a while, hasn't it," George G. Landry said and extended a calloused hand.

Jeff took it, and tried not to wince from the vise-like grip. "I appreciate your seeing me," Jeff replied. He didn't say "on such short notice," because it had in fact taken two months of hounding Sam to make this happen.

Landry pointed to a chair. "Make yourself comfortable," he said to Jeff. "And let's get down to business. You'd like my thinking about the space program."

Jeff nodded. The chair was indeed comfortable, but nothing else about this meeting was. The office itself looked wrong – like Landry had just put it together for this meeting. But Jeff reminded himself that although he was an historian he was certainly no expert on 20th-century office decor – certainly not what passed for it in late 20th-century California.

"I'm going to be blunt," Landry said. "You wanted this meeting; here I am; I'm going to tell it to you like it is – as some of my current colleagues like to say. You're an amateur. You don't know what you're doing. You'd be better off keeping the hell out of this."

Jeff knew better than to ask Landry who he was. He remembered Landry's non-answer at their last encounter. Nor did he ask just what this Western Coordinating Sciences Institute "coordinated" – he had a feeling he would find out soon enough. "Go on," Jeff said.

"I told you last time that you were barking up the wrong tree trying to remove Nixon on the hope that Agnew would be better for the space program. The problems with space run deeper than that. And Nixon and Agnew are both the source of other threads that need fixing."

"Some of them would have been fixed with Nixon gone," Jeff said.

"True," Landry said, "but you went about it the wrong way. You can't make history go your way by blowing away presidents – hell, you can't make history go your way by attempting to *stop* presidents from being blown away, either. You of all people should know that."

Jeff reddened. "Who the hell are you?" Now he couldn't stop himself from asking.

Landry sneered. "I'm someone who knows how to get things done in this business. We do it quietly, in little ways, when no one is watching. You know, the nail that fell off the shoe of the horse and the damn nag broke its leg and the army lost the battle and the war and the empire collapsed and all that. Except we remove the nail, or slip in a defective one – a little break-in in a hotel room, a little tip-off to a lucky security guard, that's the way you get rid of a president. Get my drift? No bullets, no bloodshed, no bullshit."

"I'm a fan of none of that," Jeff said. "But Nixon's gearing up to beat McGovern in a landslide, and still hasn't ruled out nuclear weapons in Cambodia or North Vietnam." Upset as Jeff was, he still realized that he was better off not revealing certain explicit brutal facts about the near future. Nixon's nuking of Cambodia in 1976 was the only use of nuclear weapons other than Hiroshima and Nagasaki. That secret devastating mission, no secret to Peking or Peiping or whatever it was called in the West now, had come razor close to starting a full-fledged nuclear war. Only the death of Mao that same year had sown enough confusion in China to forestall any action till the crisis had passed. "Even taking the space program out of the equation, there are a dozen reasons Nixon should be out of office," Jeff confined himself to saying.

"And I'm telling you that's exactly what's going to happen," Landry said. "Nothing we can do about the landslide, but we're on top of the nukes in Cambodia. That won't occur – I can assure you. Nixon will be preoccupied with other things. And he'll be long gone – via *legal* means – by the time the next election comes around. You'll just have to take my word for it. Watch the news next month."

"'We'?" Jeff asked.

"Never mind who we are. You and your girlfriend just stay out of our way, let us do our work. You understand?"

"What about the space program?" Jeff insisted.

"You're going about that the wrong way, too," Landry replied, tiredly. "No one's going to pay any real attention to your concerns about the shuttle's safety. You'll get through to a few intelligent engineers, they'll look into it and see what you're saying is right, but their reports will be ignored. They'll be filed away somewhere. That's the way *that* can of worms works. Too much political pressure on NASA."

"So what are you saying?" Jeff asked. "It's all hopeless? No real chance for space after all?"

George G. Landry gave Jeff a long, appraising stare that seemed to cut not only through Jeff's eyes, his brain, and his soul, but through the past nine years that Jeff had been here, years of fog in fast retreat from the sun right now.

Finally, Landry spoke. "Are you willing to do what is necessary?"

***

Jeff stepped out on the balcony of the Century Village apartment he had managed to sublet in West Palm Beach. The weather was gorgeous this Sunday – sunny and warm and just what one would expect of a late January morning in Florida. Jeff squinted at the sky, in the direction in which the Challenger would be taking off. Today would be a perfect day for the launch. Unfortunately, it wouldn't happen until Tuesday, when the weather would be cold enough to prevent the crucial expansion of the O-rings.

Jeff wished there was a way he could heat up the sky. Converge the requisite lasers over a suitable area – shunt in the sun's energy from warmer climes. But those techniques were nearly a century away from being invented. Much like Jeff himself.

But here he was. Gone from 1972 to 1986, with barely a call goodbye to Laura, via a time travel device that made the Thorne look like a Model T. Except, "don't let the glitz fool ya," Landry had advised, "the chassis may be sleeker, but the vehicle obeys the same underlying laws, the same physics of time travel, as your Thorne." Meaning it was just as subject to powerful basins of attraction. Rena's Thorne, attempting to move forward to 2084 from 1970, had been sucked back to 1963 – as had Jeff's and Laura's Thornes, traveling back from 2084 and 2094, in the first place. Those involuntary detours in time were never far from the front of Jeff's mind. "The pull of the 1963 basin is almost irresistible to vehicles traveling back from anything approaching a century or more in the future," Landry had told Jeff. So Laura and he had essentially been right in what they'd concluded in what seemed so long ago now, in 1964 – when they first had realized that perhaps their presence in the past could make a difference, and mitigate the worst of the Challenger disaster.

But the Fall of 1972 was apparently just far enough away from November 1963 that a time-travel device attempting to move forward could break free – as Rena's in 1970 apparently had not. That was Landry's theory, anyway. For Jeff, to have been drawn back to 1963 again would have been a nightmare so agonizing that he was by no means sure his sanity could have survived. But he'd held his nose, clutched his hopes, and put Landry's machine and the theory that came with it to the test. He'd been willing to do what was necessary to get this far. And here he was.

But as Jeff looked at the sky – blue as a newborn's eyes – that would soon see, hold, so much fire, so much pain – he couldn't say with certainty that he had what was necessary to finish the job.

***

"Small things," Landry had stressed, over and over, "that's the only way to get around the universe's damned resistance to time tampering. You can't do it by assassination, by preventing assassination, by causing a shuttle to blow up on television, by preventing it from blowing up. That's all beyond our reach. The most you can do is re-direct the explosion – cause it to happen a little sooner, over a different area, with a different result."

Yeah, that jibed with Jeff's experience with his great-great-grandmother Sarah in 1964. A small thing – still wonderful, hurtful, astonishing to think about. He had asked her to convey word of their brief meeting to her grandson, Jeff's grandfather, in the hope that he would in turn pass that word on to Jeff. And his great-great grandmother did, and his grandfather had, giving Jeff a tiny but irrefutable proof positive in his head that he could indeed do something in this past that could alter the future.

Small things. Landry's people had learned that two things had caused the Challenger to explode and crash into that Miami schoolhouse filled with kids in Jeff's reality – the reality that was still on cue to happen now in less than 24 hours, unless Jeff did something to prevent it.

At T plus 0.678 second – .678 of a second after takeoff photographic evidence showed a puff of first off-white then grey smoke spurting near the aft field joint of the shuttle's right rocket booster. This was the first indication that the O-rings had not slipped into place. The result would be the catastrophic explosion just after T plus 73 seconds of flight. There was nothing small about that. There was no way to stop it once the O-rings failed. And there was no way to stop the O-rings from failing. Landry had been all too right about that – every warning had gone unheeded.

But a second malfunction had caused the Challenger to veer way off course, to Miami, before the explosion. Wind shears encountered at T plus 36.990 seconds – greater than any experienced on previous shuttle flights – had defeated the adjustments of the computerized navigational equipment onboard. "The most dangerous weather phenomena affecting aviation," Ralph Nader once had written. The result would send the Challenger on its deadly course to Miami.

Landry was betting that that errant path, the result of powerful winds and impotent automated guidance, was something that human intervention at just the right moment might avoid.

A small course correction, made by a human pilot at just the right time, forewarned and forearmed. Was it small enough to escape the Universe's unblinking attention?

Small things worked. Whispers to great-great-grandmothers.

Not murders.

What Jeff still wasn't sure about was suicide.

"Jeff Harris, Western Coordinating Sciences Institute, good to meet you." Jeff extended his hand to an attractive brunette, whose press-pass fixed just above her bosom said *Cleveland Plain Dealer*. She had taken the last remaining seat next to him, at the end of a long cafeteria table.

"Mary O'Brien," she said and smiled. "Western Coordinating... I don't think I've heard of them. A new news service?"

"Sort of," Jeff replied. He sipped his tea and silently cursed the taste of styrofoam for the thousandth or more time since he'd left his century. "It's a new online service – a private operation for chief executives and other important people who have personal computers and modems."

"Online? Ah, you mean like The Source? I was talking to someone here last month who said he sends all his stories in that way – his editor has an account on the system."

"Exactly," Jeff said.

Mary nodded. "His paper got so disgusted with all the Columbia's delays that they brought him home, ruined his Florida fun. God, there were so many problems with that one that people began calling it 'Mission Impossible'. NASA was none too pleased."

"They're under a lot of pressure," Jeff said. "Hard to operate on the strangulation budget Nixon left 'em."

"Yeah," Mary said. "At least Reagan seems more gung-ho. Well, let's hope they get this one off the ground soon – those poor astronauts must have pains in all kinds of places lying out there on their butts for four hours."

Jeff didn't reply. He knew it wasn't going to happen today.

The announcement came over the loudspeakers a few minutes later, at 12:35 PM. Today's launch was cancelled – crosswinds above the runway were clocked at more than 10 feet-per-second above the highest allowable speed.

"Jeez," Mary said, and got up with dozens of other reporters from nearby tables. "Well, they're right to be careful about those wind shears, though. Brought down that Delta in Dallas last August, remember? Killed 135. And the Pan Am in New Orleans in 1982? Winds slammed into it, tossed it around like a toy. Only 9 survived that one – 153 died. I covered both those stories. One of the nice things about doing the Shuttle is we don't have to worry about those kinds of things, right?"

Jeff looked away.

"Well, good talking with you," Mary said. "Let's hope for better luck tomorrow. Maybe we'll run into each other again." She smiled.

"Sure," Jeff said, and smiled back. But he knew that wasn't going to happen, either.

***

Mission Impossible ... the press's sarcastic name for the seven-times delayed Columbia 61-C flight, the last shuttle mission before the Challenger, which indeed had finally flown a successful mission in January, though its delays had pushed back the Challenger's original launch date of December 23, 1985. That would prove to be Columbia's final mission - no space shuttle ever flew again in Jeff's reality after the Challenger crashed into the schoolhouse. He wondered if the combination of that nickname and the original TV series, or the later movies and mirrorims, had given Landry and his colleagues the idea for the plan that now was Jeff's to implement.

The plumbers and what they had done to Nixon with Watergate were after all classic *Mission Impossible*. Jeff had read up on all the pertinent new history in the several weeks that he'd been here. Impressive. He had to give Landry credit. And Landry had assured Jeff that his people would take care of all the relevant details for the Challenger.

Except, of course, the most important one.

Jeff looked in the mirror.

The use of masks to make the MI operatives look like other people had been a fundamental mechanism in all of the show's incarnations. Of course, in the early TV shows and even the first series of movies, the mask technology was more science fiction than reality. But by Jeff's time, skin weaves from DNA banks with huge varieties of features were commonplace. And Landry's technology was even better. Construction of an utterly lifelike facemask that looked like someone else was no problem at all.

Landry's team had indeed covered the other details. Jeff had studied the conversation logs of the Challenger's astronauts on this fateful day, and had memorized all of his lines. The medical records would show that the voice of the astronaut he was impersonating had had a slight cough and a sore throat on this day, and that would account for any perceived difference in voice quality. Tiny puterwafers inserted in appropriate places in Jeff's skin would generate false readings consistent with the general medical data of this astronaut. Jeff was already the same height, and the age was right. They were both about 40.

There was no way of stopping this mission. Jeff had no choice but to believe that now.

He had failed to prevent the assassination of JFK, he had

failed to kill Nixon, and he had been unable to stop this mission – the specific circumstances were different in each case, but all had hit the same unfathomable brick wall. He had spent months and months after that first meeting with Landry in La Jolla, trying in vain to get NASA, Thiokol, anyone to listen about his warnings about the O-rings. Most of his calls, his memos, his letters, never seemed to get through. And when they did, they seemed to have no effect. The Shuttle continued on its inexorable trajectory to tragedy.

In a few hours, Thiokol's engineers would recommend that the launch not proceed due to the very O-ring problem in the cold that would cause it to explode. Made no difference – the managers outvoted the engineers anyway. Jeff was certain that had he been there with a videotape of the explosion, those plumes in the sky, that burning schoolhouse in Miami, would have made no difference either. Somehow the launch would have proceeded anyway.

Small things. That was all he had left. Like being inside the Challenger, after its launch, to make a little, manual course correction so that, when those vicious winds began blowing with the O-rings gone, the Challenger would go nowhere near those kids in Miami.

Jeff had trained intensively for ten weeks. The simulation had been exactly like the inside of the Challenger, with the wind shears projected in all of their force and fury. Far too strong, and sudden, for the nav computers to handle – even if they were performing at peak efficiency, which Jeff knew was no sure thing, given the spotty record of so many other systems on the shuttles. NASA had been right to postpone the launch yesterday. And today's wind slam would be even more overwhelming – and unexpected. Microburst out of nowhere, down-draft from the base of the cloud, wind smacks the ground and comes back up like an inverted mushroom and the Challenger's hit fore and aft by headwinds and tailwinds, spun around indeed like a toy to Miami, a toy with grievous tons of explosion. But Jeff with the wisdom of hindsight – this time all too terribly clear – would know just what to do.

Landry's people would help Jeff take the pilot's place. Jeff was glad at least that one of those astronauts, fallen heroes to the rest of the 20th and the 21st century, would survive this.

But not Jeff.

He looked again in the mirror, tears in his eyes, and saw the face of Michael J. Smith.

***

Jeff waited in the bathroom. Souped-up security passes courtesy of WCSI and a mask of his own face worn over Smith's had gotten him this far.

Mike Smith, Jeff knew, was finishing his breakfast. Soon the Challenger pilot, anticipating his first trip in space, would make a quick last pit stop in the bathroom. Jeff carefully peeled off his own face so that he once again looked like Smith. As soon as the shuttle pilot entered, Jeff looking like Smith would hustle out of the bathroom and join the others in this mission. Landry's people would see to it that the real Smith was safely and quietly escorted out of the bathroom and off the premises.

Jeff heard a noise at the door and tensed.

Someone walked in. The height was right, but from what Jeff could see of the man's face, as he turned to the urinal, this was not Smith.

Jeff looked at his watch. Mike Smith should be here any minute. He hoped the man at the urinal concluded his business quickly.

The goddamn guy was humming now as he finished up. Jeez, the voice sounded familiar. Jeff tried to stay focused. He'd heard lots of voices around here as he'd checked out the place as best he could in the last few days. But something about the glimpse he'd caught of this guy's face, just a quick profile at most, was really bothering Jeff now. He'd studied photos of hundreds of NASA people who worked here, and of course of all the astronauts, but this guy seemed none of those–

The humming man flushed, rinsed his hands in the adjacent sink, and dried them. Then he turned and looked straight at Jeff, who was standing in a half-open stall near the door.

Sweet God Almighty!

"Hello," the man said. "There's no easy way for us to be introduced, so let's just leave it at here I am."

Jeff was unable to speak.

"The first thing I need you to acknowledge is that my being here shows your plan to go up in the Challenger won't happen," the man said.

Jeff could see that was true. But he also knew that some aspects of the future were nonetheless subject to change. He might still be able to get on the shuttle, sacrifice himself as planned, and then the older version of himself that he was now confronting would never have been here. "This must be very painful for you," Jeff said. "I still carry the turmoil everyday of what it was like to change my – our – memory when I met our great-great-grandmother."

"Yes," Jeff's older self said. "It's painful, though I prepared myself as best as I could for the sudden rush of memories I knew I would have when I met you. It's like I'm living this twice, for the first time." He shuddered. "Let's get out of here now, shall we?"

"If I go with you," Jeff said, "if I don't take Mike Smith's place today, then the Challenger will kill all those children in Miami, and the future of the space program too. We'll have my future, not Laura's. But that's what I've been working for these past 10 years to change. Please. You already know that. Don't destroy the last chance we have."

The older Jeff shook his head. "There's no time for me to spell it out to you now. Just come with me." He took a few steps towards Jeff, and pulled out some sort of weapon.

"Keep away!" Jeff moved a pace towards the front door. He offered a derisive smile. "I *know* you're not going to kill me with that. And if you stun me – how are you going to explain lugging Mike Smith's body around?" But Jeff knew he was on shaky around. He had to stay conscious if there was to be any chance of his making the switch with Mike Smith. He couldn't even afford a rip in his outfit which might attract attention. He looked out the door. Smith should be here any second. Jeff looked back at his older self, who was still approaching.

Jeff had to do something quickly. Now he smiled weakly at his older self, as if acquiescing, then turned on him with a ferocity he never knew he had. He smashed his older self's arm against the wall, then battered it with his fist until the weapon fell. He punched him repeatedly in the solar plexus. His older self sagged, blue-faced and breathless to the floor.

Jeff walked out and closed the door the behind him. For a moment he hoped he hadn't hurt his older self too badly, then realized how absurd that concern was: what he was about to do would eliminate his older self from existence entirely.

But how would he make the switch now? He couldn't continue waiting in the bathroom. But neither could he just burst in on the Challenger crew at breakfast with Smith still there. Where was the pilot already anyway? Why wasn't he here?

It didn't matter.

"Please come with us, Sir."

Three men suddenly were in back of him, around him, escorting him away. One had a gun to his side.

"Where are you taking me? Look–"

Jeff received a slight but firm shove in response.

"If you're with Landry, you've got the wrong person," Jeff spoke quickly. "You're here too early – I know I *look* like Mike Smith, but he isn't here yet. I'm Jeff Harris."

No reply.

Jeff savagely elbowed one of his escorts and broke free of another.

The third pointed a small, snub-nosed pistol in his face.

"Listen to me," Jeff said as slowly and deliberately now as he could, "you're making a very big mistake." He looked the man in the eye. The expression he saw was even less compromising than the barrel of the gun.

Then he felt a twinge of something in the back of his neck,

and all he saw was a swirling, darkening blur of red, brown, and black.

***

"Jeff..."

He opened his eyes to a series of faces, like a carousel of corneas being fitted to his eyes, except each showed a different frame, a different face...

Rena ... Laura ... Landry ... Jeff at 10 ... Jeff at 50 ... Jeff at 40 ... Michael Smith ... Rena ... Christa McAuliffe ... JFK ... Bobby ... Dion ... Laura ...

"Jeff..."

The spinning slowed ...

Rena ... Laura ... Landry ... Nixon ... John Lennon ...

I'm just rapping with my friends, Ron...

No need to be afraid...

And slower still...

Rena ... Laura ... Jeff at 40 ... Rena ... Laura ... Laura ... Laura ...

"Laura," Jeff said. But she looked different, older. "What's–"

"Shh, baby." She put a finger, cool, to his lips. Jeff felt tears on his cheek. He realized they were hers.

"I missed you so much," she said.

"I'm sorry," Jeff said. "I know."

"I tried to track down Landry," she said. "No way I could do it in the 70s – he and that Western Coordinating Institute left no trail. So I had to take the long way home to you – live these 13 years day by day. But I never gave up hope I would find you."

"I'm sorry, angel, so sorry," Jeff said again, and he hugged her. "What time is it?" He pulled away.

"It's 11:30," Laura said. "The Challenger lifts off in a few minutes. We'll be able to see it from here."

Jeff looked around, saw he was in the front seat of a car, passenger's side, parked along some field with shrubs. "We've got to stop them!" He moved to get out of the car. His body ached all over.

"It's too late for that," Laura said, tears in her voice as well as her eyes.

"It's *not* too late," Jeff insisted, and opened the car door. He turned back to Laura. "All we've been struggling to accomplish – limit the damage of the Challenger, save those little kids! We can't let it happen!"

Laura appeared not to hear. "I tried so hard to stop the whole flight – call it off – get the O-rings fixed. I tried so hard, so many things. But it just wasn't possible – something always seemed to get in the way." She shook her head, looked back at Jeff, put her hand on his. "But I think I may have headed off the worst."

"How?" Jeff looked at his watch. It was past 11:30 indeed. No way that either of them could stop anything having to do with the Challenger now.

"I spoke to Mike Smith years ago," Laura replied. "He thought I was crazy – this mission hadn't even been scheduled then. He wasn't even an astronaut then. But you know, I guess if you're cut out to become an astronaut, you have a sense of what science can accomplish not only now but in the future. So I told him who I was, about the Thorne, how I got here, what would happen to the Challenger one day, everything. I'm sure he still thought I was crazy – then. But he heard me out. And when the wind shear hits 37 seconds after lift-off, he'll see it on the instruments, and I think he'll remember what I told him. And he'll do what needs to be done. He'll make sure the Challenger flies far away from Miami." And she broke down into sobs and tears.

Jeff came over to her side of the car, pulled her out and into his arms. They both were crying.

"How'd you know where to find me?" Jeff asked. "I mean, Landry's people–"

"I finally managed to break through to part of Landry's operation just a few months ago. I saw some of the plans. I knew you'd be here. I knew Landry's men would be kidnapping someone – you, an astronaut, I couldn't get to that piece of the plan. But I figured I'd hire my own team, intercept Landry's, and see whom they'd taken. Maybe it would be you. And I got lucky." She touched his face. "That mask only fooled me for a moment."

Jeff touched his face too, realizing that the mask was off.

They turned in the direction of the Challenger. It was starting its liftoff.

And they looked at the sky, hands clasped, eyes singed from the smoke that would soon plume far from the Earth, far from the schoolhouse, close to the heavens.

LATE LESSONS

Sequel to "Loose Ends" and "Little Differences". First published as a novelette in Analog, October 1999.

Jeff and Laura walked hand in hand past lush Victorian vines, in the Haupt Conservatory of the New York Botanical Gardens in the Bronx.

"There's a timelessness about this place," Jeff said. Antique gardens always held a special attraction for Laura and him – perhaps because the gardens reminded them of that night long ago, in Wave Hill across from the Palisades, in the 1960s.

Laura just smiled. They entered a room with a skylight dome, slightly cloudy and cracked now with age. A keen blue sky shone through anyway.

Jeff breathed in the honeysuckle and looked at the dome. "Hard to believe it's finally up there again," he said. "They took their time."

"They had to be careful," Laura said. "The Discovery has to fly a successful mission. It was worth the 32-month wait. It'll deploy its communications satellite and come back home with its crew safe and sound. And the space program will slowly recover."

Jeff shuddered. He recalled the last launch they'd seen – the Challenger. They hadn't the heart to see this one launch in person. And they had tried to stay far away from the space program after the Challenger – let the world take its natural course, the course Laura remembered. That was the best way to get back on track in space.

"There are some terrible things coming up soon that I'd like to stop," Jeff said. "The Pan Am plane blowing up over Scotland is the worst, I think – that's due to happen right before Christmas – but I guess we have no choice but to leave well enough alone for the sake of the space program. At least 1989 looks to be a pretty good year."

"Yeah," Laura said, patting her belly and smiling. "I'd say a *very* good year." She was six weeks pregnant with Jeff's child.

"It'll be a good year to be born," Jeff said, and pulled Laura close for a gentle hug. "Berlin Wall comes down, beginning of the end for the Soviet Union. Not the greatest for space – though that should be ok now with the US program in gear again. But a good year for freedom."

"Don't be so sure about the Soviet Union," Laura said. "Andropov's a pretty tough customer."

***

"Loser," Laura shut off the television. "His voice is like – what's that numbing stuff the dentist gave me last year? – Novocain." Michael Dukakis had just been talking about the economy.

"He's the least of our problems," Jeff said, aggravated. He had just returned from a microfiche historical research session at the NYU Bobst Library.

"Don't worry, honey," Laura said and kissed him. "They'll have it all online in the next decade or two."

"Right," Jeff said. "But that's not what I'm worried about. I checked the newspapers almost day by day. Brezhnev died all right on November 10, 1982, and Andropov succeeded him. But that's it! In my timeline, Andropov dropped dead in 1984, some old guy Chernenko took over, he died in 1985, and Gorbachev came in – with glasnost, perestroika, and the end of the Cold War. It's in every book on every world history screen."

Laura shook her head. "None of that at all where I come from. The Soviet Union's still going strong a hundred years from now. They play a major role in the space program in the 21st century–"

"How could I have missed that?" Jeff barely heard her.

"I mean, I've just been assuming these past few years that Gorbachev would be in power."

"You weren't here doing the crucial time," Laura said. "Remember? You took Landry's damned device straight from 1972 to 1986."

There always was an edge in Laura's voice when she spoke of that, and Jeff couldn't blame her – he had left her alone for 14 years, living through realtime the hard way, while he had made that desperate attempt to get himself on board the Challenger. He had been willing to sacrifice his very life for the space program. Was that truly the only thing that mattered in his world?

"And after the Challenger, you were still thinking day and night about the space program," Laura said, almost reading his thoughts, like she always did. "You still think about it day and night."

"Did the Soviet Union do much damage in your 21st century?" Jeff asked.

Laura made a face. "Not so much the Soviet Union. But, yeah, a few of its client states, especially in the North Atlantic dome."

***

George G. Landry walked along the beach and squinted at the dawning sky.

"So quiet, so clear," his companion said, a woman with carbon hair and violet eyes, in her early 20s. "Hard to believe a hurricane's roaring up the coast – they say it'll hit us here on the Cape in a couple of hours."

"There's a storm roaring through the Soviet Union right now," Landry said. "Much worse than a hurricane. Human backlash... They say it could wash away everything that we've worked for."

Karina put a toe in the water. "Warm as a bath," she said. "There's nothing you can do about Moscow now. It's out of your hands. We'd better get back to the cottage and start boarding up the windows – Hurricane Bob could blast it to pieces."

"Yep, out of my hands," Landry said. "Pity you can't board up timelines as easily as windows."

"Well, you've done more than most," Karina said. She took his hand and steered him back in the direction of their little cottage on the bay. "And all of this may yet turn out your way anyway."

"Hey folks," a man called down from a cottage near theirs. "Gonna be a nasty one – I'd get out of here to a shelter if I were you. The Brewster Elementary School has one – and I believe Ocean Edge is taking people in."

"Thanks Gil," Karina shouted back. "I see you and Chris got most of your rentals boarded up already."

"Ya," Gil answered. "This one's gonna be one to remember – the hurricane of August 19, 1991."

***

Sam McKenna had aged remarkably well in the past sixteen years, Jeff thought – though not as well as Jeff had appeared to age, of course, because in fact Jeff had only aged two years, from 1986 to 1988, having travelled instantly from 1972 to 1986 courtesy of Landry and his fast track to the future.

Sam had apparently accepted Jeff and his story when he'd reappeared after the Challenger explosion – the corrected but still tragic explosion, the one that didn't veer off course and take out that schoolhouse filled with kids in Miami – because professors after all were like that, aptly known for their penchant to suddenly take a special last-minute appointment in some other part of the country, even the world, that started for a year but grew into a decade or more. At least, that's what Jeff assumed Sam believed. For all Jeff knew, Sam really thought Jeff was a madman and was just humoring him. But that was ok too.

Sam certainly always played along with Jeff as he spun out what must have seemed to Sam to be wild what-if scenarios ... What if Nixon had nuked Cambodia, what if the space program had died a total death in 1986?

Now Jeff sat on a bench with Sam in Washington Square Park – not far from where Jeff had first hustled into the past, to November 1963, all those years ago – and spoke of a new what-if, of a Soviet Union headed towards disintegration and freedom, of a dictator named Gorbachev who paradoxically used his totalitarian powers to order his society to be more open, his people to be more democratic. And of a people who thusly directed and inspired had indeed removed that totalitarian system, including its benevolent dictator, altogether.

"And this revolution proceeded without a hitch?" Sam asked. He was a political scientist, so this discussion was catnip for him.

"Well, nothing in this world proceeds without a hitch," Jeff replied. "You know that. But this one unfolds pretty smoothly – the only serious threat crops up about two and a half years from now, in the summer of 1991, when the hardliners stage a brief coup against the liberating dictator."

"Against Garbage ... chef?"

"G O R B A C H E V," Jeff spelled out the name. "Gorbachev – though, if I remember correctly, it was pronounced something like Gahr-bah-chawf."

"If you *remember correctly*?" Sam asked, and laughed.

Jeff returned the laugh. "Yeah, I really get caught up in these alternate history scenarios–"

"Right, you're a regular *Man in the High Castle*," Sam said. "You oughta write some of this stuff up. But ok – what do you see as the result of this hypothetical coup against this hypothetical self-effacing dictator?"

"In the reality I'm sketching, it fails."

"Hmm ... ok, so you have your access point," Sam said. "You remember the article I had in the *Atlantic Monthly* last year – "Other Choices"?

"Yeah..."

"Well, its thesis is that people with clear agendas and some kind of power do best not to stage a revolution themselves, but wait until a time of turmoil – when someone else has incurred the great start-up risks of getting the turmoil underway – and then strike. In fact, that's how the Bolsheviks came to power in Russia in the first place – riding on the coattails of the democratic revolution against the Czar."

"And the relevance of this to the failed coup against Gorbachev in my alternate history would be?" Jeff pressed.

"Obvious," Sam said. "If there's some sort of coup against Andropov in 1991 in our current reality, that's the time to get rid of Andropov and install Gorbachev. The Soviet Union turns out just the way you want, except a few years later."

"Right," Jeff said. "But how can we know if there'll even be a coup against Andropov?"

"We can't," Sam replied. "But I know someone who might know – Yelena Grinko. She's used to be Professor of Philosophy in Minsk – she's got the Soviet political climate down pat. She'll be in New York next month. Shall I arrange a meeting?"

Jeff nodded, and thought: the last friend of yours that you arranged for me to meet was George G. Landry.

***

"Dammit, I can barely hear you." Landry pulled the phone away from his ear, and shook it. "Damn Soviet Union – I'd have a clearer connection to Mars."

"Take it easy, honey," Karina said. "It's the Cape Cod service – full of static in the best of times." She stroked his shoulder.

Landry turned his attention back to the phone. "Yeah, that's a little better. No, I'm not in the car – we've got bad weather here, and the car phone is useless. I'm in the basement of some school. No, no point in my giving you the number – I don't know how long we'll be here–"

"Excuse me, Sir. Will you be on much longer? One of the campers needs to make a call–"

Landry started to curse–

Karina spoke over him. "He'll be off in a minute," she said, soothingly. "It's a business emergency."

"Ok," the woman said. "I'll come back in five minutes. Please have him off by then. Otherwise–"

"Absolutely," Karina said. "I promise."

"Ok," the woman said. She gave Landry a glare, then strode away.

"Nothing like a counselor who takes her campers' needs to

heart," Karina remarked.

Landry was straining to hear what was coming through the phone. "Ok, you got him, good. Right. That's good. Ok. No, no – you don't do a *thing* to him until you get the go-ahead from me."

***

"The Soviet Union is a sick country – we suffer from an illness, an illness of the spirit, that was introduced into our country more than 70 years ago. That's what you must remember when you deal with us – you are dealing with a society not in its right mind." Yelena Grinko ended her talk to a round of sustained, impressed applause.

"She's brave," Jeff said over clapping hands to Sam, who had just returned from the bathroom. "To talk like that and not be worried about retribution back home."

"She's not going back home," Sam said. "Her dream is to land a job in a philosophy department over here. That's what every Russian academic in America wants."

They left the Tisch Hall auditorium, and adjourned to Gavin's. "One thing I can say about NYU," Sam said, "the food's a lot more exotic than up at City College. Too bad Laura couldn't join us."

Jeff nodded. "But you used to love the soul food up in Harlem."

"I did, but it always laid heavy the next morning."

"You sound like my great-great-grandmother," Jeff said.

Yelena joined them a few minutes later. Sam made the introductions.

"That was a courageous speech you gave," Jeff said.

Yelena smiled over the top of her menu. "I deconstruct my country."

"I think I'll have the escargots to start," Sam told the waiter.

Yelena frowned. "I had them with Derrida in Paris last May – they gave me, how do you call it, the hives."

"Try the shrimp," Jeff said. "They're delicious."

"Yes," Yelena said, "very fresh. I had them here last time." She looked at the waiter, who took down her order, and looked at Jeff for his.

"I'll have the calamari," Jeff said, and looked back at Yelena. "So do you see any chance for improvement in your country?" Jeff asked her, as the waiter scurried away with their orders. Not a single one for a main course with a backbone, Jeff thought, for no apparent reason.

"No, I'm pessimistic," Yelena said. "Andropov is a very ruthless man – far brighter than Brezhnev. He's consolidated his power in the past seven years."

"And the stirrings in Poland? And Hungary?" Jeff asked.

"Andropov will crush them." She shattered a breadstick on the table. "Just like he did in East Germany last year."

Jeff sighed and shook his head.

"You see, Yelena," Sam said, "my friend has an idea that there's a new regime under the surface in the Soviet Union – that somehow something in your recent history went wrong to suppress it, but that maybe there'll be a chance in a few years to get it back on course."

Yelena looked puzzled, then laughed. She turned to Jeff. "Ah, you are a science fiction writer then – like Isaac Asimov! He was born in Russia, you know."

"Yeah, I know," Jeff said.

Yelena put her hand on his. "I'm only making a joke at your expense, forgive me." She smiled, then grew very serious. "But, you see, there is nothing bubbling under the surface in my country now, except for more illness. Even if there was a revolution tomorrow, no one would know what to do. My people are all quite happy being children."

"No talk at all of openness, of a new vision?" Jeff asked.

"A new openness? You mean glasnost? Shevardnadze talked about glasnost during his leadership of free Georgia in March of 1985, but..."

"Andropov ended that and had him killed that September," Sam said.

"Yes." Yelena nodded, gravely. "And I left my country then for the last time, never to return. No, the last chance we had for any freedom was maybe 1982 to 1984, before Andropov fully mastered his office. By the time poor Shevardnadze made his stand in Georgia in 1985, it was already too late."

***

"God damn you! I'm almost five months pregnant! Doesn't that mean anything to you?" Laura turned away in a fury.

"Of course it does," Jeff replied. "It's just–"

"Just what?" Laura whirled around. Her eyes were brimming with tears. "It's always something with you. You think you can change the world, perfect it to your ideals. Don't you get it yet? Haven't you learned anything in all of these years? Nothing in this insane loop of a universe we're in ever turns out the way we plan it. If were lucky, very lucky, maybe we find we're in the right place at the right time, and somehow tip the balance in our favor."

"We tipped the balance in favor of a Challenger explosion that didn't destroy the space program," Jeff said. "Actually, I tipped nothing – *you* tipped the balance–"

"That's what you wanted! That's what *we* wanted, remember?"

"Yes," Jeff said. "That's what we wanted. A world in which space exploration had some chance in the 21st century. The world you knew. The world I wanted. But what I didn't know was that that world was somehow tied to the Soviet Union continuing on into the 21st century. I didn't want *that* world – it may be too much of a price to pay."

"Maybe the Soviet Union is necessary to keep humanity in space in the 21st century and after," Laura said. "You can't know that it isn't. Maybe it is – after all, Sputnik and Gagarin and the Soviet Union started it all in the first place. And before that, Hitler and the V2s. Those origins are the same in both of our realities. Maybe space needs some kind of totalitarian hand to help push it forward."

"No." Jeff shook his head. "I can't accept that. We've got to try for something better – the best of both of our realities. A vibrant space program in the 21st century *and* a world free of sick dictatorships. You should have heard Yelena Grinko–"

"I don't care about Gringo," Laura said. "You can't just splice two different realities together like they were pieces of tape."

"I can't just leave the world like this," Jeff said.

"How do you propose to get back there? Landry's vanished, his Western Coordinating Sciences Institute's been replaced by some sort of online psychiatric center. Even if you went back in time, you don't speak a word of Russian – you'd be arrested as a spy and sent to some frozen gulag hell the minute you set foot in Moscow."

"I know. I haven't figured it all out yet. Yelena has some ideas–"

Laura stalked out of the room. Then she stalked back in.

"You want the best of both of our realities – here she is." She pulled Jeff's hand, and put it against her midsection.

Jeff kept his hand there. Then he got down on his knees, and put his ear to the same place. Amnio had told them just last week that their baby was genetically fine – at least, according to the dim lights of 20th-century science – and she was a girl.

"I love you," Jeff said softly, to Laura and the baby.

***

"I don't like conducting business this way. Strangers all around us, I feel like someone's listening to my every word, it's absurd." Landry looked fitfully around the hall.

Karina followed his gaze, stopping on a nearby couple. "That guy's hand is halfway up her shorts – they couldn't care less about our business."

"All it takes is one – one person, one act, one word at the wrong time – and what we set in motion will be as out of control as this hurricane. This place is far too public."

"The hurricane is precisely the reason we're stuck here now," Karina said.

"It wasn't here the last time," Landry said.

"Weather patterns are even less predictable than people – you say so yourself in the primer–"

"Ok folks," a voice boomed down the hall. "I think it's safe to go home now. Watch out for fallen trees and downed wires. It's a real mess out there. Bob took his toll."

Landry and Karina eventually made it to their car, and on to Route 6A.

"Jeez," Landry said, as they turned on to Ellis Landing Road. A huge locust tree was on top of the pretty yellow cottage on the corner, crushed now in the center like a piece of rotten layer cake. The road around it looked like the floor of some insane giant's barbershop, strewn with cuttings and clippings and trees pulled out from the roots.

They made their way through the debris. "Our cottage looks all right." Karina pointed to the "Sea Piper," silhouetted at the end of the road against the bay.

"So far, so good," Landry said.

But on closer inspection, the view was less promising. A thick branch had taken out their overhead phone wire, and they discovered once they were inside that their electricity was gone.

"I thought I heard someone at the school say that they were shutting off the power for this whole part of the Cape," Karina said, as they settled in and took stock, "a safety measure, until the central cables are repaired." She handed Landry a glass of wine.

He sipped slowly, said nothing.

"Well, it is romantic in a way," Karina said, lighting a hurricane lamp. "Food in the fridge will definitely be good this evening. If we don't open the door too often, most of it should still be ok in the morning."

"I'm more concerned at this point with food for thought," Landry said, scowling. "I can't command the situation if I have no information." He sat down on the couch and began fiddling with the small transistor radio he'd taken out of the bathroom. "Nothing but static and more weather gibberish about the hurricane," he grumbled.

"Well, keep trying," Karina said, and pushed over a stool so she could reach the top cabinet. "I'm pretty sure I saw another kerosene lamp up here somewhere."

"Ah, wait a minute," Landry said. "Here's something..."

"–no further word as yet on the fate of the Soviet Premier," a crackling voice on the radio intoned, "though the BBC says–"

Someone rapped sharply on the front door.

"Looks like some kids from the school," Karina said. "Maybe we left something there."

She opened the door.

She saw a fist.

But instead of hitting the door it veered towards her face–

***

Her head throbbed, her stomach ached, her eyes felt like broken glass–

She lifted herself up slowly from the floor. Across the room, a bunch of people were around Landry, slapping him around, talking angrily – in Russian. They all had their backs to her, except Landry. One had a knife.

Landry caught her eye for a second, and gave her a signal, a subtle signal, but as clear as day for her. It said: get the hell out of here.

"You idiots," Landry said loudly, perhaps to distract their guests. "You can't do anything to influence events over there by beating on me over here. Everything's already in motion–"

Karina bolted out of the door. Her only chance for escape was the beach, which stretched for miles in either direction, with houses all along the shore, at the bottom of their long flight of stairs.

But a big ugly man was standing on top of the stairs, blocking her egress, turning slowly around now to face her–

She rushed towards him, shoved him with all of her might, before he had turned fully around. She caught him off balance, and he fell, startled, backwards, down the weathered wooden stairs.

His head hit the big rock that served as the stepping stone at the foot of the stairs, making a sound like a cantaloupe that had slipped off a car seat onto the pavement. Karina stepped over the rock and the head, and ran in the direction of Orleans on the sand.

She ran and ran. The beach felt crusty under her feet, sand half baked in the sun that had prevailed after the hurricane. It was easy to run on.

She looked behind her several times. Not a soul on the beach – unless she counted the terns and the sandpipers.

Finally she saw the cottage – set off on a rise, about a quarter mile past the old Linger Longer by the Sea resort. The bleached grey cottage was their fallback place, George had said, in case anything went wrong.

She'd never been here before, but now she'd have to trust her fate to the people within. A nice couple with a little boy, as she recalled. And an old grandmother, named Sarah.

***

Three thousand miles away, two and a half years earlier, near another beach, Jeff joined Yelena for lunch at the Valencia Hotel in La Jolla.

"The fish in this restaurant are delicious," Yelena said. "Very fresh!"

"Yep," Jeff said. "We go for fresh fish in this country."

"And the vegetables," Yelena said, carefully cutting a piece of cauliflower. "So fresh, especially for the winter!"

"Well, it's never really winter in southern California, even in February."

"Yes," Yelena said. "I looked out of my window this morning and said to myself, 1989 is on its way to being a beautiful year in California."

"Your room is comfortable?" Jeff inquired.

"Oh yes," Yelena said. "The bath was hot, and the little bottle of vodka was cold – perfectly chilled! Thank you!"

"I'm glad – you can thank the Salk Institute for that." Jeff had arranged with Jonas Salk for an invitation to Yelena to come to La Jolla and give a series of lectures at his Institute. Jeff had met the creator of the first polio vaccine years ago at a AAAS Conference – and had found him, in addition to being a brilliant scientist, an equally brilliant, if unrecognized, philosopher of science. Salk's face seemed to shine like a light bulb when he talked about his theories of human survival – and Jeff saw in him, much as he did in Sam McKenna in another way, someone who perhaps was willing, and able, to understand at least a bit of the whirring paradox that was Jeff's life.

They had stayed in sporadic contact over the years. But today, Jeff was focused on another institute in La Jolla – the one that had once been the Western Coordinating Sciences Institute, that had housed George G. Landry and a time-travel machine, much sleeker than Jeff's original Thorne, that had whisked Jeff from 1972 to 1986. That had been the last Jeff had seen of any time-travel device. And the last Jeff had seen of Landry and WCSI as well.

He reminded himself that the building it had been in was now home to some kind of online psychotherapy seminar group. A small change compared to some of the other changes he had seen over time, except–

"And how did your expedition go this morning?" Yelena asked, as if she were peering into his mind.

"Odd," Jeff said. "Bizarre. Some of the people sitting at their computers were there in 1972 – they admit it! They remember Landry, but are vague on just what happened to him. They remember WCSI, but say it merged into some other organization. So what are they doing there now – what are they, specialists who come with the office building?"

Yelena laughed. "I've seen stranger things in this world, believe me!"

Not as strange as what I'm about to tell you now, Jeff thought. So far, all he had told her was that he had arranged for the Salk Institute to invite her to La Jolla, so she could be here as he tracked down Landry and WCSI, because they had some crucial relevance to the Soviet Union. No Russian could turn down an invitation like that – for that matter, few American academics would, either.

"How badly do you want things to change in the Soviet Union?" he asked her.

"Very badly. But I told you, it's hopeless now. Andropov is too strong."

"Yes, I understand that," Jeff said. "But you also said Andropov was vulnerable when he first took over – from 1982 to 1984."

"True," Yelena said. "But – forgive me – so what?"

"Don't ask too many questions just yet," Jeff said. "Just play along, ok?"

"Sure – ok – I like games."

"Do you think that, if someone had a mind to do it – if someone really wanted to, and had the connections – that someone back in 1982 to 1984 could have forced Andropov from office – could have replaced him with someone perhaps not so dictatorial?"

Yelena considered. "Yes, it is possible. Of course. But I wouldn't make a bet on it. Our system is very stable, as you know – usually death is the only sure way to get someone out of office. Of course, Khrushchev was forced to leave, and Kosygin had to move over, but that was back in the 1960s – still lots of instability then, with Stalin dead only a decade. But by the 1980s..." Yelena shrugged. "No, by the 1980s, death is likely the only way."

"That's what I was afraid of," Jeff said. "So if we really wanted to do this job – still playing along with my game – someone would have to kill Andropov, inject him with something that gave him a fatal heart attack, preferably in his first few years in office, before he'd had the chance to strengthen his central authority beyond even what Brezhnev had."

"Yes," Yelena said, clearly relishing even the hypothetical prospect of a murdered Andropov. "I would agree. And who would you select to implement this ... assassination?"

"Someone who really knew her way around back then in the Soviet Union," Jeff said. "Someone with the knowledge to appreciate the benefit that Andropov's death could bring to the Soviet Union – and the world. Someone with the courage to stand up to such a dictator. I was thinking of you."

***

Yelena's eyes widened, her lips struggling between laughter and some darker emotion. Whatever she was thinking, Jeff counted it as a good sign that she hadn't thrown down her fork and walked away.

"This isn't really a game, is it?" she asked. Now her face was just ashen.

"I'm not going to insult your intelligence and say I know you'll think this is crazy but I'm a time-traveler. You deserve better than that standard speech, and frankly, I find it boring already." Actually, Jeff had said something like that only once before – to Laura, back in 1964 – but it indeed bothered him to contemplate that declaration, the time-traveller's classic confession.

Yelena just looked at him.

"So here's what I *will* tell you," Jeff continued. "Yes, I'm a time-traveller. Yes, the science is possible – that's how I'm here. But there's nothing crazy about it – paradoxical, oh yes, paradoxical, more than enough self-defeating loops to make you crazy, that's for sure – but on its own terms it's quite logical. You can go back in the past and change events. It's not easy, but it can be done. I know that, because I've been there and done that. I spoke once to my great-great-grandmother, and she relayed a message about that to my grandfather – when he was just a little boy on Cape Cod – and he relayed it to me, *after* I'd travelled back in time, and already lived through part of a life in which he hadn't said anything like that to me the first time. And I've also changed a larger event – a much larger event. Or helped to change it. The universe puts up a lot of resistance to these things, and..." Jeff became aware that Yelena had yet to say a word in response. "Is any of this getting through to you? I mean, I know English isn't your native language, and–"

"I assure you, I'm understanding every word of it," Yelena said. "I read H. G. Wells, I read Dr. Isaac Asimov, I read Mr. Robert Heinlein. Most of their works aren't available in the Soviet Union – but I have read every one since I've been in the West. So I know about time travel. We Russians know a lot of things – don't let your propaganda fool you. In some things, we know more than you."

"Ok," Jeff said.

"So. You want me to go back in time and kill Andropov. For me, the thought of my killing someone – anyone – is far more crazy than going back in time. What would you have me do? Shoot him in the head? Put poison in his tea? You said inject him – how would I get close enough to him to do that? I'm not a doctor. I'm not a murderer. But somehow, I don't think the problem will even arise. Obviously this George Landry and his coordinating group have something to do with your time machine, but you say neither of them are anywhere to be found. So how could anyone even get back to 1982 from here?"

Jeff smiled. "Music is my guide."

"What?"

"I was a professor of popular culture in the 21st century, and cultural history of the late 20th is my specialty," Jeff said. "I know the music from the current period – when each hit record was released – like the back of my hand."

"I love rock 'n' roll music," Yelena said.

Jeff nodded. "When I first came here in 1972 – to see George G. Landry – there was a guitarist sitting in front of the building Landry was in, singing a song by John Lennon. No big deal about that. Except for one thing: the song was 'Real Love,' not released by the Beatles until 15 years after Lennon's death, in 1995."

"And your point is?"

"My point is that there obviously was some cultural contamination from 1995 in 1972 – which means there had to have been some backwards contact in time. In fact, I'd guess that there have been time machines cutting this way and that way in time, touching just about every year, emanating from that building in which the Western Coordinating Sciences Institute was located, for years. Think about it. It was *once* a time travel facility – but there's no such thing as just 'once' when it comes to time travel. If the building housed a device that went, say, from 1972 to 1995, then that same building housed a time travel device, for however short a time, in 1995 – regardless of what other purpose the building may have served then. My guess is that if we staked out – kept an eye on – that building long enough, sooner or later a time machine would appear right before our eyes. I could probably arrange for a more permanent appointment for you somewhere out here in La Jolla. Perhaps at the University of Southern California–"

"You want us to watch that building for six years, until 1995?"

"My guess is we'll find a time machine there much sooner than that–"

"Forget it," Yelena said. "It's still impossible that I would go back in time and kill Andropov. Like I told you, I'm not a murderer."

***

Sam McKenna was at Laura's door, humming a Beatles song.

She let him in, then gave him a long hug. The two had grown very close during Jeff's 1972-1986 leave of absence in time.

"He'll be back soon," Sam said, taking off his winter coat. "It won't be like last time."

"I don't know," Laura said. She took the coat and put it in the closet. She liked the piney smell of it.

Sam closed his eyes and hummed the Beatles' refrain again.

"You love that line, don't you?" Laura asked.

"Not so much the line, but the word – 'awoken' – and the D minor 7th chord swelling restlessly underneath it," Sam said. "C, D minor 7, G is a very common progression, really. But in John Lennon's voice it's magic."

"Jeff loves it too," Laura said. "All of Lennon's music. It crushed a piece of his heart when Lennon was killed."

"As it did us all."

"We heard an advance cut from the Travelling Wilburys album last month," Laura said, finally showing Sam to a seat and fetching him his customary ginger beer. "It made us cry."

"Wilburys?"

"Yeah," Laura said. "A temporary, studio superstar group. Bob Dylan, George Harrison, Roy Orbison, Jeff Lynn, and Tom Petty – extraordinary sound. Spanning the 50s to the present."

Sam sipped his soda.

"Jeff said the group was unreal," Laura continued. "It existed, in a manner of sorts, in our world. But it was really a glimmer, a bleed-through, of something else entirely, from an alternate universe."

Sam smiled. "I think we should have another talk."

***

Felice Montag met Jeff and Yelena at the evening door of the pastel grey building on Silverado in La Jolla. She frowned. "I was hoping you wouldn't come."

"That's the thanks I get for helping you unravel that packet-switching problem, huh," Jeff said, with a smile. The primal plan – the very first of so many plans he had been working through for so many years – had been for Jeff to have arrived a few months before the Challenger explosion in 1986. He had thus been trained in 2084 to be thoroughly adept at personal computer technology in the 1980s – no telling when and how that might come in handy. It of course had been no use to him at all when his Thorne had unexpectedly landed back in 1963. But here in 1989, in an early online scholarly network centered in this building in La Jolla, Jeff's antique computer savvy had been just the thing to ingratiate himself with a harried programmer over her head in too many packets of traffic and too few lines to handle it.

"Well, yeah, you did save my butt yesterday, and I really appreciate it, and that's why I'm here." Felice ushered Jeff and Yelena in, looked out and around the parking lot to make sure no one was watching, and closed the heavy door sharply behind her. "All right. The deal is I take you upstairs, you've got 30 minutes to look around and your photographer takes any pictures she wants, and then we're all three of us out here. And let's hope this is my one and only excursion into industrial espionage."

Jeff had worked with Landry and his colleagues back in 1972 on the first floor of this building – the same floor that Felice and her people now occupied, and which Jeff had visited three times since he'd arrived a few weeks ago in La Jolla, including the propitious occasion when he'd overheard Felice cursing at her computer and he'd offered his helpful suggestions. The second floor, however, was the one he wanted to carefully inspect. This was the one he had seen just twice in 1972: once when he'd first talked here to Landry, one more time when he'd entered the neo-Thorne for the instant temporal elevator to 1986. This was the upstairs to which Felice now took Yelena and Jeff. "So I'll see you downstairs in half an hour," Felice said, and left.

The layout was, unsurprisingly, nothing like what it had once been. Landry's office and the section behind it that had housed the time-travel device were simply gone – dissolved now into rows of primitive 286-computers, each attended by a chair upon which someone could sit and address the computer from the front, and a modem with a phone jack through which the computer could talk to the rest of the world from the back. That world was already in the first stages of the revolution that would let people do all of this from their homes and places of business, soon from their pockets and palms and earlobes, but this current world still clung, even at this late date, to the penny-arcade amusement-parlor set-up that harkened back to Edison and his kinetoscopes. Old ways of doing things died hard, like the heartbeat of recalcitrant history itself, which Jeff always seemed to be trying so desperately to alter.

"You see anything here which looks promising to your needs?" Yelena asked, snapping photograph after photograph.

"No," Jeff said. "But there has to be some place for it here – some place for an artificial wormhole to open up and disgorge its vehicle without smashing all of these shiny antiques."

"Antiques? Hah! In my country, these pretty toys would be – how do you call it? – the cat's meow!"

"Well, let's see what this monocular cat looks like with a little electricity in its eye." Jeff sat next to a terminal and pressed its power switch. The beast grunted and gargled and eventually put up a C prompt on its blue-green screen. "Right," Jeff said to himself, "this would be just before Windows made its grand entrance."

He pulled a 3 and 1/2 inch disk from his polo shirt and inserted it in the lower drive. The disk was thoroughly compatible with the 1.44 mb capacity of the drive, but thanks to a special algorithm – with which it had been formatted back in 2084 – it could hold a million times that data. The key was that the disk always looked to the 286 write-head as if it was empty, and thus could be written to with more data. Jeff was sure that this mirage feature would be more than enough to capture all the text on any medieval network this knight in glittering armor might be connected to. The puterwafer back in his hotel room could easily search the download for any relevant information, then decompress and display it for him.

But that was not the disk's most impressive feature: it was also intelligent enough to read 20th-century encryption systems as if they were block letters on a kindergarten blackboard. If Jeff was right that this building still served as a port for Landry's time machine – and this seemed more than likely, given that Thornes and their descendants, as far as Jeff knew, traversed time not space – then these computers and their networks might well bear some trace, some notation, of the time-travel operation. Jeff doubted that these information machines, creaky as they seemed on the surface, served no part in Landry's schemes. It wasn't like Landry to lavish his time on thoroughly useless window-dressing.

Soon the intelligent agent in Jeff's disk was in every corner of this primordial virtual universe, cracking codes it encountered like eggshells, transforming the data regardless of its size into superslick packets that were downloaded in just minutes on these arthritic 2400 bps modems. Jeff was assuming that Landry had used 20th-century codes for encryption – Jeff was betting that Landry wouldn't have risked calling attention to himself by use of a code that wasn't of this century. "Camouflage in contemporary culture is your best defense," Landry had advised before Jeff's departure to 1986.

"Okeydokey, all done," Yelena said.

"Good, same here." Jeff removed his disk from the computer. If he was lucky enough to find in the data some schematic of this floor that indicated where the neo-Thorne materialized, Yelena's photographs might provide additional essential details.

"Let's go," Jeff said. They were back on the ground floor, thanks and goodbyes to Felice, with ten minutes to spare.

They had their answer – or part of it – two hours later.

Yelena was on the couch, half asleep, a glass of wine in her hand and a lock of blond hair over her eye. Jeff was at his puterwafer, soft as a bar of chocolate, a tenth of a kilogram – but, as the advertisements said from where he came from, the human brain itself was only a kilogram, and look at all that *that* had done.

"Damn it!" Jeff exclaimed.

"No results from your search?" Yelena asked, groggily.

"No, I have a result. I found part of the schedule. There was an arrival here this past December. None in 1989. Goddamnit – I *knew* I should have gotten on this sooner."

"Ok," Yelena said. "But that's progress–"

"No, wait. I was searching for arrivals. Let me try this a different way. Let's see ... Departures ... They're just as good as arrivals – a departure means a machine will be on hand. Ok. What's this?"

"What?" Yelena asked.

"There's a departure scheduled for mid-March – just two weeks and five days from now–"

"But–"

"One of us – I hope you – is going to take that machine back to November 1982, or sometime right after, at the beginning of Andropov's reign," Jeff said.

"Listen," Yelena said, now fully awake. "I haven't agreed to anything. I told you. I'm 38 years old – too old to become some kind of hitman in time. I don't even know yet if I entirely believe you. But let's say I did. If what you're saying is true about time travel, and how it can change yesterdays, how can you even think about just kidnapping a time machine and keeping it from its original mission? For all we know, the only reason that you and I are here talking right now in America is because of something that the original mission made possible in the past. Fooling around with just history is bad enough. Fooling around with the history of *time travel* – the history that *makes* the rest of history, if there is such a thing – is just insane."

   ***

"Communism," Sarah Harris said. "After what the Czar did – pogroms, *gutenyu*, you shouldn't know from such things! – I don't worry about Communism. Anything is better than the Czar!"

Karina drank a cup of tea, lemon and sugar, with hands that still quivered.

"Would you like a sandwich?" Sarah started to open a package of rye bread. "You look hungry."

"No, please, Mrs. Harris. You've done enough just letting me into your cottage for a few minutes to rest. You need the food for your family."

"There's more than enough to go around!" Sarah said. "Yitzhak – my son – and his wife Marilyn and my granddaughter Rachel are stuck in Hyannis because of the hurricane. It's just me and Eli, my grandson, here. How much can a five year old eat? And I'm a 96-year-old lady – how much can *I* eat, I ask you? Please! I insist! Have a little something!"

"I eat a lot, grandma," Eli piped up. "Mommy says I eat a horse!"

Sarah laughed. "Eat *like* a horse, *tatteleh*. Anyhow – in my country, in Russia in the old days – a loaf of bread would last for a week! Even when I first came to this country, to Ah-mer-ica, for a penny I could buy a roll, for another penny a piece of herring, and eat like a queen!" She kissed her fingertips in a gesture that said how good it all was.

"Ok." Karina relented. She was very hungry, another few

minutes couldn't do any harm. She had covered her tracks very carefully from the beach to here. The texture of the sand had made it easy. She had seen no sign on anyone in pursuit... The thought that she might be attracting Landry's attackers to this unprotected, very old woman, not to mention the little boy, was too awful to even contemplate. She'd just wolf down the food, for strength, and leave–

"Here you go." Sarah gave her a plate with a sandwich. It was delicious – smoked white fish with some sort of old-fashioned potato salad.

"It's wonderful," Karina said. "Very fresh!"

Sarah smiled, and placed another cup of tea right next to the plate.

Karina noticed that although Sarah's hands shook, they had an underlying strength – like an aged willow trembling in the wind, with taproots that reached to the center of the Earth.

"That rain was really something today," Sarah said, as if she was on the same weather wavelength as Karina.

"Yes, it was. But I guess I'm used to it."

"You don't come from this part of the country," Sarah said.

"Well," Karina began, then thought the better of it and bit again into her sandwich.

"You come from Russia, no?" Sarah asked.

"Is it that obvious?" Karina asked. She thought she had her American accent down cold. "I mean, lots of Americans use the name Karina."

"To me, anything Russian is obvious," Sarah said. "I lived there when I was a little girl, for the first ten years of my life."

"I didn't spend that much longer there," Karina said. "My mother was Russian – but she also spent lots of time in America–"

"Was she a spy?" Eli asked, scooting out of the bedroom on a tricycle.

"Eli!" Sarah exclaimed, with just the right mixture of remonstration and pleasure.

"Yes, she was," Karina replied, in a hoarse, mock-conspiratorial whisper. "And she spied on many things."

"And your father?" Eli asked. "Was he a spy too?"

"Well, I don't know," Karina said, slowly. "I never knew my father."

"Ok, Eli, let's play with that puzzle," Sarah interrupted whatever Eli was about to say. He ran off to get the puzzle box.

"I'm sorry–" Sarah began.

"It's ok," Karina said, and smiled. "He seems like a very bright little boy – I love intelligent children."

Sarah beamed. "Eli is a *mitzvah* – a blessing – I don't have to tell you that. Marilyn is Yitzhak's second wife. His first wife – what's the use of talking – the doctors *killed* her, and it was supposed to be just a simple operation. Then, thank God, Marilyn came along. Yitzhak started his family late in life. But now they have Eli and Rachel."

"He's a beautiful boy," Karina said. She touched her mouth with a napkin and stood up. "I'm feeling much better now – your tea and sandwich and conversation were the perfect restorative."

"You're not leaving so soon? Not in this weather," Sarah protested.

"The hurricane's over – I'll be fine."

"No, I insist–"

"No, Mrs. Harris, *I* insist this time. You've been very kind. But I have to leave now." I can't jeopardize your family a moment longer, she thought.

Sarah held up her hands in an exaggerated motion of frustration. "All right," she finally said. "But let me give you a little something before you leave."

"Ok." Karina could see there was no point in arguing about this. "Can I just use the bathroom before I leave?"

"Of course!" Sarah pointed her in the right direction.

The package Sarah gave to Karina as she left contained another white fish sandwich. "Please. I insist. Give this to George."

Karina nodded and squeezed Sarah's hand.

There were tears in her eyes as she walked swiftly away on

the beach – but in a direction not towards but further away from George's house.

He was most likely dead. Just like the vile Soviet Premier whose death had been announced on the radio when she'd first entered the cottage of Sarah Harris. But Karina took no joy in that: his successors would be indescribably worse, with George unavailable to pull the strings. The future of that part of the world would make the hurricane seem, as Sarah might say, like a spritz on the beach.

And what of herself?

Her greatest vulnerability lay in the 20-minute walk on the beach ahead to Orleans. Her footprints wouldn't last, but she would be plain as day, likely the only person on this part of the long empty beach after the hurricane.

If she could just make it there now, and the buses were running after the storm, the money in her wallet would get her to Logan Airport in Boston. There she could use a credit card to book the next flight to La Jolla.

There was nothing more she could do here in this August of 1991, except die at the hands of Landry's executioners. Her only chance was in the past.

**

"I've been wracking my brains, and I've come up with two possibly pivotal events at the end of March." Jeff was on the phone with Laura. He yearned to see her face – the nuance of her lips, the catch of her eyes. A conversation like this without the benefit of sight to guide him was maddening. He could never get used to the lack of phone screens in this century. "I want to be as sure as we can be this time that something I do doesn't inadvertently flip my history into yours, or yours into mine, or wipe them both out – so let's check our recollections of history for March and see if they coincide."

"I'm listening," Laura said, tiredly. "I'm not sure I remember anything *specifically* happening in March 1989 anyway, but go ahead."

"Ok. Bear with me. Both events are very well known. I

wouldn't dare interfere with a time-travel arrival right before either of them, but I don't see how a time-travel *departure* – away from this time, right after this time – prevented by me, could affect these events. One is the Exxon Valdez – which spills eleven million gallons of crude oil off the Alaska coast on March 24."

"Right," Laura said. "That's in my history too. Serves as a high water – or oil – mark of the danger that fossil fuel can pose to the environment."

"Good," Jeff said. "So we're ok on that one. The other event is Fleischmann and Pons–"

"Who?"

"Drs. Martin Fleischmann and Stanley Pons – they announce the first evidence of cold fusion at the University of Utah on March 23. I remembered that date as soon as I pegged the Exxon Valdez. The two dates are a classic in techno-cultural history – the solution to fossil fuel pollution unveiled but one day before the most publicized incident of pollution in the century. Every school kid knows it. There's a famous *Analog Magazine* article about that coincidence by Mallove that everyone reads in the 7th grade–"

"Never heard of it," Laura said.

"Never heard of what – *Analog Magazine*?"

"Of course I've heard of *Analog*," Laura said. "But Fleischmann and Pons mean nothing to me."

"How about cold fusion?"

"Nope," Laura replied.

"So what do people do for energy in your version of the 21st century?" Jeff asked.

"Pretty much the same as in the century we're in right now," Laura said. "Fossil fuel. Some solar. A little fission and fusion here and there – but fission's frowned upon because it's deemed too dangerous, and fusion rarely makes sense economically."

Jeff shook his head, then realized Laura couldn't see it. "So let me get this straight," he said. "In my reality, the Challenger takes out a schoolhouse and the space program along with it. But the Soviet Union starts collapsing at the end of that same decade, and a universal, low-cost, safe and reliable fuel is discovered. In your reality, the Challenger tragedy is more limited, but the Soviet Union continues, and the world is still smarting from all the soot in the air?"

"Sort of adds up, doesn't it," Laura said. "In my reality, the Earth is more irritating, more inhospitable – politically as well as physically – so there's more of a motive to get off of this planet and out into space."

"I'm not sure I like your reality so much anymore," Jeff said.

"Well, I guess you should have thought of that before you nearly sacrificed your life to alter the course of the Challenger," Laura said.

Jeff sighed. "There's got to be a way to get the desirable elements of both."

"Maybe. Maybe not," Laura said. "You're trying for an alchemy of time – to create the perfect world, the golden age, out of the two different timelines each of us has. But we don't know if that can be done – we don't even really know what the elements, the building blocks, of these realities are. So, if anything, we're worse off than the alchemists. Maybe we should just leave well enough be now–"

"No! We've been over that already."

"Just listen to me for a minute," Laura said. "We've already changed the Challenger part from your reality to mine. So, when you're born in the 21st century, the Challenger will never have reached Miami. You'll be a different person in that century – with no motivation to come back and alter time. And yet you're here right now, talking to me on this phone. That means that you – the person you are now – has survived our tampering with time. And I'm here with you in this time. And we have our baby – you've already felt her inside me. Soon you'll be able to hold her. Can't we just have that? Haven't we earned the right to enjoy our lives now? Sam says that–"

"I don't give a damn what Sam says – this is none of his business!"

Laura was sobbing.

"Angel, I'm sorry," Jeff said. "You know I love you. I'm going to try very hard not to be the one to go back–"

Laura hung up the phone with a slam.

The emptiness rang in his ear.

He thought of nothing for a few minutes.

But his mind edged, of its own accord, towards images of Laura. He could see her sitting in the back of his classroom in City College, on that very first day in 1964, with him stranded in the past after the Thorne had pulled him back way too far.

He called her back. "Ok," he said. "I promise you it won't be me – I'll figure out a way, I'll make sure it's Yelena or someone else who goes back. Let's talk about names for the baby."

***

Karina slipped into an air-conditioned cab at the San Diego Airport. "I'm going to La Jolla."

The driver turned around and gave her a smile through his big moustache. "You'll be right at home there, Senorita."

"What makes you say that?"

"La Jolla's filled with beautiful, narrow-bodied women like yourself."

"Why thank you." Karina smiled. She enjoyed the compliment, as well as the great way the cabbie pronounced La Jolla, with the guttural 'ch'.

She leaned back and closed her eyes. She figured she was safe now – or, at least, as safe as she could be, given the ever-present inherent dangers of travel in the past. Sometimes she wished she could be like other people – recline on a beach somewhere in La Jolla, thong bikini riding up her backside, ogled by decent, uncomplicated men like this cab driver. But that was not her lot in this universe.

The cab pulled into La Jolla. Its streets were quiet in the dusk, much as she remembered them, muted pinks and ochres, stucco gateways to other worlds. "When you get to California, you're at the end of the world," she recalled her mother once saying. "The only way further is up." That was true enough. California represented the end of expansion ever westward – to go any further in a conventional way was only to go back east, back to the Far East, back perhaps to some of the very origins of humanity.

Yes, space – outer space – was one way out. Some people thought that outer space was what everything was really all about. She had never been in outer space. But she was adept at traveling through inner space – the space between years – the liftoff into time.

"We're on Silverado Street, Senorita. Tell me where."

She pointed to the pastel grey building, and paid for her ride.

She looked for the guy singing John Lennon songs. He had been here the last time. *It really is*, he had sang. Yeah, it really was – but what was it? Not John Lennon – he was gone, and she was pretty sure no one could save him. His death in prime time – in original time – had left too many markers. Just like JFK's. You could only change secondary things, shadows on the Platonic wall, without major damage to history, if you could change them at all. Of course, the trick was telling which was the shadow, and which the wall.

She knew just which nondescript place on the door to place her palm upon. A minuscule scanner recognized her print. A bolt slid open. She looked around to make sure no one was watching. She quickly entered.

The inside seemed empty of people, too. She hurried up to the second floor. She knew just how to elicit the time machine from its hiding place.

Its destination was already set. She pondered for a few moments. It would take her hours to recalibrate for a different arrival date – those settings were a complicated business. And she might do damage by arriving somewhere – some year – she was not supposed to be. On the other hand, if the destination on this machine was already set, she might be stealing someone else's ride. Whose? George Landry's? That could be a blessing, at least for him, if it kept him from being killed on Cape Cod.

Her head throbbed. "Don't get too close to the contemplation of paradox – therein lies the path to complete paralysis," George himself had always said. She thought again about George in that room, in that chair, in their cottage on the bay. She thought about that knife at his neck. "Everything's already in motion."

She wiped a tear from her eye, and started the sequence. Her arrival date would be in December, 1988, specific day and time variable, to be decided by the machine and its scan to make sure there were no witnesses to its materialization.

***

"So what are we going to do if this key created by your computer doesn't work?" Yelena asked.

"No problem," Jeff replied. "In that case, I'd invite Felice out to dinner. Talk her into coming back to my hotel room for a little drink. Slip her a Mickey Finn – that's the name for that here, isn't it? – and while she was in dreamland, I'd duplicate the key. Easy as a A,B,C."

"You have lots of confidence."

"Yes."

"Who was Michael Finn? A Mark Twain man?"

"Huh? No – Mickey Finn is an it not a who." Jeff laughed. "It's a drink with, you know, a sleeping pill mixed in – I thought the usage was appropriate to this decade. Or maybe it is, but you don't know it because you're Russian. You're a confusing person to be around in these kinds of circumstances."

Yelena smiled. "You seem like a nice man. Would you really do that – knock a girl out with a drink just to get a copy of her key? It's hard to tell when you're joking."

Oh, I'd do much more than that, Jeff thought. I was this close – *this* close, he pressed his index finger against his thumb – to killing Richard Nixon. As Laura never tires of reminding me.

They reached the evening door on Silverado. No one was around. Jeff slipped in the key. Among the informational assets his intelligent agent had brought back from Landry's net was a diagrammatic of this building's security system, including this door. That information, fed into his puterwafer and its key-making module, had produced this little celluline key.

Which worked. The bolt slid open. Too bad, a libidinous part of his brain noted. Felice in his bed in his hotel room after she awoke was by no means the worst scenario in the world.

"Let's get upstairs," he said.

"Looks the same as last time," Yelena said, gesturing to the rows of 286-computers as the two walked into the room on the second floor.

"Yeah," Jeff said. It was one week prior to the departure date that Jeff had discovered on the downloaded schedule. "There are only two possibilities here, assuming the schedule is right. One, the time machine is already here, camouflaged in some way. Two, if it's not here now, it has to get here some way in the next seven days, so it can be here one week from now for the departure. Its likely arrival time in that case would be in the evening, or on Sunday, when no one was around."

But the room indeed looked the same as last time, which meant there was no sign of the time machine that Jeff could see. Yelena's photographs had come up empty in that regard too.

They stayed the night, but saw nothing. They went through the same routine for the rest of the week – up all night in the computer room, grabbing what sleep they could during the day in their hotel rooms – with the same lack of results.

"Pray it shows up tonight or tomorrow," Jeff said wearily on the Saturday night before the Sunday departure date. "If not, there's something very wrong in our calculations."

"Ok," Yelena said. "But remember, I make no promises–"

"Yep, got that. I understand." But Jeff thought to himself: She makes no promises, but she's not accompanying me on this night after night because she's not intrigued on some level about the time-travel possibility. Take my hand, I'm a stranger in paradox. More than intrigued. Likely consumed – as Jeff had been, back in the 2080s, when he'd first been drawn into this, into that cool orange continuum of a control room. The sherbet room, Rena had always called it.

"Jeff!" Yelena whispered sharply.

He focused his eyes on the present, on this room with its ancient computers before him, and saw someone walk in on the far side. He hadn't even realized that line in the wall was a door.

It was Landry!

Yelena looked at Landry, her eyes wide open. Those eyes suddenly looked a tiny bit familiar – this was the first time Jeff had seen her with that expression. He put his index finger up to his lips and caught her attention to indicate silence.

Landry did something with one of the computers that seemed to turn the others on. Of course, they were networked – Jeff knew that already. He had searched and searched for some indication of a time machine in all of these computers, individual and networked, and had found nothing. Not even a hint of a digital temporal manipulation imprint.

All of these 286s – there were more than 20 of them – functioning as one integrated, mutually catalytic, self-augmenting unit could be powerful indeed. But if Landry had a tiny amplifier in his hand that made their combined computing power exponential, rather than additive or even multiplicative, the resulting capacity would be truly extraordinary. There were already exponential combiners you could hold in your hand in Jeff's time. Landry no doubt had access to much more.

But extraordinary capacity for exactly what? Surely not enough to haul a person through time. All the computing power in the world could not in itself create an artificial wormhole like the Thorne.

Landry pulled something out his pocket. It looked vaguely like Jeff's puterwafer, except even thinner, more sharply delineated, smoother. Landry waved it around, like a magic wand. Obviously, it was communicating in some way with the 286 network, operating in tandem with it.

Jeff realized that his intelligent agent and his puterwafer, for all of their sophistication, had done little more than capture what was on this network, hold its shimmering information in their digital shells. Landry's wand was interacting with it and commanding it. The screens of the 286s pulsed in synch with his swaying hand, their innards seeming almost to hum in accompaniment.

And out of this electronic procreation something indeed took shape. At first, Jeff wasn't quite sure what he was seeing – he'd never

seen a time-travel machine from this end, on the outside looking in, neither his Thorne nor Landry's fancy drive, in his two previous journeys.

It came like something out of the rain. A shiny new car fast approaching in a blinding grey-white storm, a sleek silent helicopter in a hurricane. Except the glimmer had nothing to do with water.

Where had Landry been keeping it? Surely these computers, powerful as they now no doubt were in exponential synergy, had not just created this machine on the spot out of atoms in the air.

No, of course not. The answer was obvious.

Landry must have had this machine – and perhaps others like it – not someplace else, but some*time* else. In another month, another year, who knows, another century – in this place – to be called back to this time, or whatever time Landry was in, by a remote command generated by this computer network now in amplified exponential gear. A signal would be intrinsically easier to send through time than an object. Light, electricity, whatever the format of the information, weighed nothing.

Jeff's original Thorne, as far as he knew, had no such automatic feature – it required a human pilot to make it work. But Landry's machine was far more than a Thorne.

Jeff became aware of Yelena squeezing his hand.

Landry was approaching the machine – clearly the same sleek module Jeff had taken from 1972 in 1986, in this very place.

Time to find if Jeff could put a new little rewind into time.

"Hello George."

Landry wheeled around, startled. "Who the hell are you?"

***

"Don't tell me you don't know who I am," Jeff said.

"I don't, but if that's what you want, ok, I won't." Landry looked at the small stun weapon Jeff was pointing at him. "I certainly know exactly what *that* is, though, if it makes you happy."

"Well, that's something." The truth was that Jeff's little stun-gun, which he'd brought along in his suitcase from the future in his unintended trip back to the 1960s, had never worked back here. Jeff had tried it on a squirrel or two in the park, even on the neighbor's cat once, to no avail. Fortunately, Landry didn't know that.

"So, I gather you're not from around here originally," Landry said, still looking at the weapon.

"You really *don't* know who I am, do you?" Jeff asked. Landry might have looked a little younger than Jeff remembered, and so for Landry this experience might well be happening prior to what Jeff thought was their first meeting – in Washington, in 1969 – but Jeff couldn't be sure. He hadn't seen Landry all that many times, and when he had, the circumstances had been tense and trying–

"Look," Landry said, "I can't prove to you that I don't know you – I could be feigning ignorance – how can anyone prove what they don't know? So let's get to the more important question: You're obviously from the future. You obviously know this is a time machine. You've obviously used it or something just like it to get here. So – just what the hell do you want?"

Jeff raced through his options. He hadn't expected to find Landry here. Perhaps this opened up new possibilities.

"Let's start by your telling me just where you're going in that," Jeff said and pointed to sleek machine.

Landry shook his head no. "Sorry. I make it a point never to reveal my destinations. As a time-faring man, you no doubt understand why – our work is complicated and dangerous enough, without expanding the circle of people who know where we are going."

Jeff brandished his weapon.

Landry laughed. "Come on. You're not going to use that if you want information from me. Unconscious people are very uncommunicative. The dead even more so."

Jeff tried to stare him down.

Landry made a sarcastic sound, turned around, and took a step towards his machine.

"I *will* render you unconscious if you take another step in that direction," Jeff said quietly.

Landry turned to face Jeff again. "Ok, that's progress. Part of what you want here is for me not to get into that machine. Why?"

"I want the ride myself."

"Ah, I see," Landry said, his eyes lighting up. "And what happened to your machine?"

"Short answer is, long story," Jeff said, "assuming you don't already know it."

Landry smiled. "And you expect me to just turn over my machine to you – not having any idea what you intend to with it? You really think I would do that, given what I've just told you about how serious all of this is?"

"Sorry, I can't tell you what I'm going to do with it either–" Jeff began.

"He wants me to go back in time and change a crucial event or two in our country," Yelena said, revealing herself for the first time.

Jeff turned around to tell her not to say anything more, then noticed she too had a weapon in her hand. Except it was the old-fashioned kind – a pistol, that fired bullets, the kind that ripped into your heart or brain.

"Yelena, what are you doing?" Jeff demanded.

"I brought this along in case a situation arose," Yelena said. "I think one has arisen–"

Landry made a dash to the time machine.

Yelena fired a single shot, which went clean through the baggy edge of Landry's trousers.

Well, that at least answered one of the questions Jeff had – unlike his weapon, Yelena's worked.

Landry stopped, shaken but apparently unhurt.

"The next one will hit flesh and blood, I assure you," Yelena said. "Maybe even your balls."

Jeff looked at her. "Who the fuck *are* you?"

"Never mind me," Yelena said. "This man you call George Landry is KGB."

"What?" Jeff asked.

"Absurd," Landry said.

"You deny that I saw you at the University of Moscow in 1987?" Yelena asked.

"I thought you've been here in the United States since 1986," Jeff said to Yelena.

"Yes, I was in Moscow in 1987, but that doesn't make me KGB," Landry said.

"I'll soon find out the entire truth, with my own eyes," Yelena said, and began walking towards the machine.

Jeff looked at her eyes again, and again saw something, some flicker, something deeply familiar there–

"Don't let her do it!" Landry shouted at Jeff. "You've got the damn stun-gun, use it!"

Yelena sneered. "It's a toy."

Landry erupted, lunged towards Yelena. She stepped back, coolly leveling her gun at Landry's head. "Walk away from me," she barked. "Last chance."

Landry backed off, shuddering with fury.

"Yelena, please–" Jeff began.

"Don't worry, don't worry – I'll take care of everything," she said. "It was good to see you again." She smiled and entered the gleaming machine.

Its doors closed a split second later. And a split second after, it disappeared in the same glimmering almost-rain that had delivered it into this room.

"She used the pre-set destination," Landry muttered, still shaking with anger. "No other way she could have gotten out of here so fast."

"And just when is that?" Jeff asked, throwing his worthless stun-gun on the floor in his own frustration.

"December 1982 – a month after Andropov takes over. I was

trying to go back to stop that."

***

It was February – 1989 – when Karina finally arrived in New York. She shivered. Much colder than La Jolla, she thought to herself as she buttoned up her thin jacket, all the way to the top, even though she was indoors.

"Thirty years ago today that Buddy Holly died," Bob Shannon said on CBS-FM Radio. But who was Buddy Holly?

She settled into her room on Patchin Place, in the Village. "A prime sublet," the agent had told her. "A science fiction writer usually lives here – lots of interesting books you can read, if you don't get ketchup on them."

She'd earned enough money waitressing in La Jolla – in two different restaurants, almost night and day – to keep her going here in New York for at least a few months.

She considered her options, and warmed her hands with a hot cup of tea. Its steam soothed her face.

She picked up the phone and called Sam.

"Karina! Where are you?"

"Here in New York."

"Yes – you sound close. Wonderful! Where's George?"

"I ... I don't know. I left him in 1991." She started crying.

"Are you ok? Is George–"

"I don't know," Karina sobbed. "I think he's dead."

"Oh my God, that's what I was afraid of. What happened?"

"I don't know," Karina said again for the third time, helpless. "He had in motion a plan to kidnap Andropov, threaten to kill him, kill him if he had to. Chernenko's dead since 1985, so Gorbachev would have taken over." She was crying again.

"Yes, I know," Sam said as gently as possible. "What went wrong?"

"Everything, everything! A hurricane on Cape Cod – in the summer, two years from now – cut him off from his contacts. Some people found us at his cottage – I'm sure they were KGB. I think they killed him–"

"George is a resourceful man. Don't count him out.

Remember the way Dick Atwick fooled us all and survived? George is far superior."

"I know," Karina said, "but ... you didn't see him in the chair. And ... Andropov's dead – I'm sure of that. I heard it on the radio before I left 1991. And his successor's no Gorbachev – it's Vladimir Putin, that KGB weirdo."

Sam gasped. "That's what happens when we let these things get out of our control. I told George: you've got to stay on top of these things, beat by beat."

"It wasn't George's fault," Karina said. "I told you – we had a hurricane."

"I know, I know, it's no one's fault," Sam said, sincerely. "But this is a grave situation – or will be, in two and a half years. We've got to figure out, the two of us, what can be done to prevent it."

"I don't know if I can do this anymore," Karina said. "That's the main thing I called to tell you. And ... I found some old papers in George's cottage. They say my mother's in New York now. I – I want to see her."

"I don't think that's wise at this moment," Sam said.

"I don't care anymore about wise."

***

"Look, I know you don't trust me," Landry said, "but the only way I can see out of this is for both of us to lay our cards on the table."

Jeff had consented to a late dinner with Landry at the Valencia in La Jolla. The waiter now brought their poached salmon to the table.

Landry tasted, and made a face. "Not very good," he said. "I guess the future has spoiled me."

"Yelena loved it," Jeff said. "She said it was very fresh."

"Not surprising," Landry said. "Compared to what they serve you in the Soviet Union, a piece of stinking tripe over here would seem fresh."

Jeff shoved a piece in his mouth and washed it down with wine. "All right," he said. "Here's the world I'm trying to create for the 21st century: a vibrant space program, democracy in

Eastern Europe, and, oh yeah, Fleischmann and Pons start cold fusion."

"Who?"

"Ok, never mind about them."

"I'm with you on the other two," Landry said. "That's the world I'm after, too: strong space, no Soviet Union. But as you may have already discovered, that's a hard play. The Soviet Union was, after all, as much responsible for humanity in space as the Nazis and the United States. Maybe even more so – Sputnik, Gagarin, they were crucial in picking up the lead of the Germans, and egging the US on. Von Braun was already here in the US, but without those Soviet accomplishments, JFK would have been much less willing to follow Von Braun's cues. And the Soviet Union did lots of good in the 21st century too – Mir 2, the red settlements on the Red Planet, the Oort stations in the 2090s..."

"A little ahead of my time," Jeff said. "In fact, even *in* my time, in the 21st century I come from, we have no space program and no Soviet Union. I assume the reality you're talking about has strong space programs in both the US and Russia – I mean, in the Soviet Union."

"Right," Landry said, "And in Europe, Japan, and China as well. But I agree with you that the world would be better off with a strong space program spearheaded by the US at the end of the 20th century, with ensuing worldwide involvement – and no Soviet Union in the 21st. But it'll be tough sledding bringing that combination about."

"Maybe Yelena–"

"Forget it," Landry said. "She's on the other side. If anything, she's going back there to strengthen Andropov's hand – to see to it that he lives at least another decade."

"How can you be sure?"

"She's already back there, right? If she'd succeeded with *your* plan, Gorbachev would be in power right now – not Andropov. It's March 1989 now, right? Hold on." Landry turned to a passing waiter. "Who's the Premier of the Soviet Union? Can you tell me?"

The waiter shrugged. "I don't know. Lenin? Nikita?"

Jeff and Landry both waved their hands in disgust.

Another waiter, who had been listening, came over, laughing. "It's Yuri Andropov, right? Hey, there's an article about the Soviet Union right here in the paper. Says Andropov spoke out today about the execution last month of Boris Yelstin. He said there was no place for capitalist sympathizers in the new and improved Soviet Union."

Jeff looked at the paper and shook his head, sadly.

"Thank you," Landry said to the waiter.

"Sure," the waiter said. "Hey, you can keep the paper."

"Thanks," Landry said. He turned back to Jeff. "Satisfied now?"

"Hardly satisfied," Jeff said, "but I take your point." He pushed his food away, mostly uneaten. "The salmon wasn't that bad, but that news story made me lose my appetite."

"I don't blame you," Landry said.

"So what do we do now? Yelena took your time machine."

"Suppose I told you I had another one."

***

Lord, the streets of New York were cold in this century. She was afraid to look at anybody too carefully, lest they take offense, or mistake her gaze for an expression of sexual interest that she wasn't in the mood for just now.

But Karina couldn't help but stare at everyone she passed, scrutinizing their faces, assessing their eyes for some sign that they were of her kind.

Her kind ... What kind was that? Someone born out of time, conceived in one century, gestated in another, raised in a third. "You're three centuries old," George always teased her, especially when they lay in bed together after making love, he running his fingers down the small of her back, giving her one last hot chill. God, she missed him. He was old enough to be her father in biological age – but what did that mean to people like George and her? He was the only man she'd ever known who really understood her. The only man she'd ever felt herself with.

She didn't feel that way about Sam. She didn't really trust him. She'd declined to meet him in the ten days she'd been here. She dyed her hair and cut it so Sam would have trouble recognizing her if he'd decided to show up and press the point.

Her kind ... The theory was that a tumble through time had no adverse affect on the fetus. But as long as she could remember, she had always felt on the brink of paranoia when she contemplated what was going on around her. Except when George was around.

Her mother would understand. She was a child of time herself, in her own way. It had been ten years since Karina had last seen her. She didn't even know her name anymore – names changed too quickly in this business. But Karina had an inkling, based on those papers she'd seen on the Cape.

She stopped at the NYU Student Union Building. There was history here! She looked up, and sought out that student lounge, as she always did when she walked by this corner.

But the path to her mother was elsewhere today.

"Excuse me," she said to a security guard, who looked like Charles Manson in a uniform, lounging against a lamppost. "Is that Tisch Hall over there?" She pointed to a likely building.

Manson smiled and nodded, revealing a set of teeth that looked like Mayan maize.

"Thanks." She hurried off. Her breath felt sticky in her chest. The talk would begin in about 20 minutes.

***

"I had three machines in stasis – pre-set for 1982, ready to be called into service here – when we started this escapade a few hours ago," Landry said. They were back on that second floor of the pastel grey building on Silverado. "Yelena the Great took one. I propose to call forth a second, and take it back to 1982 myself to see if I can accomplish what she either failed to do or more likely deliberately prevented."

"How can I be sure you'll do as you say?" Jeff asked.

"Because I'm going to give you one of these little eels – much more powerful than your wafer – and show you exactly how to call forth the third machine, in case you need it."

And Landry did just that with a supple device no bigger than a finger.

"Allow a minute or two for settlement after I leave," he continued. "You know the drill. Call up the local radio station – here's their number–"

Jeff frowned.

"–then get the number yourself, if you still don't trust me."

"Ok, I trust you," Jeff said. At least, I trust you at this point more than I don't, he thought. And what other choice do I have?

"Good," Landry resumed. "And if the radio station tells you Comrade Drop-off is still head of the Soviet Union, you'll know what to do – go back to 1982 and give it a shot yourself. Maybe the two of us will prevail over Yelena – or over the enemies of all three of us back there."

"You don't seem all that confident," Jeff said.

"Confidence? No such thing in this line of work – you should know that."

"Yeah, but I don't speak Russian," Jeff said. He was also thinking of Laura, and their baby.

"Not to worry, most of the important people over there still speak English. It gets much worse in the next century, of course, if we're unable to change this – they were speaking Russian in northern Canada already the last time I was there in 2060, for crissakes."

"Ok," Jeff said. "I get the picture." Laura would never forgive him, he was sure. What he wasn't sure about is if he could ever forgive himself if he left her again.

"All right, buddy – I'm off to the races, then." Landry walked towards his machine. He turned around. "You have a look on your face that we'll see each other again – you obviously recognized me when you laid eyes on me here a few hours ago. Since that was the first time for me, this obviously means that we'll be meeting again later in my life, earlier in yours. I'll try not to upset you unduly then – give too much away that we'll be

meeting again in your future. I'll make it hard for
you – play the hard-ass to your neophyte – to make it easier
for you." Landry smiled. "But you already know that. Till the
next time, then – whenever it may be!" And he walked into the
machine.

It disappeared in the silver-grey pseudo-rain.

Jeff didn't have to call the radio station – he could feel the
lack of change in his bones, the stasis of standing in an elevator
when it should have been moving but wasn't. Or maybe worse –
moving down when it should have been moving up.

He called the station anyway. "Yeah, right, thanks." Yuri
Andropov was now not only General Secretary of the
Communist Party but President of the Soviet Union, as of March
22, 1989.

Jeff looked at the remaining machine. His eyes burned and
his mouth was dry. There were dozens of good reasons he could
think of for not going. Yelena and now Landry had failed to turn
the red tide, why should he be able to do any better? And there
was Laura, Laura, Laura.

And there was just one good reason he could think of that he
had to go, one goddamn worm that wouldn't stop moving inside
him: this world with the Soviet Union ascendant, this world
that he had perhaps somehow unwittingly midwived into being
with his Challenger tinkering. No, there was nothing uncertain
about it – he *had* created this world, this wrong world, and it was
unacceptable – it wasn't meant to be.

He took a step towards the machine and stopped. He took
another unsteady step–

"You're not going to break your promise to me, are you?"
Laura's voice asked, in his head.

"I don't want to," he said aloud.

"Then don't," Laura's voice said.

Not in his head.

He spun around.

"My God – how long have you been here?"

"Long enough to hear the little chat you and George had,"

Laura said.

"I was thinking of you – and the baby," Jeff said. He looked at her. She looked more pregnant now than the last time he had seen her. "Are you ok? I mean, the both of you."

"Oh, we're fine," Laura said, and patted her midsection. "The plane ride was smooth – though I bet they were glad to get me off the plane without a special delivery."

Jeff smiled, weakly.

"You know, you didn't mention to Landry the most important reason that going back to 1982 to kill Andropov or whatever you expect to do back there is a bad idea," Laura said.

"I – I didn't feel comfortable talking to him about you and our baby–" Jeff began.

"That's not the most important reason," Laura said.

Jeff looked puzzled. "What, then? That murder is bad? We've been over that already, with Nixon. You and I don't see things exactly the same on that."

"No, not murder in general. Murder of *Androhpawf*!" Laura said. Her voice had an odd intensity – an odd accent – that Jeff had never quite heard before.

"Ah, I see you're beginning to understand now," Laura continued.

"You said you loved me," Jeff was barely able to speak. "That's our baby–"

"I do, and she is," Laura said. "But you loved me too, and that didn't stop you from doing what you needed to do to save the Challenger, remember?"

"Yes, but–"

"And your loving me, and the baby – would that have been enough to stop you from going back to try to change things in the Soviet Union even now? You were about to walk right into that machine and leave us behind, weren't you?"

"I hadn't made up my mind and you–"

"The Soviet Union is a great country," Laura said. "*My* country – the country of the 21st century, yes! Of the world! Of space beyond the world! We launched the Sputnik! We had the first living organisms in space – and then the first man to circle the globe! We had our losses, too – three brave cosmonauts died in Soyez 11! But we pressed on in space. And we do great things in the next century! If we're allowed to continue-"

"But Andropov's a murderer," Jeff argued. "You don't believe in that – I know you."

"I believe in sacrifices, tradeoffs, weighing the choices that sometimes have to be made," Laura said, her eyes wet and shining with resolve as well as sorrow. "I stopped you from killing Nixon not because I was so much against murder, but because Nixon alive was helpful to my country – we needed Nixon so Brezhnev would react against him, cooperate with him – Nixon was the perfect American for my country!"

"No! I don't believe it," Jeff insisted.

"Believe it," Laura said. "And believe that, yes, I do love you." And she stepped into the machine – a second before Jeff realized how close she had moved to it, a second too late for Jeff to do anything about it.

He tackled the machine, but all he got in his arms was the rain that wasn't moist and a faint electrical tingle.

His body was soaked with perspiration anyway and his face was slick with tears.

Laura was gone.

And Jeff knew, not only that he might well never see her again, but that she was going back to 1982 to stop Landry and Yelena – to make possible the very Soviet dominance of the 21st century that he had been trying so hard to prevent.

And that, Jeff understood at last, and after all of these years, had been her mission all along - her real reason for tracking and meeting Jeff in 1964, maybe even for staying with him all of this time, even after he had left her. Just as his had been to save the Challenger. She had helped with that because a vibrant American space program was a good source of competition, a powerful stimulant, to the Soviet space effort in the 21st century.

***

"Karina? I hardly recognized you, with that new hair! Good

thing the call of nature brought me back here!"

Karina had been concentrating on the talk from the back of the auditorium, eyes dilating with every word. She turned to face the intrusion, and her eyes dilated even more – with a different emotion. "Sam!"

He smiled. "Come." He put an arm around her. "Let's go over there." He gestured to a descending flight of stairs outside of the auditorium. "I think we can find a bit of privacy there."

She hesitated, not wanting to leave the talk. But with Sam right here ... "Ok," she said, and reluctantly allowed him to lead her to the staircase.

"You know, I told you this wasn't a good idea," he said, when they'd settled in, about a half flight down, backs against the wall. "Meeting people you're not supposed to, unexpected intersections in time, they can cause trouble, *big* trouble. You see, we have no *record* of your being here, of your meeting your mother in this time and place. That's the problem."

"Stop talking to me like a child," Karina snapped. "I know about trouble. I saw George–"

"I know, I know, believe me," Sam said, as soothingly as possible. "But whatever happened to George two years from now – and, again, we can't be sure, he may still turn up ok after all – there's surely no point in making things worse by twisting up the threads back here, in 1989. Surely you see that?"

"My mother's the only thing I can see," Karina insisted. "I'm sick of this time-travel depravity – I want a normal life, a family, my parents, a husband someday – people weren't meant to live like this! Jumping around through time, crossing wires, tying their souls up in knots to the point of not knowing who or where or even when they are when they take the simple human action of looking in a mirror? It's enough already! I'm going to meet my mother, tell her the truth of what I've been through, what the future has in store for her–"

"Of course you will, my dear." Sam had removed an embroidered handkerchief from his vest pocket while Karina had been talking – one he always carried for occasions such as this. Now, without the slightest warning, he put it over her face and nose with one hand, and brought the other around the back of her head, pressing her face into the handkerchief, so that she was immobile. The chloroform derivative worked almost instantly. Within 15 seconds she had crumpled into his arms. In 15 more she was utterly unconscious.

He propped her head up as gently as he could against the wall. He lifted her left eyelid, and looked at her pupil – ring of sweet chocolate, dilated, unseeing. Unremembering too, he hoped – though that was not sure a thing with this quick-acting drug. He let the eyelid droop slowly closed, and kissed her on the forehead. "Of course you will, my dear – of course you will."

He walked quickly up the stairs and out of the building, and summoned the security guard on the corner. "There's a girl who seems to have passed out on the lower staircase," he told the guard. "She may need some medical attention."

The guard bared his stained teeth. "Drugs, goddamn drugs," he said. "These kids are killing their mortal souls with those drugs."

Sam nodded sympathetically, then hurried back into the auditorium. Yelena's talk was just ending. Jeff was already applauding. Good – everyone would be out of the building and long gone before Karina awoke.

***

Jeff walked up the stairs of his Eastside brownstone in New York. He hadn't felt so utterly alone, so entirely out of place, since he had first set up residence here after his stranding in 1963.

The news on the TV was uniformly depressing: no Chinese students in Tienanmen Square, no sign of Gorbachev anywhere. And May was even worse: Yuri Andropov further consolidated his power by crushing for good the rebels in Afghanistan.

Well, at least the US space program seemed somewhat back on
track. A report said six shuttle launches were planned for 1991.

Jeff shut off the TV and tried to call Sam. His phone machine said he was out of town.

Jeff took the subway down to NYU. Sometimes, when he was half asleep, rocking to and fro with the train car, he felt as if he were a hundred years in the future, back where he belonged … back where, if he opened his eyes, he was sure he would see the soft holographic ads all around him, the mirrorims of products new and bold, the smooth smiling service that only robotic engineers could reliably render. But when he opened his eyes, the ads and the people were always garish, dirty, and two-dimensional – the ubiquitous greeting card of the 20th century.

He walked around Washington Square, and daydreamed of Rena. He thought of Laura, and yearned for his baby. But all he saw were faces which seemed to look at him as if they knew him, even though he knew they did not.

He pondered his situation. There had to be some logic, some path he could follow to influence events. He'd tried to call forth more time machines in La Jolla, but Landry had been telling the truth when he'd said there were only three. Worse than that, the schedule he'd downloaded from Landry's network revealed no further arrivals or departures at later dates. It was as if, with Laura's departure – back to 1982 and the Soviet Union if she was telling the truth – Landry's whole time-travel project had concluded and vanished.

But there had to be others.

Something had to have been the source of all the time travelers to 1963 that had caused the JFK vortex that had pulled him back into the 1960s in the first place – assuming, of course, that he and Laura had been right about that.

Laura … the key was with her. He still couldn't believe that she was a Soviet communist, bent on keeping that system in place through the 21st century. He knew her. She believed in freedom. Maybe she would have a change of heart back there, and help Landry after all.

But if she had, wouldn't Jeff have seen the evidence already? All he saw was Andropov.

Still, he looked through Laura's papers. She had left New York to fly to La Jolla in a hurry. Lots of half-scribbled sheets were still around.

He came upon a sheet with doodles and names. Jeff smiled and grimaced at the same time, crumpled the sheet in his fist and then put it under his heart. The names were the ones he and Laura had been discussing during one of their phone calls – possible names for their baby.

Jeff uncrumpled the sheet and looked at the names. Some were the ones they had talked about. Names based on parents and grandparents and ancestors ... names based on no one's names, just names they liked ... and there were some names that Jeff hadn't recalled Laura mentioning at all.

At the bottom of the sheet, two names were circled, with arrows pointing to penciled explanations.

"Karina" –> "because my favorite grandmother was named Karen, and because I think a part of Jeff still loves Rena"...

"Yelena" –> "after Jeff's grandmother, Eleanor, who was Eli Harris' wife"...

And then, in smaller letters on the right-hand side of the sheet: "Karina Yelena Harris" –> "because our daughter should always know she is Russian, whatever may happen".

Jeff hugged himself and cried: I lost my daughter not once but twice to those cursed machines in La Jolla.

***

He taught classes in the 1989 summer session at NYU – mainly so he could be closer to the streets around Washington Square Park. He felt more at home there these days than at home. It was easy to get a job at NYU, with his forged credentials ratified now by real teaching spanning decades.

One afternoon after his class, a student was waiting for him outside his office.

She looked familiar, but he'd learned not to get too excited about that. He let her in, and bade her to a seat.

"Would you like admission to one of my Summer Session classes?" He pulled out a pen and looked for an admission form. "I'm too egotistical to ever refuse a student willing to pay money to hear me talk."

The student laughed. "Actually, I was hoping you could admit me to your life, now that I've finally found you."

"Oh?"

"I'm pretty sure I'm your daughter."

The pen fell to the floor.

"I've located another time machine," Karina continued, "and I think I know how to get Mikhail Gorbachev back in power."

LAST CALLS

First published in 2015 as a novella by Connected Editions. Sequel to "Loose Ends", "Little Differences", and "Late Lessons".

"W hat's the *matter* with you?" Jeff screamed up at the sky, the closest he could get to the universe, which seemed to twist every good deed he'd attempted into something horrendous.

He wished he could just reach up, get his fingers into the sky, and pull a piece out of it. Maybe the rain or cosmic light or whatever poured out would cool him down, settle his psyche, and steady this careening world, just a bit.

He looked out across the Hudson at Ground Zero. It had been nearly two years since September 11. He'd seen this absence of skyscrapers many times since then, and the emptiness still was as raw and traumatic as the very first time on the very first day. Like the hole in your soul from the loss of a loved one, this hole in Manhattan was something that would never go away.

He'd managed to get rid of Andropov and get Gorbachev in power. But the declining Soviet Union had left Afghanistan in the hands of the Islamic fighters and Osama bin Laden. And they had caused that hole across the Hudson.

That wasn't the way it had been in Jeff's original timeline. September 11 had not happened in Jeff's history, the world with the Soviet Union falling apart and no space program -- the one that Jeff had worked most of his adult life to change.

And, somehow, Jeff's meddling with time, to get a 21st

century with no Soviet Union but a strong space program, had led to this crater in Manhattan. Holes like that belonged on the Moon, not in his hometown of New York City. Tears of rage and self-pity blurred his vision. Why hadn't anyone from any damned future warned him about this?

No, he had learned a long time ago, or should have learned, that he couldn't rely on any one from any time to get things right. He could rely only on himself. He rubbed his eye looked again at the cold pit across the river. He had caused this. September 11 was ultimately his fault more than anyone else's.

He had known this the moment he had turned on his television on that beautiful Tuesday morning in September, and had seen the report of that plane crashing into the first World Trade Center tower. He had known at that moment that this was due to him. And that he had to do something to change that, to make sure those planes never flew towards those towers. He had known he needed to do that for almost two years. And now, finally, he had a plan.

***

Karina hurried along the shore. Sandpipers, newly returned after the hurricane and ravenous, skittered along the sand, sifting the grains for an insect meal. One set of delicate prints in the sand caught her eye. They ended abruptly. Either the sandpiper had died, exhausted after the storm, its body carried away by a lucky crow -- or the piper had managed to take wing to more promising climes.

As she had done, three years ago in her lifetime.

She looked quickly behind her, at the receding slick of blacktop and sand that was Skaket Beach in Orleans. Good. The highest form of life between her and the empty parking lot was a lone seagull.

Three years ago in her lifetime, as she'd approached this place in a final sprint from the opposite direction, she'd noticed a few kids and their parents already back on the beach, quick to reclaim what was left of their summer vacation from Hurricane Bob, which had ripped apart Cape Cod in the summer of 1991.

Now she needed to be here at some time before that instant -- before her earlier self, still frantic and panting, had traversed the stretch of shore from the cottage of Sarah Harris to here.

In fact, she needed to be here precisely one hour and twenty-three minutes -- seconds, at least, were not crucial -- before her earlier self. Any tiny bit later, and she risked arriving too late at their cottage in Brewster to save George. Any earlier, and she risked paradox, with utterly unforeseeable consequences, by running into her earlier self at their cottage.

She shuddered. Timing was truly everything in this business.

She turned her attention again to the shore ahead, to Brewster, and quickened her pace. The sand felt good and compact against the soles of her bare feet. There was something odd about having weapons in her hands in the pockets of her windbreaker, and no shoes on her feet. The weapons in her hands seemed to intrude upon her connection to the sand. She could have run with shoes or sandals but barefoot was the best way of making time with the least amount of noise.

A small creek -- more an awning of sand and sea grass than a flowing creek -- opened up ahead of her, followed by the iron-red sand that was the welcome matt of Linger Longer by Sea. She looked for the weathered little grey cottage off to the left, half obscured from this vantage point by drooping locust trees. If her calculations were right, her earlier self would be in Sarah Harris's little cottage right now, finishing her first cup of tea. Karina fought off the urge to get a peak of her earlier self through the window -- and the little boy she now knew to be her great-grandfather, Eli, and the woman who was her great-great-great-grandmother Sarah.

She had to get to George as soon as possible, and he was still at least 10 minutes further ahead on the beach. The image of him sitting in that chair, KGB swarming over him, was as clear in her mind as it had been three years ago. One of those killers had a knife.

The safest course of action, in terms of saving George, would have been for her to approach their cottage in Brewster not from the beach, but from the forest side. That way, there was little danger of her running into any KGB who had might have set out after her, after her escape from the cottage three years ago in her lifetime, just a few minutes from the time it was now. But she couldn't be sure that the forest path was clear enough to walk upon after the hurricane. And there was another reason.

She had somehow managed three years ago to make it first from their cottage to Sarah's, and then from Sarah's to Skaket Beach in Orleans, without any interference from the KGB. That always struck her as strange -- there had been at least five KGB in the cottage, in addition to that pig she had pushed down the stairs. Surely one or two of them would have come out after her -- standard mop-up procedure for the "wet affair" they no doubt had in mind for George. And yet, she had made her escape to Orleans without seeing so much as a shadow on the sand.

The explanation seemed obvious: KGB had indeed followed her, but someone had intercepted them before they could intercept her earlier fleeing self. And, given that she was here right now, the best candidate for that someone was: she, herself, right now.

A scan via binoculars down the beach towards Brewster now provided the first confirmation of her hypothesis: two bobbing figures, no bigger than sanderlings even under extreme magnification, were approaching. Her instinct was to use her weapon, and render them unconscious. The stunner would work fine at this range. But she couldn't be sure who they were -- they after all were not wearing tee shirts that said KGB. At this distance, and with the mist from the bay distorting the light, she couldn't even be 100-percent positive they were people not birds.

She slowed her pace. She had the tactical advantage. The goons were expecting a fleeing girl with her back to them. She could afford to wait at least bit longer before she dropped them--

She heard a noise from behind her -- back near Linger Longer, near Sarah's cottage. She whirled around and focused her binoculars. The figure that came into vision was -- her earlier self! Younger Karina was at the foot of Sarah's cottage, looking towards Orleans, away from where Karina was now!

The current Karina took a breath to steady herself. Ok, there was no harm done. As long her younger self didn't turn around and see her, there was no chance of that vague nagging paradox to undermine her now, the one that came of memories suddenly in residence where none had been before. Younger Karina now seemed to half look in current Karina's direction, but without binoculars there was no way she could see her. Her younger self turned and started jogging away, towards Orleans, exactly as she of course had done three years ago.

Current Karina exhaled. Good. Her mind was still sharp, not blurred by new-born impossible memory. But seeing her earlier self just leave Sarah Harris's cottage brought into focus another problem: she was here a bit later than expected, which meant she had less time now to get to George.

She turned around to look again at the two approaching figures from Brewster, and two things happened immediately: She now could see what she was almost certain were weapons in their hands. And a scalding burst of air seemed to rip through her sleeve.

She dove into the sand, rolled over and came up with her weapon, banishing most of the burning pain in her shoulder from her mind. I still have the advantage, she thought -- they don't know I'm armed.

She rolled over again -- dodging another heat blast -- and then again, coming up this time with a wide-scan stun aimed at both assailants.

They fell motionless into the sand. But how to tell whether they were really hit, or faking?

She leveled another stun at them -- let them lie unconscious in the sand for four rather than two hours. They'd goddamn survive. It was better than what they'd been trying to do to her -- what they might have already done to George.

She touched her shoulder, winced, and hurried on. Likely

not more than a second-degree burn. Fortunately, the singed area wasn't much bigger than an American quarter.

But the tide was beginning to return. Of course -- she was at least 45 minutes later than she'd reckoned. Those damned temporal meters were simply unreliable for these kinds of short hops. Everybody knew it.

She pushed ahead, water lapping at her toes. It felt cool and soothing. In other circumstances, she might have taken off her clothes,jumped into the bay, surrendered to the tug of the cosmos for a few deep minutes. As it was--

The cottage -- the one George and she had been staying in three years ago -- was now discernible through her binoculars. She looked at the foot of the stairs, right where that KGB thug she'd shoved down in her earlier escape had smashed his head. No sign of him or his head, dead or alive. No obvious sign of blood, and she didn't have time for an analytic scan. They must have cleaned up pretty quickly.

She quick-scanned the cottage. No indication of anything alive in there, either. Damn -- she squeezed the binoculars in frustration. George couldn't be dead already -- she couldn't have come back all this way just for that. Maybe the smart parts of the binoculars were broken.

She passed the two prone figures on the sand. Definitely KGB -- she remembered their ugly faces from three years ago. I hope you have bad dreams, you Communist sons of bitches. You destroyed my mother's country.

She suppressed the urge to kick them, and walked carefully on.

The cottage was now in plain view. She scanned the beach up and down one more time. Nothing. She pocketed the binoculars, took out her stunners, and approached the stairs.

All she could hear was the water rinsing the sand behind her.

She climbed up slowly, stopping on each stair. She reached the deck. The curtain was drawn across the bay window. She pushed an image of George's dead body out of her brain -- it was just in her mind, it wasn't real, it couldn't be. She touched the door -- it swung open. She looked in -- and saw no one.

The cottage seemed just as it had been before Hurricane Bob. There was no one in any room.

She debated what to do. Her heart pounded so hard she could barely follow her internal conversation. But she heard a noise out by the bushes, by the front road.

She opened the door warily, weapon drawn.

"What the hell did you do with your hair?" It was George, smile on his face, groceries in hand.

***

Karina lit the kerosene lamps, just as her younger self had at this same time and place three years ago. "Well, at least our realities coincide about the hurricane," George said, far more cheerful than she thought he had a right to be, or at least as she remembered him being the first time around.

He offered her a Swiss cheese sandwich, which she gratefully took. She turned down the glass of wine, inviting as it was. Her head was confused enough already.

"Is Andropov still in power?" She began the probe, standard in these circumstances of crossed realities. Ask the key questions --ascertain the extent of the clash. Just as George had taught her.

"Of course not." He smiled. "I took care of him personally in 1984. And our colleagues gave Chernenko the same sendoff in 1985 -- he would have died in a year or two anyway. Russian men have low natural life expectancy in this century."

"And the coup? Is there a coup going on there today?"

George sipped his wine and nodded. "Against Gorbachev, yeah. But it doesn't matter for our purposes -- the coup is small potatoes. The democratic forces that Gorbachev uncorked are already pulling the Soviet Union to pieces. It's way too late to stop that. Gorbachev will survive the coup in the short run, then he'll be swept away himself by anti-Communist sentiment in a few months."

Karina thought about the two men on the beach. "Let me show you something," she said.

She led George to the prone figures. "Where do you suppose these two came from?" she asked. "They were moving towards me from the direction of our cottage." She looked up and down the beach again with her binoculars. For all she knew, there could be more where these agents came from.

George looked them over and shook his head. "Not from our cottage, I'm sure of that. I was here all by myself through the hurricane. Quite beautiful, actually -- makes me think of what a time jump *should* be like, even though it looks so nondescript from the inside."

Karina frowned. "I guess we should get them awake -- to question them."

George shook his head again. "I don't think so. They're pretty clearly dead."

"What? They were unconscious just a few minutes ago! I gave them a second slam, but--"

George put his arm around her. "Not your fault," he said. "It's standard security for some originating sectors that a stun triggers an implant that kills you before you regain consciousness -- that way there's no danger you'll talk your head off to a captor when you awake. These guys were obviously more than late 20th-century KGB."

Karina pulled away, horrified anyway about what she had done. She looked out at the bay. It always brought her some measure of peace. Another way she was much like her father.... "Ok," she said. "Tell me more about where I was during the storm. You said you were alone in the cottage?" *That is, where I was in this different, current reality we're now inhabiting*, she thought, *because I was with you and saw you with a knife to your neck in the reality I remember.*

"Right," George said, taking her hand, looking out with her at the blue-green water. "You were in New York -- supposed to come here after the hurricane, later today or tomorrow." He squinted at the orange sun, close to setting. "Well, I guess it is later today already -- so you're right on time."

And what about the earlier version of me I saw running

from Sarah Harris's cottage, Karina thought. But she said nothing about that to George. Standard procedure in these circumstances also called for keeping at least one crucial piece of information from your partner -- because you could never be sure, in these conditions, if your partner was still really your partner.

But there was one more crucial question she had to ask. "All right, so the Soviet Union seems to be in good disintegrating shape in your -- this -- reality. What about the Challenger? Was the Miami catastrophe avoided?"

George looked at her, for the first time with a keen sadness in his eyes.

"Don't tell me it crashed into that Miami schoolhouse--" she began and stopped.

George looked out in the bay, then back at her.

"No," he said quietly.

"What is it, then?"

"You knew," he said. "I mean, yourself in this reality -- the reality with me in the cottage alone, no attack on me by KGB -- that version of you knew. I hate like hell to be breaking this news to you for the first time."

Karina could say nothing. If George was saying this was bad, that meant it must have been even worse.

"Your father -- Jeff -- prevented the Miami crash. There was nothing he or anyone could do to prevent the O-rings from going. But he got on board, in the guise of one of the astronauts, and piloted the shuttle so it came apart no place near Miami. It was part of a complex plan I hatched up with him. He perished with the rest of the crew."

***

Jeff thrust his hands deep in his fluxcoat, and looked out at the darkly flowing Hudson River from his vantage point high atop the Turoff Tower in Jersey City. The fibering of New York City cast a necklace reflection on the water. He breathed in the river breeze and savored the scent of the mid-21st century.

His fingers did a fast dance on the digital mesh in his front right pocket. He had to store these thoughts some place safe, for Laura. His fluxcoat transmitted what he typed. Weather reports, review of Sir Paul at 100 ... his words would look like common knowledge, nothing everyone didn't already know -- unless they had the encryption code, the one Laura and he had agreed upon, memorized, so long ago, back in the 1980s, when personal computers, and Laura and he, were still new.

"I know now that I made many mistakes, that I took for granted something rare and precious that we shared," is what he wanted to type, to commit to the endless memory that stretched backwards and forward in time in the grand clouds, for Laura to someday find. But business, as always -- the impossibly demanding business of time travel and making the world safe for both space travel and democracy -- took precedence. And there was barely time even for that.

He rubbed his abdomen with his forearm. His midsection felt sore in anticipation of the blow his younger self would soon mete out to him in that men's room on the day of the Challenger explosion. That would be in less than a day of his lifetime -- time to drive over to the New Jersey Institute of Technology in Newark, get into that special facility beneath the parking lot, take its neo-Thorne back to January 1986, and catch a plane down to Miami. Just enough time to derail his younger self and his plan to be on board the Challenger. Jeff supposed that the very fact that he was doing this -- that he remembered all too clearly the encounter with his older self ten years ago, when he was his younger self in his lifetime -- meant that he was bound to succeed. Still, he'd learned he couldn't be too sure of anything when time travel was involved.

But there was no point thinking about that now -- plenty of time to indulge the contemplation of paradox on the plane to Miami. He returned to his memo to Laura...

"Now in the matter of Gorbachev and Gore--" A small electric shock caused Jeff's index finger to jump, interrupting the crucial second section of his memo. The warning told him someone had opened the roof tower door, and was approaching him from behind on the cobblestone. He turned and squinted into the distance, a sudden cold breeze against his eyes making it difficult for him to see. What the hell was this? Turoff Tower was supposed to be totally secure. He put his hand on the stun weapon lodged next to the phone. He'd been meaning to get a phone that had a stun app -- they were easy to get on the dark web -- and regretted that he hadn't gotten around to doing that. Lack of time, again--

A young blonde woman who looked utterly unfamiliar hailed him. "Dr. Harris?"

"Yes?" Jeff tightened his hold on the weapon.

"I'm Heidi Cartling, Junior Programmer at NJIT."

"Yes?"

"We're having a problem with the parking lot facility. Projections said the safest thing to do would be for me to come over and fetch you. So here I am." She smiled brightly.

Jeff hesitated. Why send a person rather than an email with such a message? He did like what she looked like -- short blonde hair, long neck -- but had neither the time nor the inclination to pursue that now.

"Your knowing my name and the parking lot my car is in isn't enough," he said. His thumb de-latched the weapon.

The woman's smile wavered, then reformed. "Ok," she said. "I guess that means I'll have to trust you more than you trust me. The parking lot we're discussing contains a time travel device on a lower level. You plan to use it. You yourself come from a time later in this century, when 'the stores are open but the stars are closed' -- isn't that how President Marion put it in the last election before you left?"

Yeah, Jeff thought, and she lost in a landslide.

"So," Heidi pressed. "Is that enough for you? Or are you going to knock me unconscious with that weapon in your pocket and carry me off somewhere?"

Jeff pulled the weapon out. He felt like a fool, but kept it trained on her nonetheless. "What problem are you having with the NJIT parking lot?" he asked.

"Well, again, it's not really the lot, but the device in the area below the lot, as I explained."

"And?" Jeff prodded.

Heidi took her time to answer. It looked to Jeff as if she was carefully weighing what to tell him.

"We're getting indications that there's been too much use of the neo-Thornes, the Thornes, they're all the same at this point," she finally said. "But they've been programmed, up-time, probably well in the 22nd century, to shut down when it reaches a certain level of use. You understand?"

Jeff nodded slowly. He heard about this feature of the Thorne, somewhere in his travels –- that it was programmed to shut down as a way of protecting history from too many attempts to change it, even in the most minor of ways. "Can you tell how many more times we can use it, before it shuts down?"

Heidi shook her head no. "This is the first we've ever approached the limit, as far as I know, in our mid-21st century time. It may have been approached or triggered before, in other times. We're trying to find out when and why. We're not even sure at this point if this limit affects just our own time right now, or every Thorne up and down the timeline."

Jeff took this in. "So the upshot is I shouldn't just travel through any old time any time I want to –- I need to carefully consider my trips, as the one I make could be my last, at least a for a while."

"Exactly," Heidi said. "And if you'd like my help in working this out, perhaps you could start by putting away that weapon."

***

They buried the bodies deep in the sand at dawn the next morning, and dined on soft-shelled clams in the evening, the night after the hurricane. "Sand included, free of charge," the helpful caption on Captain Elmer's menu advised. The venerable seafood restaurant in Orleans had managed to come through the storm with no damage or loss of power, as had its supplier Farmer Jim, who harvested clams in the bay as a sideline.

The topic of conversation, as it had been all day, was how

Karina could be alive if her father Jeff had heroically died in the Challenger disaster. Karina knew the obvious, non-paradoxical answer — to the extent that anything was non-paradoxical in her time-looped life — was that Jeff had impregnated her mother Laura in 1989, before he had gone back to lessen the damage to the world wrought by the Challenger explosion. And Laura had gone back to the Soviet Union, back to an earlier time, and raised Karina.

"Except my earlier version, who left you in the cottage with a knife to your neck, believed her father was alive, as did you in that reality," Karina said.

"Yes," Landry nodded. "These are delicious," he said about the steamed clams.

"Yes," Karina agreed, "very fresh!"

"Everything tastes fresh when you come from the Soviet Union," Landry said and chuckled. "But back to your questions: perhaps a third version of you came back here, and changed the reality, so it is what you now see before you — me with no knife to my neck, but your father unfortunately dead. Or someone other than you was responsible for bringing that reality into being."

"Right," Karina said. She was well aware of how quickly even bedrocks of reality could blink in and out when time travel was afoot. One thing which had apparently remained intact was Landry's understanding of time travel — no one understood it better than he, in Karina's experience. Another reason she was grateful he was alive, maybe one of the main reasons, and odd part of her thought. "But what if I want both — my father alive as well as you?"

Landry smiled sourly — not at her, Karina knew, but about the perverse nature of reality. "You can't always net what you want — isn't that what John Lennon said? Yeah, I saw him singing that song at a concert last year."

"I thought it was Mick Jagger, and the lyric was a little different," Karina replied. And she didn't want to complicate the conversation even further by mentioning to Landry that in her reality, Lennon had been murdered a decade earlier, in 1980.

***

Jeff heard "Shannon" playing on the mono-rail he and Heidi were talking from Jersey City to the New Jersey Institute of Technology in Newark.

"Pretty song," Heidi said, dreamily.

"Yeah," Jeff agreed but frowned. The tagger on his phone said the recording was by Henry Gross. That correlated, Jeff knew, with the death of John Lennon in 1980, one of the events in history he was determined to change, if it was the last thing he did in this damn time-warped world, a hell and a heaven he was in some part responsible for continually re-creating.

"Something about that song disturbs you?" Heidi asked, focusing on Jeff's face.

Jeff explained. If Heidi was who she said she was, there was no need to keep his objectives secret. If she wasn't-- well, she would just be the latest in the long line of people who were sure Jeff was a nutcase.

Heidi nodded. "Henry Gross singing this in no way means that the recording in some way caused Lennon's murder -- you know that, right?"

"Of course," Jeff said, annoyed that Heidi felt she needed to point that out to him. "Correlation is not the same as causation. But I want to change the world in which those two events -- Henry Gross singing Shannon and John Lennon being murdered -- are correlated for whatever reason. I want a world in which John Lennon lives and the Beach Boys have the hit with that song -- hey, I want the world in which Carl Wilson's dog doesn't die in the first place. That's the way it was meant to be -- I feel it in my bones."

"Carl Wilson's dog?"

"Yeah, the song's about a dog -- Carl Wilson's Irish Setter -- that died. If ever there was an indication of a world that was the twisted result of someone time traveling, that would be it."

"What do you think the song was supposed to be about?"

"About someone's girlfriend named Shannon leaving -- the

same as what most of the Beach Boys' songs were about — Wendy, Surfer Girl, all the rest."

The mono-rail pulled into docket and the song ended. "We're here," Heidi said, unnecessarily.

***

Karina and George left their weapons from the future in their cottage, where they would be unlikely to be seen by anyone but them, if and when they returned. Taking them into a populous city like New York could contaminate the past and distort the future. Karina and George drove over the Sagamore Bridge, from Cape Cod to Route 195 on the way to Providence, where she hoped to catch a train to Newark, New Jersey, to start another journey towards the providence of time, whatever that was, she thought to herself. Amtrak had said service had resumed after the hurricane, but you never knew that for sure until you were on the train and it was moving.

"You sure you don't want me to drive you to New York, where you can easily get a commuter train to Newark?" George asked Karina again. "Amtrak also said the northeast corridor is still a mess in some places."

"Not a good idea," Karina repeated what she had already told George. "Who knows what versions of you are running around New York right now." Among the many things she didn't understand is why she had to have the same conversation with George so many times. "Not to mention running into my father," she added.

George nodded.

Karina knew he was thinking, that's not very likely, since your father isn't now alive in this timeline, but George was too much of a gentleman to belabor that point. It was moot, in any case, because that's what Karina was going to Newark to try to change — and change in a way that wouldn't unleash a cascade of unintended terrible consequences, which is what always seemed to have happened with her whenever she tampered with time. "I'm going to take a little nap," she told George, wanting more time to think. "I still haven't caught up on all of my sleep, with all of this traveling."

George nodded again.

Karina did doze off, and woke as their car suddenly slowed. She opened her eyes and saw they were approaching New Bedford, about half of the way to Providence.

George saw she was awake. "You'll miss the train in Providence, if this doesn't get any better."

It didn't. "Do we know when the next train is?" Karina asked.

"I'm not sure," George replied. "Probably a couple of hours."

The slowdown worsened to barely a crawl. "I could get off on the next exit, and maneuver around a side road, and try to get to Providence that way," George said, "though for all we know Providence could be the source of this problem."

Karina considered. She knew, on the one hand, that it didn't matter what time she arrived in Newark, since the Thorne at the New Jersey Institute of Technology would get her to the future at the time she designated, whatever time she entered the artificial worm hole now, in the present. But there was the matter of her own state of mind -- plain old impatience, she had to be honest with herself -- which made any delays between now and getting to the future intolerable.

She sighed. "You win -- drive me to New York," she said to George. And a part of her thought, could he be so powerful, so well versed in the manipulation of reality, that he had caused this traffic jam, because he had wanted to take her to New York all along? No, she couldn't see how he would have been able to do that.

***

Jeff had used the Thorne and neo-Thorne facilities at the New Jersey Institute of Technology more than in any other place, but he felt the least at home here. The New York University Thorne, where he had started this journey -- more like this life -- decades ago in his lifetime, still seemed like the way a Thorne facility should be, even though he had used it only once. He often wondered if the fire that had destroyed the Student Lounge and with it the Thorne had been deliberately set by someone, maybe Jeff himself at some time in the future of his life. He could at least be sure that so far in his life, at least, that had not happened.

Heidi led Jeff not to the Turoff Lab with the Thornes, but the Weizenbaum conference room. Murray Turoff, who had done most of his work at NJIT, had won the Nobel Peace Prize in some timelines in the late 1990s for his pioneering work in computer mediated communication, also known as computer conferencing, and prelude to all the social media of the 21st century. The people who built this gleaming facility in Newark and its outpost in Jersey City obviously had some knowledge of Turoff and his accomplishments. They also knew about Joseph Weizenbaum and his MIT program Eliza, an early AI which mimicked a Rogerian psychologist, and came close to passing the Turing test for an AI being indistinguishable from a human being. Jeff smiled. There were a lot of "Tur"s in this business.

Heidi sat with Jeff in front of the big screen. "Jeff Harris," it said to Jeff, and didn't bother to acknowledge Heidi's presence.

Jeff nodded.

"We've reviewed your plans," the screen said to Jeff, "and find them mostly ok. But, before we proceed, please tell us why you came here to the future, rather than traveling straight back to 1983 to stop yourself from dying in the Challenger."

"I wanted to confirm that the Twin Towers had still been destroyed -- that their destruction has really taken, this far into the future, before I undertook to make sure that didn't happen," Jeff replied.

"Make sure?" the screen asked.

"Give it my best shot, right," Jeff replied. "I know there are no certainties in this business."

"And your other plan is to stop John Lennon from being killed?" the screen asked.

"Yes," Jeff said. "A personal thing, I guess -- I grew to really love the Beatles, and especially John Lennon, when I was living through the 1960s." And Laura singing Lennon's "Yes It Is" before it had been written is what put Jeff on to Laura being a time traveler, he thought, but didn't say to the screen, because he didn't know if this program knew that, and, if it didn't, he saw no reason to inform it.

"And if I told you that Lennon's life and death had profound social consequences, would that make you change your mind about changing that reality?" the screen asked.

"Probably not," Jeff replied. "Obviously, any songwriter and singer of Lennon's caliber had some important social impact."

"This is not just some important social impact," the screen replied and quoted Jeff. "This would be about as big a social impact as you can get –– as in, there may be a connection between Lennon not living and September 11, 2001 not happening."

For the first time in this conversation, Jeff looked at Heidi. She was as surprised as Jeff was about this announcement, though nowhere nearly as upset, likely because she hadn't lived through the 1960s, and obtained Jeff's first-run love of Lennon.

"You want to tell me how that could be so?" Jeff turned back to the screen.

***

The drive to New York was tiring, and Karina and George were hungry, so they stopped for a sushi dinner at Japonica in the Village, on the way to the Holland Tunnel, which would take them across the Hudson River to Newark and the New Jersey Institute of Technology. Thinking about the Holland Tunnel even in passing made her uncomfortable, because it reminded her of September 11, even though she was pretty sure that the Tunnel had not been seriously damaged in that attack. Knowing the future made a hell of a way to live life, and not hell in a good, exciting way, someone somewhere had told her. Maybe it was her mother, maybe it was father, maybe it was George, maybe it was someone else whose words not name or face she now remembered.

After placing her order for chirashi –– it was incredibly fresh in this restaurant, even for someone who hadn't just come from Russia, she was sure –– Karina excused herself and went to the lady's room. Her bladder was bursting after the long drive.

She returned to an empty table. She knew instinctively that George hadn't left the restaurant or gone to the bathroom himself. The waiter confirmed that when he arrived with her order, asked her if she wanted anything else, and didn't say a word about George, who had ordered chicken teriyaki.

She knew what had happened. Something -- someone -- had changed her history. She now remembered arriving at George's cottage on the Cape, finding no one there, and driving his car, with the keys she had found in their dresser, right here to this restaurant in New York City. That memory, in fact, was more vivid, more up front, than her recollection of finding George in the cottage and his driving them to to New York. That's the way it was with these changes in history wrought by time travel -- if you were player, an active participant, in creating events or changing them, you had a recollection of before and after the change. The most important question now was what else had changed in this new world.

She summoned the waiter and asked if he had a copy of the newspaper. He nodded and returned with today's edition of *The New York Times*. Judging by its front page, all was it should have been -- George Bush was President of the United States, Gorbachev was fighting for his political existence, Yelstin was surging.

But what else had changed that was not on the front page? And what had happened to make George Landry wink out of this existence?

***

Jeff found the click-clacking of the 7th Ave subway oddly comforting. Maybe that wasn't so odd. He had always found the rhythm of train tracks soothing -- like in that Arlo Guthrie song -- in synch with what he was feeling, always at least as far back as 1963, when he'd first started riding these antique underground and elevated rails.

But he did feel genuinely comforted -- and energized at the same time -- by what he had accomplished, and by what he was about to do. The first goal of his three-part journey had been successfully negotiated in 1986. He had confronted his earlier self in that bathroom, and stopped him from sacrificing his life on the Challenger. And the shuttle had indeed exploded, but not into the schoolhouse filled with kids in Miami. That was a big victory, of sorts. And obviously he had survived, because he was still here.

He had then returned to the New Jersey Institute of Technology, and taken a Thorne backward in time, to December 8, 1980. This was the date of John Lennon's murder, the second event which Jeff was intent on stopping. The digital nomenklatura in Newark were on board with this, and had helped Jeff put together a plan. They had misgivings about Jeff then doing something to prevent September 11, and had advised Jeff not to attempt that, but that didn't faze him. The programmers of the Thorne had no control over what Jeff did in the past or the future or at any time. The most they could do was prevent him from using the Thornes, by making them inoperative for him. But Jeff was more than willing to save Lennon and then work on his own to stop September 11, without the Thornes in Newark or anywhere else. He had a plan for that. But first things first: making sure John Lennon lived, and "Real Love" was a record released by all four living Beatles in the mid-1980s, after a brief reunion.

Lennon's killer, Mark David Chapman, had gotten Lennon's autograph, as John and Yoko walked to their limo which would take them to the Record Plant studio, a few hours before Chapman would shoot Lennon in the back at the Dakota, goddamn sicko that he was. Photographer Paul Goresh had captured that autograph.

Jeff had gone through a dozen plans in Newark, ranging from warning Lennon to tackling Chapman as he waited in the shadows with his gun, later in the evening. But stopping Chapman now, before the autograph, seemed the safest way to proceed -- if Jeff failed to do that, for any reason, he'd have a second chance, before 10:50pm, at the Dakota.

The No. 1 train that Jeff was on pulled into the 72nd Street and Broadway Station. Jeff looked at his analog watch that he always had around his wrist -- the least obtrusive timekeeper for a traveler to the past. Good -- the trip on Amtrak from Newark's Penn Station to New York's Penn Station, plus the trip on the subway up here, had taken under an hour. More than enough time for Jeff to get to the Dakota ahead of Chapman.

***

Karina decided to stay another day in New York City, so she could research the history of this timeline beyond what she could see in a copy of *The New York Times*. She booked a room in the Washington Square Hotel down the street on Waverly Place -- she was fortunate to get a room in this small, historic place, which she paid for with the copious local cash she had obtained with her current 1991 Citibank card waiting for her at NJIT when she'd arrived two days ago -- and woke up reasonable well rested and energized the next morning.

She checked out of the hotel and made her way to New York University's Bobst Library, just a few steps away. She still had her student ID card from her previous sojourns here, and it worked perfectly in gaining her admittance now.

She keenly missed the capacity to look up info instantly on her phone, but this library was a workable alternative, and, hey, it was the way people had done research for millennia prior to the 21st century. Within less than hour, she was convinced that this timeline was in accord with what she recalled and expected: John F. Kennedy had been assassinated in 1963, the same for John Lennon in 1980, and the Challenger had exploded in 1983 but nowhere near the schoolhouse in Miami. These were all events in which her father had been or would be involved, had tried or would try to stop or mitigate in one way or another.

Karina walked out into the mid-day August sunshine and smiled. The world was as she'd expected -- not what she wanted the world to be, but which meant she had a stable foundation upon which to act and help her father change this world. Washington Square Park was bursting with colors and sounds and life. A radio was blaring familiar music. "That's 'Real Love,' and this is Bob Shannon on WCBS-FM. The last song — at least of this date — that the Beatles recorded together. But did you see the interview with Lennon in *Rolling Stone* last month? He says they might do another reunion in 1993, on the 30th anniversary of "I Wanna Hold Your Hand".

Karina leaned on a big tree for support. The rough bark hurt her hand. Her world had just changed again.

***

Jeff walked slowly to the northwest corner of 72nd Street and Central Park West, where the stately Dakota stood. It was 4pm. He had plenty of time. All accounts said that Chapman didn't get Lennon's autograph until 5:40pm today.

Jeff thought again about his conversation with the powers-that-were at NJIT. Jeff had left them believing that he had reluctantly concluded that it was more important to him, and the future of humanity, to stop Lennon's assassination than the destruction of September 11. Lennon's survival was indeed important to humanity, if only for the songs unwritten after Lennon's death, like his sublime "Windows Unlimited" in 1999, having nothing to do with software but everything to do with the cosmos at large.

But NJIT was wrong to think that Jeff could choose that over the survival of thousands of souls in New York, Washington, and Pennsylvania. No, this was a choice Jeff was not willing to make. He was going to stop both.

Fortunately, the AIs or whatever they were called in this era at NJIT didn't know Jeff all that well, or as well as they supposed. Neither did Heidi, who had been sitting right next to him, and who seemed very perceptive, but, after all, they had just met less than an hour before.

So Jeff had been allowed to go on his way, to do two tasks in the past — the Challenger and Lennon — but not the third. But Jeff didn't need a Thorne for the third, and so didn't need to go back again to NJIT. He could live in real time from now until 2001, just as he had with Laura in the 1960s and 1970s, waiting for the Challenger. And he would do what was needed to alert the authorities about Mohamed Atta and the other terrorists closer to the time of their horrendous attack.

Jeff looked up at the Dakota. He had arrived at his destination. He looked around and saw no one worth noting. He crossed Central Park West, took a seat on a green-painted splintery bench, and waited.

***

The minutes passed slowly and the day grew cold. Jeff was glad he had bought a winter coat in Newark before boarding the train to New York. He kept his hands deep inside his pockets and scrutinized the Dakota.

Fans of John Lennon slowly began to appear, like in a time-lapse motion picture. None of them was Chapman. This bothered Jeff -- Chapman was supposed to have been hanging around the Dakota all day today, even touching Sean Lennon's hand at some point, according to the boy's nanny. Well, maybe she or the reports were wrong.

It was now 5:30pm, and still no sign of Chapman. Where the fuck was he?

Jeff decided to cross the street to get a closer look at what was happening at the Dakota. Probably Chapman was lurking in some shadows, and Jeff had missed him when Jeff first arrived here, more than an hour ago. But Jeff had surveyed the area pretty carefully.

Paul Goresh the photographer stepped out of the limousine that pulled up. He had with a big old-fashioned camera in hand. Well, every camera from this era and well into the 21st century looked old fashioned to Jeff.

Chapman was no more visible to Jeff close to the Dakota than Chapman had been to Jeff across the street. Chapman was supposed to give Lennon a copy of his *Double Fantasy* album, which Lennon autographed. Lennon was then reported as saying to Chapman, "Is this all you want?"

Jeff looked carefully all around. There were five people, in addition to him and Goresh, now standing on the sidewalk.

Three were women. Two were men, and both had albums in hand, but Jeff couldn't tell if they were *Double Fantasy*, and the people looked nothing like Chapman. Should Jeff try to stop them now, anyway? Was he witnessing the prelude to an assault on Lennon by someone other than Chapman?

The five now turned to the entrance of the Dakota, from which John and Yoko emerged. Both were smiling. Lennon signed albums. Jeff watched like a hawk -- no one pulled a gun or any weapon.

Lennon now turned to Jeff. "No autograph?" Lennon asked Jeff, with a laugh. He extended his hand for a handshake with Jeff. "Is this all you want?"

***

Karina sat on a bench in Washington Square Park, and steadied her nerves with a coffee she had obtained from a vending cart. The breeze was cool, and that helped calm her, too.

She thought she knew her father pretty well. They had spent almost two years together, just a few blocks from here in his apartment, before he had left for the future and she for the Cape, to save George Landry from a fate she remembered, but which turned out to no longer have happened.

Jeff her father had told her lots of things about the future, and lots about the past, including his desire to save John Lennon. If Lennon was now alive, that could only mean that somehow her father had succeeded. But at what price and unintended results?

She wept silently with joy, anyway. Damn the consequences, right? It was wonderful and miraculous to save someone you loved, save him from the cruel fangs of history, wasn't it? A deep part of her soul nodded in satisfaction.

But she was still concerned. She had come to New York on her way to Newark to meet her father, wherever he might be, in the future. And if he wasn't in the future, she'd have a better chance of learning where he was at NJIT than she would here, on this bench in Washington Square Park.

She looked at her analog watch, another little habit she had picked up from her father. It didn't matter in the slightest what the time was now. The Thorne at NJIT would take her to any time she wanted to go. But it was time to leave New York.

She stood, turned west, where she would catch the train to Newark, and froze. She could tell who he was, well before she could make out his face. He had an unmistakable walk.

"I know, it's difficult," George Landry said, as he reached Karina and touched her shoulder with something almost approaching tenderness.

***

Jeff staggered back, in shock, and tried not to show it. Those were the very words Lennon was reported to have said to Chapman in their next-to-final encounter.

And this meant, what? That Jeff would somehow murder John Lennon in the Dakota archway later this evening? No, no, that couldn't be. It wasn't that Jeff was incapable of pulling a trigger -- he had been this close to killing Nixon at the Lincoln Memorial, and would blow away Chapman right now, if Jeff thought that was the only way to stop that maniac.

But Chapman was not here -- even though he was supposed to be -- and Jeff didn't like those fateful words being said by Lennon to him. Jeff looked around. Was Chapman somewhere in this vicinity, just beyond the edges of Jeff's vision?

Jeff did notice the photographer, Goresh, who was standing by the limo, as John and Yoko climbed in. Goresh looked for a moment at Jeff, and maybe smiled at him. Had Goresh taken a photograph of Jeff and Lennon? Would that photograph go on to become world-famous, like the one of Lennon and Chapman? No -- that had happened only because Chapman had killed Lennon later this evening, and Jeff was positive that he could and never would do that.

But Chapman had, according to every history Jeff knew about, so where the hell was he now? The fact that Chapman wasn't here now of course didn't mean that he couldn't and wouldn't show up here later with his cowardly, despicable gun. Jeff had to make sure he wasn't distracted from stopping that.

He looked around again, as the limousine with John and Yoko pulled away, to take them to their recording session at the Record Plant, if that part of history was still holding true. Jeff thought he saw a glimpse of someone across the street. Could that be Chapman, arriving here later than recorded, for whatever reason? The figure was now walking quickly away, west towards Broadway, and there was a truck in the street that was blocking Jeff's view.

There was no sign of the figure and the future when the slow-ass truck had finally moved on. But Jeff crossed the street, and walked as fast as he could, in the direction he thought the figure had gone.

***

Karina told Landry everything that had happened to her, since his disappearance in Japanica, just a few blocks north of here, last night. What was the point of keeping anything secret from this man? He seemed to know everything anyway. And she was relieved to find that, in his reality, John Lennon had not been killed in 1980, which meant the two were at least on the same historical page.

"The frequent changes in reality you've been experiencing are sometimes evidence that your future life is not certain to continue, in a variety of timelines," Landry eventually told her.

That, certainly, was no relief. "And where have you been, and how long in your lifetime, have you been since we last met, that you picked up such good tidings about my future?" Karina asked Landry with a sour smile. He likely wouldn't tell her much, if their personal history was any guide, but it didn't hurt to ask.

"Cairo, and then Hamburg," Landry answered, matter-of-factly. "And it's been about two years for me since last we met. Cairo has a lot to commend itself, I love walking amidst the antiquities, a kind of time travel in itself," he added, almost dreamily.

"Pretty far from the Soviet Union," Karina said. "Is Egypt still its ally?"

"Egypt's more an American vassal now," Landry replied. "But

THE LOOSE ENDS SAGA

that's not why I was in Cairo."

"Which was to ..."

"Establish a relationship with Mohamed Atta," Landry replied to Karina's uncompleted question.

"The September 11 terrorist?" Karina asked.

Landry nodded.

"Why not just kill him outright?" Karina asked.

"Because if it hadn't been him, it would have been some other terrorist with big ideas who put together the attack," Landry replied. "No, my goal is to leverage Atta to sabotage and derail the attacks from the inside."

***

Jeff, still shaken by what had happened, got to Broadway and 72nd Street, and looked around in all directions. A part of him wondered why he should he should feel so inside-out now, spun around like a top, given all he had gone through before. He should be used to this by now, right? But he wasn't. Maybe it was John Lennon and his music, and the special impact that music had on the soul. Jeff breathed in deeply, in an attempt to steady himself that was only partly successful.

He looked north and south, east and west, and on the basis of no evidence crossed the street and headed south on Broadway. He walked by the Pink Cloud, a greasy spoon of a diner on 69th Street, and got very lucky. He entered, to get a tea to go to calm his nerves, and there was Chapman sitting at the counter nursing a tea or coffee or whatever in a thick beige cup himself.

Jeff quickly turned his head away so as not to alarm Chapman, and considered his options. There were a few empty seats at the counter. But he'd have a better view of Chapman from a table. Jeff sat an empty, stained formica table between Chapman and the door.

Unfortunately, two of New York's finest were yapping it up with the pretty cashier with Styrofoam coffee containers in the their hands. If Jeff approached them and told them about Chapman, Jeff would be arrested on the spot -- the perennial predicament in trying to alert authorities about murders or other bad events that hadn't yet occurred.

A waiter came over and asked for Jeff's order in a thick Greek accent.

"Orange juice -- large -- a tea with milk, and scrambled eggs, but with tomatoes instead of potatoes," Jeff told the waiter, who nodded and walked away.

Jeff looked at the counter. Chapman was still leaning over his cup, and the cops showed no indication of moving. There was a blonde with a ponytail and nice body also at the counter, but Jeff didn't have the luxury of looking at her now.

The waiter arrived with his orange juice and tea. Jeff slowly sipped the orange juice and kept his eyes on Chapman. He'd have to just wait this out, at least until either the cops or Chapman left the restaurant.

***

Karina looked out at the estuaries as she and Landry made their way to NJIT on the commuter train the two had boarded in New York City. She had no way of knowing the temperature of the water, but it reminded her of the cold fluid pulse of the cosmos in Cape Cod Bay, as her father called it. She could feel it tugging at her now.

The trouble with Landry, she always knew, is that she ultimately had no idea who he was, and what was his agenda. She had slept with him, sometimes loved him, had risked her life to save him, but she couldn't trust him. He came in and out of her life, like a strange dream, and yet she had no choice but to rely on him, because she had no one else to rely upon.

The train pulled into Newark's Penn Station, which ended Karina's reverie. She took Landry's hand as they left the station, as much out of a desire to keep him from vanishing as out of affection, though she knew full well she had no control at all over the vanishing. They hopped in a cab and told the driver to take them to NJIT.

The New Jersey Institute of Technology in 1991 was just a suggestion of the sparkling center of digital technology it would become by the middle of the 21st century, a rival to MIT. The cab left them off on Martin Luther King, Jr. Boulevard. Landry tipped the diver handsomely, and the two walked, Karina's hands around Landry's arm, to the computer center.

The Thorne in this period of time, they both knew, was housed in a small room off the "refrigerator," the main-frame computer that hosted NJIT's global computer conferencing facilities, as the educational and social networking that was conducted in this decade was called, at least by Murray Turoff and Roxanne Hiltz, who ran these programs for the university.

Landry's palm print opened the door — a handy palm to have, Karina thought, as she always did in these circumstances.

The room with the Thorne was low-key and non-descript, as were most of the Thornes themselves on the outside. This always struck Karina — how a device that looked like so little on the surface could do so much with what it had and did to time and space on the inside.

Landry felt the same way. "Inelegant, un-plush," he said and gestured to the Thorne before them. "A triumph of physics, to be sure, but not of visual design or comfort."

Karina nodded. Definitely a triumph, this whole operation at NJIT, which always had a least one Thorne at the ready, pulled instantly from wherever it was in the timeline, past or future, to this room, a split second after anyone entered.

"You want to go the future, to help your father," Landry asked, running his fingers over the control panel of the Thorne.

"No, I've changed my mind," Karina replied. "I want to go to the past, to help my father make sure that John Lennon survives."

Landry looked at her. "And the Challenger?"

"I can talk to my father in 1989 about not going down with the Challenger," Karina said, "if that happened later than saving John Lennon in my father's lifetime. If it happened earlier — well, that shows my father was not killed in the Challenger explosion, after all."

Landry smiled, impressed, and set the Thorne for December 6, 1980, two days before Lennon's murder in most timelines.

Landry gestured to the time machine. "All yours," he said to Karina. "I'll have to step outside the room, of course, for safety's sake."

Karina hugged and kissed him on the lips. "And where will *you* be headed?" she asked, as she entered the Thorne. She knew a new one would appear, a moment after hers departed and Landry re-entered the room.

"I'm really not sure," Landry replied.

***

Jeff had nursed two orange juices and three refills of his tea -- "yes, with a new bag, please" -- which still tasted like rusty dishwater, though he was pretty sure he had never actually tasted anything with rust on it. The cops and Chapman were still very much in evidence. Only the blonde with the nice body had left. Fortunately, she was wearing a winter jacket that went only to her waist, so Jeff was able to get good glimpse of her tight blue jeans as she walked out the door.

He focused on the matter at hand, and gradually became aware of something he hadn't realized before. Lennon had not been killed in 1980 in Jeff's lifetime. He had briefly reunited with the Beatles in the mid-1980s, and recorded "Real Love" and several other songs then. Jeff Lynne had produced that session, because George Martin's hearing had already gone. Suddenly, Jeff was able to remember all of that, as well as that in his original timeline, the one he was back here to change, Lennon would be murdered by Chapman tonight.

But if that wasn't going to happen, where did that leave Jeff with Chapman, drinking yet another cup of coffee at the counter, right now?

As if to answer Jeff's question, the cops received a staticky call of some sort on their walky talky, looked at each other, and quickly left the Pink Cloud.

It was just Jeff and Chapman now in the restaurant, and some presumably anonymous diners and staff. Jeff stood and walked towards Chapman. Killing him now seemed a little drastic, seeing as how Chapman in Jeff's current, on-top memory had not murdered John Lennon, would not murder Lennon this evening. But how could Jeff be sure that this memory would hold, that it wouldn't change a moment from now to what it had been until just a few minutes ago, a recollection of an historical record of Chapman killing John Lennon?

Jeff strode right up to Chapman, who looked an odd combination of smug and frightened. "Mark David Chapman? My name is Jeff -- can we talk?" Jeff seated himself next to Chapman at the counter without waiting for a reply.

"Is this about John Lennon?" Chapman asked.

How could Chapman know that that's what this about? Also, Jeff realized that if Chapman pulled a gun on him, Jeff was a sitting duck seated at this counter. "Yes," Jeff answered carefully. "I understand you're a true fan."

"Yes, I am," Chapman replied, maybe relaxing just a little. "And I would never do anything to hurt him, please believe me!" Now his voice was up again with emotion.

"I believe you," Jeff said, trying to be soothing. "But why would that even occur to you?"

"Because she told me what happened -- she spelled it out for me. But it wasn't me -- it must have been someone else!" Chapman insisted.

"Who told you?" Jeff asked, somewhat surprised.

"I didn't get her name," Chapman said. "She was here in the restaurant when I arrived." He looked around. "She isn't here now."

"The blonde woman who just left?" Jeff asked.

Chapman shook his head no. "I don't think her hair was blonde. And she was older." He looked around the restaurant. "Her!" He pointed to the woman who had just come through the door.

***

According to the historical records that Karina had been able to examine, Mark David Chapman flew from Hawaii to New York City and arrived December 6, 1980, two days before he murdered

John Lennon. The records said Chapman had checked into the Sheraton Hotel, on Seventh Avenue, between West 52nd and 53rd Street, near Times Square. That was where Karina was headed now.

The leap back in time in the Thorne had gone instantly, with no problem, as had the trip via train under the tunnel from Newark to New York, although that had taken a little longer. Karina walked up the grimy stairs of the Times Square subway complex into the dark early December evening.

Her plan was straightforward. The best way she could help her father was to dissuade Chapman from his demented mission before he ever showed up at the Dakota. Of course, she was acquainted enough with the stubborn resilience of history to know that, even if she removed Chapman from the equation, someone else might show up to kill John Lennon, if it was his fate to die. Not that Karina believed in fate -- far from it, otherwise she never would have gotten so involved in time travel -- but she was always struck by that writer from the beginning of the 20th century, and his stories about not being able to escape your fate. What was his name, Ambrose Bierce? No -- O'Henry.

She entered the lobby of the Sheraton Hotel, looked around, and, seeing no sign of Chapman, went straight to the front desk. "I'd like a room for three nights," she told the clerk, a young man with a moustache, about 25. "Is it ok if I pay with cash?"

"Of course," he replied, graciously. "I like money in the hand better than plastic, myself," he added and smiled.

Karina returned the smile. "Has my friend Mark David Chapman checked in yet?" She hoped the question wouldn't arouse too much suspicion. She was a young, unassuming woman, and she was pretty sure people weren't all that security conscious in 1980.

But the question caused the clerk to lose a little of his smile. He looked at a big screen in front of him, the size of television screen, no doubt connected to some kind of primitive database, and typed on his keyboard. "C-h-a-p-m-a-n?" he spelled out the name.

Karina nodded.

"No, not yet," the clerk said. "And you are?"

"Karina Harris." No point in using a fake name. Her real name would mean nothing to this clerk, or to Chapman.

"Should I tell him to contact you, when he arrives?" the clerk asked.

"No, I want to surprise him." Karina put on her best shy, slightly flirtatious face.

That brought back most of the clerk's smile. "Of course," he said. "Please fill this out." He handed her a clipboard with a form, along with two sets of keys. "You're in room 403 – I think you'll like it."

Karina filled out the form, scooped up the keys, thanked the clerk, and headed to the elevator. Along the way, she passed by the café, and looked in, on the chance that Chapman was there and hadn't yet checked into the hotel.

No Chapman, but something -- someone – caught her eye as she started to walk on. She turned back, looked again, and caught her breath. No way -- couldn't be!

The last thing she wanted was running into her later self -- which would cause her later self nothing but grief. She walked into the café and looked more closely. The woman at the table saw her smiled.

Oh my God, Karina said to herself, and she was a committed atheist.

***

Laura Chapin Harris walked into the Pink Cloud. She saw two men at the counter. They were looking and gesturing at her. Jeff Harris and Mark David Chapman.

Jeff saw Laura, and suppressed the urge to run and hug her. He didn't want to let Chapman know how much Laura meant to him.

"She's the one who talked to me about John Lennon," Chapman said, again, in an exaggerated whisper, in a tone that sounded to Jeff almost like fear.

It had been almost eight years in Jeff's lifetime since he had last seen and held Laura. She looked maybe a tad older than what Jeff recalled. Mostly she just looked good, so good, as she always did to Jeff. As far as he knew, she and Jeff's younger self were now in New York, living on the East Side, near York Avenue.

Laura joined Jeff at the counter, so he was sandwiched between Laura and Chapman, one of the best and one of the worst things in his life. Had Chapman been seated between them, Jeff would have been unhappily part of a sickeningly perfect shit sandwich. Laura took Jeff's hand, likely to calm him, and it mostly worked.

"Have you been to the Soviet Union?" Jeff asked her. Laura had gone back to the Soviet Union at the end of the 1980s, presumably to help Gorbachev and Yeltsin end Communism, so if she answered "yes," this meant she was a little older than the last time they had been in contact.

"Yes," Laura answered.

"I'll take the check please," Chapman asked the waitress with an Afro behind the counter, and made to leave.

"Please don't," Jeff said, in a quietly commanding voice.

"It's ok," Laura said, softly. "I've reported him to the police. He won't get anywhere near John Lennon tonight. Or any other night."

Chapman looked stricken. "You said you wouldn't!" he said to Laura.

"I know," Laura said, "but, you know, belt and suspenders. You can't be too careful with lunatics like you."

The waitress arrived with Chapman's check.

This wasn't sitting well with Jeff at all. He knew the only way to guarantee that Chapman didn't murder John Lennon was to kill this piece of sicko shit right here and now.

Laura picked up something of Jeff's emotion, and tightened her grip on his hand. "This is the best way," she said to Jeff. "What you have in mind will do who-knows-what to the timeline, and could well lure other monsters out of the woodwork. Not to mention that you're not--"

"--a murderer," Jeff finished the thought and said the word to himself. He'd heard this from Laura before, about his plan to kill Richard Nixon.

Chapman put a five-dollar bill on the counter to cover his coffees and tip, and slid off his stool. "I was nowhere near him, I assure you," he said to Laura, in a quavering voice.

She glared pure hatred at him. "Even this is far too close. I'd strongly advise you to leave this city and never come back."

She looked at Jeff with eyes that were slightly moist for a different reason. "If you want to stop September 11, this is best way," Laura said very softly to Jeff.

   ***

"Momma," Karina said, trying without much success to control her volume, and walked quickly to the table.

Laura rose, put her arms around Karina, and kissed her repeatedly all over her head. She pulled away and touched her daughter's face. "How long has it been, for you?" she asked, her voice brimming with emotion.

"Five years, I guess," Karina said, unable to hold back her tears.

"Longer for me," Laura said, now crying, too. "Why do we do this to ourselves?" She gestured Karina to sit, which she did.

"The greater good, as Poppa always says," Karina answered.

Laura nodded. "Have you seen him?"

"Yes," Karina replied. "I mean, here in New York, at NYU, after you left to go back to the Soviet Union, but that was almost three years ago in my lifetime, too."

Laura took Karina's hand. "Are you hungry?" she asked and looked around for the waiter.

"I'm fine," Karina said. "I'll just get some water."

Laura pushed her glass, still full with water, across the table to her daughter. "I know where he'll be, two days from now."

"That's the day of John Lennon's murder," Karina said. "You know for a fact that Poppa will be there?"

"Yes, Heidi Cartling told me, at NJIT, in the future," Laura said, and unconsciously frowned. She didn't like the way the

Cartling girl talked about Jeff. She could see Jeff's lips on that long blonde neck, she knew from first-hand experience how women in academe were attracted to him, but maybe that was no longer any of her business. She and Jeff hadn't seen each other for years in their lifetimes.

Karina either missed the frown or didn't care, because she had more pressing things to think about. "So you're here for the same reason I am -- and Poppa -- to stop Mark David Chapman from killing John Lennon."

Laura nodded again. "I think I already took care of that."

"You killed him? That's the only way to know for sure that Lennon will be safe."

Laura frowned again, long and broadly enough that Karina couldn't miss it. "You're just like your father -- killing isn't the only way."

"So what did you do with Chapman?"

"I met him at the airport and told him I told the police all about him," Laura replied. "Which I did. They've assigned an undercover cop to guard Lennon -- a kid, your age, looks like just another fan. He'll stop Chapman if he gets anywhere close to John Lennon."

Karina considered, and slowly shook her head. "I don't know," she finally said.

"Think about it," Laura said. "As far as you know, John Lennon was alive and well, well into the 21st century. You've been there, isn't that right? There was that Beatles re-union concert in 1985, Paul McCartney was the last to come aboard, but he eventually showed, right? And all the Beatles including Lennon were there."

"Yes, I recall that," Karina replied. "And I also have an earlier memory of Lennon being killed, and of—-"

A waiter showed up, and Karina stopped talking. "I'll have a roast beef sandwich, with tomato and mustard, on a deli roll, if you have it."

"We do," the waiter said, and left.

Karina returned her attention to her mother. "So you're right that what you did stopped Chapman from killing Lennon the day after tomorrow. But you and I both know that could change in a heartbeat."

***

Jeff looked at Chapman as he walked, seemed to slink, out of the restaurant. "I won't be comfortable until 10:50pm tonight passes and Lennon's ok. And even then ..."

"There'll be police around Lennon — as I told you, I alerted them. They're protecting him right now," Laura said.

"I just came from the Dakota — Chapman was there to, I followed him to this restaurant. I didn't see any police."

"They're undercover. They look like his entourage," Laura said.

The two decided to get a room at the Empire Hotel, above O'Neal's Balloon, a few blocks down the street. Jeff was insistent on staying in the area, staking out the Dakota in the evening, and doing what was necessary to stop Chapman, should the police fail.

Jeff was exhausted and stretched out on the big bed, his head against the burnished brass rail. Laura joined him, but both were too preoccupied with Chapman to do more than cuddle and talk.

Or maybe not. Jeff put his hand inside Laura's shirt and gently stroked her back.

"We should talk about September 11," Laura said.

"Yeah," Jeff said, but left his hand on the small of her back.

"I assume the voices in the future told you the same thing they told me," Laura said, "that saving Lennon and stopping September 11 may be incompatible."

"They did," Jeff said. "Did they tell you why?"

Laura shook her head no. "They never do. But Karina says Landry is trying to work some angle with Mohamed Atta."

"That obviously hasn't worked as yet. I'd love to see her," Jeff said, and moved his hand further down Laura's back.

She removed it. "I don't where she went after she left the Sheraton, like I told you."

"I know," Jeff said. "Who the hell is he, Landry?"

"I don't know that, either," Laura said.

"We don't know a lot of things," Jeff said, softly. "But I know I think about you every day, about the first time we kissed when you spilled that wine, about doing this, even though you're a Russian spy or whatever agenda you're really serving." And he kissed her and he put his hand on her back again, and this time she didn't remove it.

"You sure you want to do this?" Laura murmured.

"No," Jeff replied, but by then they were mostly undressed, and proceeded to put the plush bed to best use.

***

Karina walked north on Broadway and considered her options. She could return to her mother, who had told her she was staying at the Sheraton at least two days, through December 8th. Or, Karina could hunt down Chapman herself, and make sure in whatever way was necessary that he did no damage to Lennon. She could try to meet up with her father -- her mother had told her that she had information that he would be at the Pink Cloud restaurant up on 69th Street, at 6pm on December 8th. Or she could she turn around, head south, and return to NJIT and New Jersey right now, where she could try to connect with Landry, and see if she could help him derail the September 11 attacks.

She wanted to go back to her mother, but she didn't know if she could trust her. Not that her mother would ever deliberately do any anything to hurt Karina -- Karina knew implicitly how much her mother loved her - and loved her father, too, for that matter. It was just that Karina could never be sure what ultimate goal her mother was pursuing. For some reason, she had more confidence about that in her father -- what she saw in Jeff Harris was usually what she got.

Could she believe her mother that Chapman's threat to John Lennon had been neutralized? Well, Lennon was still alive and well for decades to come in her memory, which told Karina that maybe her mother indeed had succeeded in stopping Chapman.

She passed by the Pink Cloud and kept walking. She stopped by the Papaya place on 72nd Street. She'd developed a taste for this juice drink from her father. She ordered a small-size container, sipped it slowly as she leaned on the counter, and did a little experiment.

Ok, she decided she would go back to her mother, and made a definite commitment to do that in her head. Then she thought about John Lennon, and all four Beatles singing "Real Love" in 1985. Good. The memory she had of that recording, seeing videos of it years later on YouTube, was clear and unmistakable. Ok. Now she changed her mind, and decided with equal conviction to head south, past the Sheraton and her mother, to Penn Station on 33rd Street, where she'd catch a commuter train to Newark. Yes, she was definitely going to do that. And she thought about Lennon, and saw the same video of the 1985 recording of "Real Love" in her head. Lennon and McCartney were laughing and mugging for the camera. Yoko and Linda were dancing some kind of drunken waltz together. It brought tears to her eyes. Then the camera panned and there was Ringo and Barbara, and George and Patty. Hmmm . . . this video, she realized for the first time, showed a reality a little different from her original memories, in addition to Lennon being alive. In her original memory, of Lennon being murdered in 1980, Harrison and Patty had split up. Harrison had earlier written "All Things Must Pass," Patty had later married Eric Clapton, and George married Olivia. None of that existed in the reality of Lennon reuniting with the Beatles in 1985. She wondered whom Eric Clapton had married instead.

Karina ordered another papaya, large size, and deliberately changed her mind again. She would go back neither to her mother nor NJIT -- she would hunt down and kill Chapman. She started thinking about John Lennon but was interrupted by someone who walked in and ordered a papaya too. He looked exactly like Mark David Chapman.

Her mind and world and everything inside and outside and all around her seemed to freeze for the next few minutes, until

Chapman took the container of papaya juice he had ordered and walked back out on 72nd Street, east, away from the Dakota. Yeah, he not only looked like Chapman, he was Chapman, she was sure of that. And he was walking away from where John Lennon and he would be, in her original memory, in two days.

That, of course, guaranteed nothing. Chapman could take a plane to Los Angeles tonight and return tomorrow, in more than enough time to kill Lennon the day after that. There was no certainty that the psychotic weasel bastard, sweating a bit even in the December cold, wouldn't turn around and head right back to Lennon's residence in the next few minutes.

She had no idea where Lennon was at this moment, or what Chapman intended to do. But she had learned something crucial in this instant, and she maybe had grown up, was now fully an adult, for the first time in her life.

She wasn't a killer. She knew that now about herself. No matter how much she wanted to kill a deserving target, with every ounce of her essence, no matter how logical that seemed, she knew could never bring herself to do it. Not in this way -- not when the target was even someone as horrible as Chapman, when he was just standing at a counter, waiting for his damned papaya. Maybe if she caught him going with a gun at Lennon it would be different. Maybe if it was a KGB pig trying to kill her or someone she loved. But not this way, not when he was just standing there. She just didn't have it in her, no matter how much she wished and fantasized and assumed she had.

She wondered if her father and mother were the same way.
***

Jeff and Laura took up a position across the street from the Dakota at 10pm, in case Lennon and Chapman for some reason showed up earlier than Jeff and Laura's history had recorded. Their spot afforded them a good view of the Dakota and its infamous archway, where Chapman shot and killed Lennon as Lennon walked past Chapman and nodded at him.

Chapman was nowhere to be seen, including around the block, which Jeff had walked a few times. Lennon's limousine pulled up to the Dakota's 72nd Street entrance at 10:50pm, exactly as in Jeff and Laura's history.

"If Chapman shows up, I'm going to strangle him with my bare hands," Jeff almost growled from a place deep in his soul.

"If he has a gun, he could kill you," Laura replied.

"He won't expect me," Jeff said. "I'll grab him from behind."

But Lennon and Yoko had already exited the limo and were now in the archway, and the only other person with them was a guy who looked to be in his 20s, and had the aura of a fan. But he looked everywhere, repeatedly, including possibly at Jeff and Laura across the street.

"He must be the undercover cop," Laura said.

Jeff nodded. The Lennons and the cop were now inside the Dakota, and out of sight.

"What if Chapman is waiting inside?" Jeff asked. He knew out of sight was by no meant out of danger.

"First, why would the doorman have let him in?" Laura replied. "And, second, the undercover guy is still keeping his eyes wide open for Chapman."

Jeff nodded again and relaxed a little.

"And most important, I still have the prime memory of Lennon surviving," Laura added. "Do you?"

"Yes," Jeff said, and a permitted himself a smile –- it seemed, for the first time in a long time, at least days.

Laura took his hand. "Let's walk back to the hotel, and focus on our other problem."

"Let's wait here a few more minutes, and make sure our good memories of Lennon are still intact," Jeff replied.

They waited about twenty minutes, and walked slowly back to Broadway then south to the Empire Hotel.

"Tell me more why this wonderful thing you just made happen may be incompatible with our stopping September 11," Jeff asked Laura.

"It's a song Lennon performed at the 1985 concert. Landry says it inspired Muhamed Atta," Laura said.

"You mean like 'Helter Skelter' inspired Charles Manson?"

"Yeah, maybe, apparently," Laura said.

"That was a McCartney song, if I remember correctly," Jeff said. He had been a young professor of popular culture, especially music, from this era, and in other circumstances this conversation would have been a real pleasure. "What got to Atta? 'Real Love'? That's a gentle, beautiful song."

"No, I don't think it was that one," Laura said.

"Lennon performed lots of songs at that 1985 concert -- and all were peaceful – 'Revolution,' 'Imagine,' 'Give Peace a Chance,' 'War Is Over'. How did Atta even see that concert? 2001 was before YouTube, wasn't it?"

"Yes, but the 1985 concert was widely shown on CNN, HBO, and national television networks all over the world at the time. The Beatles re-union was a very big deal."

Jeff nodded.

"'Free as a Bird'," Laura said. "I think that was the song in the concert that inspired Atta, according to Landry."

"But that's a beautiful song, too," Jeff objected, realizing the absurdity and futility of objecting to history if that's the way it went down.

"I know," Laura said. "But something about the sky and going home triggered something in that terrorist brain."

The two reached the Empire. "So what do we do to stop it?" Jeff asked.

***

Karina walked outside the papaya place, looked west down 72nd Street to make sure Chapman wasn't returning, and made a decision. She finished the last of her frothy juice, enjoyed the slurping sounds she made with her straw, and confirmed that John Lennon was still alive in her future in her primary memory.

She looked one more time towards the west and the Hudson, and hailed a cab. "Penn Station," she told the cabbie.

Her timing was a good. A train was practically waiting for her at Penn Station in New York, which she boarded. The ride to Penn Station in Newark was smooth and swift, as was the cab ride from the train station to NJIT.

Heidi Cartling was seated on maple bench, outside the room with the Thorne. This was the first time she had seen Heidi this far back in time, at the end of 1980. Karina liked what Heidi looked like. She could easily imagine the long-necked junior programmer naked and in bed. Karina liked women as much as men, but this was egregiously not the time or the place.

Karina told Heidi where -- or when -- she wanted to go. Karina also thought Heidi caught what Karina had just been thinking about her, and maybe Heidi was inclined to similar feelings, but, again, not today.

"The space-time fabric is wearing thin in this era," Heidi said, "and we've been told to limit our jumps to the absolutely essential. I said the same to your father, the other day."

"Stopping September 11, if it can be prevented, seems pretty essential," Karina replied. "Only bad things resulted from that -- no silver linings at all."

"Agreed," Heidi said. "But we both know that the surest way of stopping that is making sure the Soviet Union triumphed in Afghanistan, and killing bin Laden right in the cradle, as it were."

"True," Karina said, "but we both know that damned ship has sailed already, too."

Heidi accepted the point. "So what year do you want to visit? Choose wisely -- this may be your last opportunity."

"What happens if the space-time continuum unravels and stays open?" Karina asked.

"Unknown," Heidi replied. "But at the very least, it would confound our Thornes. Their travel is predicated on the natural time-space continuum, before we started plying it apart."

"Ok," Karina said. Her plan when she arrived here had been to travel back to 1991, and do what she could to meet up with Landry and help with his plan to dissuade Muhamed Atta. But with opportunites for time travel now headed for some absolute limitation, 1991 seemed too far away from the event she wanted to stop.

"The summer of 2001," Karina said.

***

Jeff and Laura were back in their bed in the Empire Hotel, very much awake, and continuing the conversation they had started at the Dakota an hour earlier.

"We could contact Lennon and ask him to remove 'Free as a Bird' from the 1985 set," Jeff suggested.

"When, now? Five years before the concert and probably almost as long as Lennon's decision to do the reunion?" Laura asked and shook her head no. "He'd think we were crazy — always a problem when you try to tell someone about their future — and if not, he'd be unlikely to respond very kindly to our meddling with his life."

Jeff shook his head, too, at the ironies that seemed baked into the fragile pottery of time travel. "And of course he'll never know about the meddling from you that just saved his life tonight."

"Didn't Elton John have a song like that," Laura asked, playfully, and rubbed Jeff's abdomen. "'Someone Saved My Life Tonight'?"

Jeff got up to get some water. "You're becoming almost as much of an expert about 20th century music as I am."

"You taught me a lot," Laura said, truthfully, and smiled. "But even if we were able to get Lennon to take 'Free as a Bird,' out of the concert, Atta would likely find his dark inspiration someplace else."

Jeff nodded.

"In one of most common timelines," Laura continued, "Lennon is murdered tonight and September 11, 2001 happens anyway, right?"

Jeff nodded again. "All right, let's look at this another way." He finished his water, put the glass on the night table, and rejoined Laura in bed. "I suppose you wouldn't want to go back to the Soviet Union, do what you can to keep Andropov in power at least through the 1990s, so the Russians kill bin Laden in Afghanistan before he can do any damage?"

"Right, *nyet*," Laura replied, and moved a bit away from Jeff, so she could make her point to him face-to-face. "The Soviet

Union surviving into the 21st century would stop September 11, and would be good for humans in space -- the goal that started you on all of this in first place -- but it would be awful for the world in all kinds of other ways, as you well know."

Jeff sighed. The sad strains of the Soviet national anthem played in his head. A 21st century world armed to the teeth with nuclear weapons and using them, nukes of space stations and missions in the solar system, yeah, he had gamed those scenarios, and had to agree that even stopping September 11 wasn't enough to risk making them come true. "Let's get some sleep, and see what we think about all of this in the morning," was all he said.

"Good idea," Laura said, and put her arms around Jeff and her head on his chest.

Jeff fell asleep, thinking he was glad indeed that John Lennon had been saved, the options for stopping September 11 were very limited, and they likely would have to travel much closer to that time to have any chance of stopping that attack. But that assumed there was still some juice left in the Thornes, because, if there wasn't, the two would have to live 20 years in real time to get within striking distance of preventing those planes that crashed into the Twin Towers and the Pentagon and Pennsylvania from ever getting off the ground.

***

Karina left an anonymous tip with the FBI about the impending attacks as soon as she arrived in July 2011. But nothing changed in her memory, which meant her tip had not been taken seriously by an important enough person. When she was sure that her warning to the FBI had had no effect, Karina set off on her Plan B to stop September 11, which in her heart she had always known was Plan A.

She booked a flight to Miami, Florida, to stop Muhamed Atta in his tracks directly. History had recorded that Atta had driven Ziad Jarrah, another terrorist hijacker who would be part of the September 11 attacks, to Miami International Airport on July 25, 2001.

Karina arrived in Miami a few days earlier. As she left the airport, she reflected on the parallels that seemed to proliferate in her family of time travelers. Her father had delighted in the papaya juice in King's Papaya, on the East Side of New York, in the 1960s, and she had sipped papaya juice and seen Chapman in Grey's Papaya on the West Side just a few days ago in her lifetime, two decades ago in world history. And here she was now in Florida, where her father in 1986 had prevented the Challenger from demolishing a schoolhouse filled with children.

She awoke in her room in the hotel near the airport early in the morning of July 25, and began to put her plan into motion. She hand-printed her message clearly on a piece of hotel stationery, then tore off the name of the hotel just to be safe. She folded the paper in half. Her note said, "I know what you're planning to do with the planes."

She figured this couldn't give Atta any specific ideas, in case he wasn't planning his multiple plane hijacks. The last thing she wanted was to be the worse than bitterly paradoxical cause of what Atta and his hijackers were going to do. She was determined to stop not trigger that, in any way.

She walked to the airport entrance and took up her post standing near the door. Security was light, because, after all, this was before not after September 11.

Atta and Jarrah should be arriving any minute, if her facts were correct. She put a dark nylon scarf around her head and tied it under her chin. This, she hoped, would make Atta more receptive to her message. She thought there was a good chance that just reading what she had written would throw the hijackers off, at least postpone what they had planned for September 11, which would give Karina more time to alert and with any luck mobilize the authorities.

A cab pulled up to the curb, and much to her satisfaction, Atta and Jarrah indeed emerged. Her history was right. Her pulse was pounding. Now she would see if she could change that history.

She strode up to Atta. He looked in her eyes, with a

combination of a leer and perhaps some surprise and confusion on his face. She thrust the folded paper into his hand, quickly turned and walked away. She stopped and waited behind a white pillar, so that she could see Atta but he couldn't see her.

Atta looked at down at his hand— at the very moment a kid, in pursuit of a runaway balloon, smashed right into him.

Atta said something that sounded like a curse in Arabic.

"Jimmy!" a mother's voice called out. "Watch where you're going! Apologize to the man!"

"I'm sorry," Jimmy, about eight years old, said sheepishly to Atta.

Atta scowled but patted the boy on the head.

Now the mother, with two other energetic children in her charge, reached Atta. She apologized again.

"Let's go," Karina thought she heard Jarrah say to Atta, and the two nodded courteously to the mother, and walked through the airport into the lobby.

Karina had no idea what had happened to the note she had given to Atta, but she was 100% sure he had not looked at.

***

Jeff awoke the next morning, ordered room service breakfast for Laura and him, and made a decision while she was still sleeping.

She awoke while he was finishing his breakfast. She stretched, rubbed the sleep from her eyes, and felt happy -- until she saw Jeff's face.

"What's wrong," she asked Jeff, put on the robe from the hotel that had been at the foot of their bed, and joined Jeff at the table.

"Nothing that has happened, as far as I know," Jeff replied, and poured Laura a big glass of orange from the pitcher he had ordered. "But I just don't feel comfortable assuming Lennon is totally out of danger from Chapman as yet. I think we should go keep on eye on the Dakota, at least another day or two.

Laura knew better than to argue. She finished her juice, toast, scrambled eggs, and tea in a few minutes, dressed quickly, and left with Jeff for the Dakota.

They hailed a cab. "We don't know John Lennon's schedule today," Laura said. "With him not being killed yesterday, I doubt there are any historical records of what he did, where he may have gone, today."

"I know," Jeff said, as the cab pulled up to 72nd Street and Central Park West. He gave the driver a $10 bill for a fare that was just over a dollar. "Keep the change."

"Thank you, sir," the driver said, brightly, in an Indian or Pakistani accent.

Jeff and Laura waited across the street, spelled each other as one went to fetch tea or water, and walked all around the Dakota, for several hours.

"Maybe I'm worrying for nothing," Jeff said, a few minutes before noon. They had been at the Dakota since shortly after nine in the morning. Their memories of Lennon not being murdered were clear and intact.

Laura wasn't sure what to say. She didn't think this vigil was necessary, but knew Jeff had to come to that conclusion, feel it in his soul, on his own. "Wait a minute," she said, "isn't that his limousine?"

"Yes, I think it is," Jeff said, and stared it, and all he could see of the Dakota, intently.

Lennon exited the limo -- just himself, no Yoko, but with the same undercover cop as last night at his side.

"I guess he had an early morning recording session, or a business meeting, that took him out of the Dakota before we arrived," Laura said.

The cop looked around, noticed Jeff and Laura, and likely recognized them from last night. He said something to Lennon, who nodded, and the cop turned and started walking slowly to Jeff and Laura.

Jeff, still fixing his eyes on Lennon, thought he saw a flicker of something in the periphery of his vision. In a fragment of a second, Jeff concluded that the flicker looked like Chapman. "Mr. Lennon!" Jeff shouted at the top of his lungs and ran full speed towards Chapman.

Jeff wasn't looking at all at the cop, who had pulled out his weapon and was pointing it at Jeff.

But Laura saw this and pointed to Chapman. "He's the one you need to stop, he has the weapon," she shouted to the cop.

Chapman indeed had a gun and was pointing it towards Lennon. The cop saw this and pointed his own weapon at Chapman. "Put your gun down, now!" the cop commanded.

Chapman's response was to fire two shots at Lennon. Before he could fire a third, Jeff tackled him, thinking, I'm not going to let the resilience of history, its perverse resistance to large-scale change, manifest itself through you, you goddam piece of shit mother fucker! And the cop managed to get off a shot in Chapman's direction.

The universe stopped cold for Laura at that instant. Or maybe it was her perception that had frozen. It felt that way for what seemed like a hundred years. The puffs of smoke from the gunshots, or maybe just in her brain, slowly, finally cleared.

--and Jeff was next to her. "It's ok, I'm ok," she heard him say, and Laura got that he had been saying that to her repeatedly.

Chapman, unwounded, was being handcuffed by the cop.

Lennon, also unwounded, walked over the Jeff and Laura.

None of the shots had hit, Laura realized.

"Thank you, man," Lennon said to Jeff. "I'd hug you, but I'm coming down with a cold and don't want to infect you!"

Jeff almost laughed.

The cop walked up to Jeff and Laura, with the handcuffed Chapman in tow. "You on the job?" the cop asked Jeff.

"No," Jeff replied.

"Could you wait here? We'll need you for a statement -- a patrol car should be here in a few minutes."

"I think I dropped my copy of *Catcher in the Rye* back there," Chapman piped up. "Could someone go back and get it for me?"

"Sure," Jeff said to the cop and ignored Chapman.

The cop's response to Chapman was to push him forward, towards Central Park West, where presumably more officers would soon be arriving.

"We should get out of here now, and on to September 11," Jeff said quietly to Laura.

"That's almost nine months away," Lennon said. "What's happening then for you, a baby maybe?"

"Long story," Jeff replied, and touched Lennon's shoulder. "Keep up the great work, your music brings joy to millions and millions of people, and will for centuries to come."

***

Karina sat in the coffee shop of her Miami hotel, and laughed to herself without joy. There was nothing even remotely funny about being jerked around by the universe this way. Plans A and B had failed, whatever their order, so she was now on to Plan C.

Atta was due, according to history, to meet the so-called 20th hijacker, Mohammed al-Qahtani, at the Orlando Airport on August 6. But al-Qahtani apparently never showed. Karina could try again to deliver a note to Atta, to disconcert him and make him reconsider his planning, but she was wary of trying the same gambit again, given the universe or whatever was calling these shots another chance to throw an out-of-control kid into the works to defeat her plans.

Atta was next known to be at the Wayne Inn in Wayne, New Jersey, from August 7 through August 9. Wayne was about 20 miles from NJIT, which offered a unique advantage. She had by far the greatest likelihood there of running into someone she knew who might be able to help her with Atta –– her father, her mother, Heidi Cartling, Landry, and there were others. Indeed, other than at NJIT, she had no likelihood of crossing paths with any of them, unless it was in a place and time in which she knew one of them would be present. She booked and boarded the next available flight from Miami to Newark. The sooner she got to the air-conditioned corridors of NJIT, which felt like a dank icebox, the greater her chance of meeting someone who could help her.

She didn't have to wait too long at NJIT. George Landry walked into the cafeteria and sat at her table on July 30. His showing up here at this exact time with Karina at the table was obviously way beyond coincidence, but she was delighted to see him and thought this was a damn sight better than his suddenly popping in and out of her life the way he had the past few times.

They caught each other up on events since their last meeting, as was their all too practiced custom and the way of life for all who time traveled and worked together. She was relieved that Landry's most recent effort since she and he had talked had been his attempt to dissuade Muhamed Atta -- because that meant there was nothing new in the mix that Karina had to take into account -- but she wasn't relieved at all that Landry's attempt had obviously failed.

"I may have succeeded in peeling off al-Qahtani," Landry concluded, "though his absence won't lessen the damage in New York and Washington."

Karina nodded. "How did you know I'd be here now?" she couldn't resist asking.

"I heard Ray Peterson singing 'Corrina, Corrina' -- great song -- and that made me think of you," Landry replied, with a smile.

Karina returned the smile. She didn't know why she ever bothered asking Landry questions like this, he always gave her the same non-answers. He likely had access to some Thorne or NJIT logs, and didn't want to talk about that. "So what's your thinking about September 11?" She knew Landry was more likely to give her a more responsive answer to that question.

Which he did. "I don't think your plan of rattling Atta with your note is best way to go," he said. "I think stopping him and all the hijackers as close as possible to their boarding the planes has the most chance of succeeding."

"Isn't that dangerous in itself -- waiting until the very last minute? With no back-up if we fail?"

"Yes, it's dangerous, but it's likely still the best way," Landry replied. "That's how your father managed to stop Chapman."

"My father?" Karina asked. "I thought my mother frightened Chapman out of doing it a few days earlier." But she knew full well that she had indeed seen Chapman herself, not too far from the Dakota, after her mother had said she'd talked Chapman out killing John Lennon.

"That indeed stopped Chapman on the original night of Lennon's murder," Landry replied. "But the slime showed up the next morning, anyway. Your father tackled him after Chapman got off a few shots. Fortunately none hit Lennon or your father."

Karina took that in, feeling guilty that she hadn't even tried to stop Chapman when she'd had the chance. This made her more sympathetic to Landry's plan. "So what are you specifically suggesting we do now about September 11?"

"We wait until September 11, and stop all four hijackings at the airports."

"You're talking about four planes from three airports — in Boston, Washington, and Newark – that's a hell of a lot more than you and I would be able to handle," Karina said.

"I know," Landry said. "I'm putting together a team right now. Heidi Cartling will be able to help us at the Newark airport."

"Good," Karina said. She assumed that Landry had no idea about the fantasies she'd had about Heidi. And, actually, she didn't really care if he did. "Who else?"

"Your parents," Landry said, "who should be joining us any moment at this table."

***

Jeff and Laura had been in New York City most of 2000, and into the summer of 2001. They had not been their intention, when they'd entered NJIT with the Thorne the day after Jeff had saved Lennon on December 9, 1990. Jeff and Laura had wanted to go forward to June 2001, but the Thorne had simply refused to take their instructions, and there were no technicians around who could explain or override its balky behavior.

They two were well aware of what basins of attraction did to time travelers — one had pulled Jeff back to November 1963 when he was expecting to arrive in January 1986 to stop the Challenger disaster. That was in fact how Jeff had come to meet Laura in the first place, when she had been a student in the class he was teaching at CCNY in the 1960s.

They both had wondered, when they found in 1980 that

their path to 2001 had been blocked, if there weren't also basins of repulsion, which prevented them from traveling to certain times. But whether or not those arose of their accord -- a natural effect of time travel, as presumably were the basins of attraction -- Jeff and Laura had no idea. For all they knew, they both realized, these basins could have been deliberately created, perhaps by someone like Landry.

Jeff and Laura were glad that they at least had been able to commission transport for two to February 2000. A single Thorne accepted programming to take Laura to that time, then return to the exact time it had left in December 1980, to take Jeff forward to the exact same time as Laura. Jeff and Laura both sighed deeply with relief when Jeff arrived. The thought obviously had occurred to both of them that the Thorne could well decide or be instructed by someone else not to take Jeff forward to that moment, or anywhere, and they both knew there would be precious little in fact nothing either of them could do about that.

And the two also were glad -- delighted -- when Landry contacted them at the end of July 2001, and asked if they could meet with him at NJIT on July 30.

Jeff and Laura walked into the NJIT cafeteria, where Landry had told them to meet him, but all they saw was Karina talking with Landry at a table near the long picture window.

Karina saw them, cried out in joy, and ran to her parents. She put most of her arms around Jeff, and rest around Laura, whom she had last seen much more recently. The three hugged and kissed for a long time. There were tears in everyone's eyes except Landry's.

The four were finally seated, with teas for everyone, when Landry pointed to the cafeteria entrance. Heidi Cartling had arrived, with a tall and muscular young man.

"I believe most of you know each other," Landry said.

"This is B. W. Dunn," Heidi touched her companion's shoulder. "My boyfriend."

"'B. W.'?" Jeff asked.

"Brian," Brian replied.

"And more pertinent to the purpose of our meeting, a recent graduate of the John Jay College of Criminal Justice, and easily the best of us here with a weapon," Landry said.

"Good to meet you, glad to have you aboard," Jeff said and extended his hand to Brian, who shook it.

Laura and Karina smiled at Brian. Karina risked a quick smile at Heidi, and put what she was thinking out of her mind.

"So," Landry said. "There are six of us. It's too dangerous to bring anyone else into this operation."

"Dangerous?" Brian asked.

"The fewer people who know about time travel, the better," Jeff said. "But six still seems too few of us and too many of them."

"That's just two of us for each airport," Karina said, "and one of our teams will have to do double duty at Logan Airport in Boston, where there were two groups of hijackers."

"Shooting or tackling them isn't the only way of stopping them," Heidi responded. "Even one of us can disrupt a team of terrorists at an airport."

Karina shook her head no, and told everyone what had happened with her and Atta in Miami, in case anyone didn't know.

"That's why there will be two of us at each airport," Landry said. "And in Boston, if we can derail Atta early enough, that should give our team enough time to stop al-Shehhi and his hijackers at the other terminal."

"I still don't like it," Laura said.

"Six -- the six of us - are all we have right now," Landry said. "And with the Thornes about as unreliable as ever I've seen them, I don't know when we can expect to recruit more people to join us."

Jeff nodded in unenthusiastic, grudging agreement. "Any suggestions of who should go to which airport, and why?" he asked.

"No," Laura said, "but so far, according to my memory, all of our teams failed."

Landry looked at her. "We all have the same memory of history. That's what we're here to change."

***

The conversation continued for more than an hour.

"Tell me why we can't start by just alerting the authorities to all four hijackings," Laura said at some point, just to get this into the discussion, even though she already knew the answer.

"Because even if that got some of the hijackers arrested, it would likely not be all of them," Landry replied, "and they'd strike again, at a time of their choosing, a time we wouldn't know about beforehand -- as we do about September 11 now -- which would lose us the one advantage we have now."

"That's the lesson of John Lennon," Karina added. "Alerting the police can't be relied upon to stop a determined maniac."

"And the terrorists are probably even more determined than a psychotic fan," Heidi added.

Everyone including Laura agreed.

Discussion returned to which of them would go to which airport.

"Destruction of the Pentagon, which for all we know could still happen, could have worse consequences for America than even the Twin Towers coming down," Landry tried to sum up one part of their assessments. "I think we should send Heidi and Brian down to Washington."

Jeff and Laura had been urging that Brian, as the closest they had to a military operative, should go to Boston, where he and Heidi were the most likely to be able to stop the two teams of terrorists. They were also in the best physical condition. Karina agreed with her parents.

Heidi and Brian finally sided with Landry. Under the rules they had adopted before they began this discussion, his vote could break a tie.

"Ok," Landry said. "So Heidi and Brian are going to Washington."

"All right, then," Jeff said. "So which of us go to Boston?"

***

Jeff and Karina parked their rented car in the Logan Airport lot at 5:30am on September 11. Landry thought Karina was a logical choice to be at Logan, since she had seen Muhamed Atta in the flesh, and would have a slightly better chance than Jeff, Laura, or Landry of recognizing him from a distance, should that prove useful. Everyone had agreed. Landry had suggested that he accompany Karina, but Jeff had insisted that he be their second person in Boston, more to keep on eye out for the safety of his daughter, but hey, he felt he was entitled to that, and no one contested the point.

The two walked slowly and carefully to the American Airlines terminal. They were here at least an hour ahead of Atta and the other hijackers, who according to historical records didn't arrive at the airport until 6:45am.

Marwan al-Shehhi and his band of terrorists would be arriving a few minutes earlier at Logan's United Airlines terminal for their hijacking, but everyone had agreed that Jeff and Karina should try to stop Atta first. If they succeeded only partially, they wanted to make sure that Atta was one who was taken out of commission.

The plan for Jeff and Karina was for Karina to grab a cop or any security official as soon as she and Jeff spotted Atta, and say she saw Atta brandishing a knife or some kind of blade. As soon as that was in motion, Jeff would excuse himself and dash as quickly as he could to the United Airlines terminal, to do the same for al-Shehhi.

Jeff and Karina walked into the American Airlines terminal. There was no sign of Atta or any of the other AA Flight 11 hijackers yet. Jeff's phone rang.

It was Heidi.

***

There are bits of debris on every roadway in America, shards of glass, metal, tacks, nails, detritus of construction, on every street and highway in the world. In most cases, no one put them there. They're just there, on the pavement and under the tires, and most of the time they do no harm.

Heidi and B. W.'s taxi ran over a jagged edge of something at 6:10 in the morning of September 11, as the two were on their way to Dulles Airport to stop the hijacking of American Airlines Flight 77, which history had recorded as crashing into the Pentagon. This jagged edge did do damage. A tire blew, their car screeched and skidded into the car in front of them and made an awful, sickening, crunching sound.

Neither Heidi nor B. W. was hurt. They got out of the cab and looked around them. There was a line of cars in various mangled states ahead of them, and the same quickly coalesced behind them.

B. W. pointed to a partly overturned truck about 10 cars ahead of them. "That must've spilled whatever we just ran over on the road."

Heidi nodded and called Landry at Newark Airport. Circuits were busy. She called Jeff at Logan.

***

Heidi told Jeff what had happened. "Should I try Landry again?" she concluded.

"Call Dulles security, first, and tell them about the hijackers. Then call the Pentagon. Then call Landry," Jeff replied.

Both knew that Jeff's answer was telling Heidi to act not on Landry's but Jeff's instructions, and both knew Landry would not be happy about that.

But Heidi didn't contest what Jeff had told her to do. "I don't suppose there's any chance that these hijackers got stuck in this same traffic mess," she said.

"I'd say zero chance," Jeff replied. "If they had, we'd know about it in our historical record."

"True," Heidi said and cursed softly. "Ok, both of you take care, and luck to you in Boston," she said, with a tremor in her voice, and ended the call.

Jeff turned to Karina, who had been following his part of the conversation. He quickly filled her in on the rest.

Karina cursed, too. "Nothing ever works as expected in this business, does it? Heidi and B. J. were supposed to be our most reliable team, that's why Landry wanted them in Washington."

"Nothing is reliable in this business," Jeff said and shook his head. Then he looked at the clock on the wall. "Atta should be here any minute now."

***

Landry and Laura approached the United Airlines Terminal in Newark International Airport. Landry's phone rang.

"Yes," he said, then listened intently, deeply frowning. "No," he eventually said, "I wouldn't have done that. Right -- better to leave a specific event as close as possible to what it was in history when an attempt to change it fails. That way we know what to look for when we try change that history again.... Yeah, stay put -- sounds like you're not going anywhere anyway -- and I'll get back you."

Landry ended the call, looked at Laura -- whose eyes had been fixed on his face throughout the conversation -- and thought quickly about how much to tell her.

***

Jeff and Karina looked at every person who walked into the American Airlines terminal in Logan Airport, looked at every person twice, three times, just to make sure they weren't looking at Atta in a wig, a dress, or some other kind of disguise. Jeff hoped they didn't look too conspicuous with this looking, but, again the hijackings hadn't yet happened, so the world had yet a few more hours of what would come to be regarded in retrospect as lax security, of not repeatedly urging the public to say something when they saw something suspicious.

Jeff had had a bad feeling about airports ever since he had been knocked unconscious by a luggage rack as he rushed to save JFK in 1963. That seemed like more than a long lifetime ago, but it was always in Jeff's mind, and one of the reasons he had insisted on accompanying Karina to Logan. He was watching out now for her as much as he was for Atta and the hijackers. There was something about travel through the sky that was for some reason dangerous to those who traveled through time, as if the two just didn't mix well together.

Karina suddenly grabbed Jeff's arm and pointed. Three men had entered the terminal. "Waleed al-Shehri, Wail al-Shehri, and Satam al-Suqami," Karina said to Jeff, who nodded, and looked at the clock on the wall. It was 6:48am. According to the historical records, Atta and Abdulaziz al-Omari had flown in from Portland and landed at Logan three minutes ago. "Should we wait for Atta?" Karina asked.

They'd discussed this scenario. Their best target was Atta, since, if they took him out of the equation, the hijacking was least likely to continue. And Marwan al-Shehhi, ringleader of the United Airlines hijacking here at Logan, was supposed to be calling Atta's cell phone from a payphone at 6:52am, presumably to make sure the two hijackings were still set to proceed. If Atta was taken out of the picture in this terminal -- if ah-Shehhi's call got no response – that presumably would give al-Shehhi serious second thoughts about proceeding, too.

On the other hand—- "Let's stop them," Jeff said. "If we make enough commotion and get enough police over here, that should stop Atta, too."

Jeff and Karina ran across the terminal to the three hijackers, who were now about hallway between the entrance and the ticket counters. They narrowly avoided running into a security man of some sort, not a cop. "They're going to hijack a plane," Jeff shouted over his shoulder to the security guy, "they're armed with box cutters."

"What?" the security man wasn't sure he had heard exactly what Jeff had shouted, but had heard enough to join Jeff and Karina. The three reached the two ah-Shehris and al-Suqami, who all froze. The security man, whose named tag said Richard McCollough, turned to Jeff and Karina and held out his arms. "Let me take care of this," he commanded.

"They're armed with some kind of cutting instruments," Jeff repeated.

"He's crazy," Wail said quickly but calmly. "We have nothing, believe me." He put down his bag and opened it.

Jeff realized that he had no idea, history had no reliable

record, of which of these hijackers had brought in what kind of knives aboard this plane. He prayed to whatever force there was in this Universe that Atta and al-Omari hadn't brought all the weapons abroad—-

Karina touched Jeff's arm and gestured to the other side of the terminal. Atta and al-Omari had just entered.

She took a quick look at Jeff, McCollough, and the three hijackers, and bolted towards Atta.

"No--" Jeff shouted.

***

Karina ran full throttle towards Atta and al-Omari. The clock on the wall said 6:51am. She had less than a minute to get to Atta, and at least disconcert him enough not to give al-Shehi the go-ahead on the phone.

But the clock struck 6:52am and she was still almost halfway across the terminal from Atta. She wouldn't have minded a new reality suddenly snapping into existence, in which she was close enough to Atta to knock that damned cellphone out of his hand. But this reality with her still nowhere near enough to interact with Atta stayed stubbornly in place. She reflected on how more difficult this was than stopping John Lennon's murder, and they had almost failed to accomplish even that. They needed more people on their side. There should have been a separate team to stop al-Shehi at the United Airlines terminal directly. Landry had been dead wrong to limit the number of people attempting to stop four hijackings. Why had he done that? She wondered how Landry and her mother were faring in Newark. Had Landry deliberately tried to sabotage their mission? If so, why? They could always try this again. She shuddered at the thought.

And now she saw Atta take something out of his pocket -- godammit, a cellphone, which he put to his ear. If only she hadn't left that stunner from the future in that cabin on Cape Cod Bay in 1991, she'd fire it at Atta's head right now. She'd been too worried about contaminating the past with the future, and now she had nothing but her voice to stop this mass murderer.

Atta had no idea Karina was running towards him. He told

al-Shehi at the United Airlines terminal that everything was on schedule and fine for the hijackings.

Karina bellowed at Atta. But it was too late. He finished his call and put his phone back in his pocket. He looked up at Karina, and seemed to recognize her, but was not sure from where—-

al-Omari grabbed Karina from behind. She hadn't been looking at him at all, focusing completely on Atta. There was a men's room behind them. al-Omari put his arm around Karina's mouth, and forced her inside the men's room. Atta followed.

***

Jeff looked at Karina running towards Atta for a split second, then ran after her as fast as he could.

McCollough said something, but Jeff couldn't hear it. He swerved around a woman holding a baby, slowed a bit to do that, and resumed full speed. Karina was about half-way between him and Atta.

Jeff's phone rang in his pocket. He ignored it. He could live without stopping September 11. He had lived that way all his life. But he couldn't live with his daughter dying.

He reached the men's room just as al-Omari pulled Karina inside and Atta followed. The door closed. Jeff shoved it open a moment later.

***

"What's going on," Laura demanded of Landry.

He decided to tell her the gist of what had happened in Washington. "I have a bad feeling this is going to be bad news for all us, at all the airports today," he concluded.

"What are saying?" Laura demanded again. "We still have a good shot of stopping the hijacking here in Newark."

"Maybe, maybe not," Landry replied. "This is the least important of the hijackings. I already talked one of the hijackers out of joining the suicide mission. The plane will crash in the countryside of Pennsylvania, as you know. That will have no impact on history."

"But we can save the lives -- what's the harm in trying?" This was a combination of demanding and pleading.

"True, but if we don't, it reveals our hand," Landry said. "Maybe the best thing now is to pack all of this up and try again in a different way. Maybe with some kind of intervention further back in time."

"But you agreed that closest to the events was the best time to intervene," Laura responded.

"I did, but the facts may have proven otherwise," Landry said. "What was it that John Maynard Keynes was supposed to have said? 'When the facts change, I change my mind. What do you do, sir?'"

"Just one of four facts changed," Laura insisted. "We still can stop the other three hijackings – that will save thousands of people! Let me call Jeff and see what he thinks." She took out her phone.

"That will only distract him from whatever he's doing now in Logan," Landry replied.

Laura called Jeff anyway.

***

Heidi finished her call to Landry and looked at the traffic mess ahead. "We've got to get out here," she said to Brian. "We can't just sit here and wait for the hijacked plane to crash into the Pentagon."

Brian looked ahead and behind and began to shake his head no—-

But possible salvation or at least help showed up in the form of a trooper on a motorcycle, riding deftly between the stationary cars.

Brian flagged him down. "We have information about a hijacking at Dulles Airport," he said calmly and clearly. "Can you phone that in?"

The Maryland state trooper looked at Brian. "And who exactly are you? Do you have ID?"

"Yes," Brian replied, and gave the trooper his driver's license.

The trooper looked at the license, back at Brian, and nodded. "Ok, Mr. Brian Waters Dunn, tell me again about Dulles Airport."

Brian told him again, and added, "I expect to soon be with the

NYPD in New York."

The trooper thought for a few moments, sighed, and nodded again. "Ok, I'll try calling that in. But no guarantee my call will get through — police circuits are overloaded with everyone buzzing about this damn traffic jam."

***

al-Omari had a knife to Karina's throat, and Atta was saying something to him in Arabic when Jeff entered the men's room.

"If you kill her, the airport will be on lockdown and you won't be able to proceed with the hijacking," Jeff said to Atta, getting right to the point.

"What if we kill both of you," Atta replied, producing his own knife, and waving it in Jeff's direction.

Jeff took a step back and held us hands. "Even worse for what you're planning to do," Jeff said. "It will be just a matter of minutes until some guy comes in here to take a piss and finds two dead bodies in this bathroom. He'll tell the authorities, and every cop in the airport will be on high alert, looking for the killer. No way you or anyone will be able to board a plane." He thought he had some kind of chance of overpowering Atta if he rushed him right now, and saving all those lives. Jeff shook his head imperceptibly. All of those innocent human beings, thousands of lives, yes. But Karina's would surely be forfeit with al-Omari's knife to her neck, however Jeff made out if charged Atta.

"You'll tell the authorities anyway, if I let you live," Atta said, and moved a menacing step closer to Jeff.

"Yes, you're right that I'll do that," Jeff said. "But what evidence do I have? I'd be just another crackpot on the phone. In contrast to dead bodies in this bathroom, which will be all the evidence the authorities need to freeze everything in place at this airport."

Atta thought for a feverish second, then spoke again in Arabic to al-Omari, who shoved Karina into a stall.

Atta motioned to Jeff to get in the stall next to her. He and al-Omari took rope out of their bags, and did the best they could to tie the doors shut.

"When they find you in here like this, the police will think it's a just a joke, a prank, right?" Atta said. "Not enough to shut down the airport."

Jeff said nothing.

"You give good advice," Atta said. "Allah thanks you!" And he and al-Omara quickly exited the men's room.

It took Jeff and Karina less than a minute to stand on the closed toilet, and pull themselves up and over the stall.

They rushed outside and looked around for Atta and al-Omara. There was no sign of them anywhere.

"I'm sorry," Karina said, tears in her eyes, "I just wanted to stop him from giving al-Shehi the go-ahead for the United Airlines flight."

Jeff kissed the side of her head. "If McCollough is able to stop the ah-Shehris and al-Suqami, it's less likely that Atta and al-Omari will be able to pull off the hijacking on their own, even if they get in the plane," Jeff told her.

But when they looked across the airport terminal for McCollough and the three terrorists, there were nowhere in sight, either.

***

"Call me, as soon as you can," Laura said in voicemail to Jeff.

"These things are very deeply rooted in history," Landry was still talking about the inadvisability of continuing their mission. "You know that. Look what happened when Jeff tried to save JFK."

"I know," Laura said. "But we diminished the Challenger disaster."

"Slightly."

"And saved John Lennon," Laura said.

"Barely."

"But we're here," Laura said, "and we have to try." She thought of all those last calls to loved ones the passengers on this doomed United Airlines #93 out of Newark would be making. "We have to try."

Landry finally nodded, seeing the futility of debating this any further with Laura. "All right, we'll try it your way," he said, tiredly. "You stay here. I'll look in the bathrooms and around the corners of the terminal, to make sure the terrorists didn't somehow get past us and aren't already here."

***

Jeff noticed that Laura had called him and returned her call. She filled him on Landry's despairing view of their chances.

"Where is he now?" Jeff asked.

"Checking around the terminal to make sure Jarrah and his terrorists aren't already here."

"Don't be surprised if you never see him again, or not for a long time, and not in Newark International Airport," Jeff said.

"What are you saying?" Laura asked. "Why would he do that?"

"Because he's George G. Landry," Jeff replied. "That's what he does. He follows his own lights and the hell with everyone else."

Laura crooked her neck and looked around the terminal, but couldn't spot Landry. "He's only been gone a few minutes," she told Jeff, "you could still be wrong. You haven't told me what's happening at Logan." She looked at her watch. "Oh my God, Atta and his people should be there already -- you haven't seen them yet?"

Jeff gave Laura an abbreviated account of what had happened, but including everything about Karina.

Laura gasped and started to cry.

"It's ok," Jeff said. "Our baby's ok. I won't let her out of my sight now, I promise. And there's still a chance we can do something here to stop Atta."

But Laura and Jeff both knew that whatever Jeff now did, stopping Atta wasn't going to happen.

***

Landry had in fact slipped out of the United Airlines Terminal and headed to the British Airlines terminal, where he was delighted to find there was a first class seat on a flight to London leaving in an hour. That should be enough time for him to get out of there before all hell broke loose with the hijackings.

There was a Thorne in England. He thought he knew how to set it to arrive in the distant past, when the space-time continuum hadn't been stretched so thin. He liked ancient Egypt.

He flew out over the Atlantic, in the last minutes of peace before September 11. When he got to London, he'd take a Thorne back to 150 AD, and find a way to travel from there by boat to Alexandria. That shouldn't be too hard. The Roman Empire was still in good shape. And the Library of Alexandria was the height of civilization. He'd take up some identity back then. Events were too densely packed, came at you too fast in the hectic present, to easily change them, or change them at all. He needed the time and space, and the remove from current and recent events, to re-think all that had happened -- and not happened -- here. Perhaps John Lennon's death was necessary, after all, to stop September 11. And there were other options, other possibilities for changes more far reaching than what had just been attempted here in the 21st and 20th centuries.

###

ABOUT THE AUTHOR

Paul Levinson

Paul Levinson, PhD, is Professor at Fordham University. His science fiction novels include The Silk Code (winner of the Locus Award for Best First Science Fiction Novel of 1999), The Consciousness Plague, The Pixel Eye, Borrowed Tides, The Plot to Save Socrates, Unburning Alexandria, and Chronica. His novelette "The Chronology Protection Case" was made into a short film and is on Amazon Prime Video. His alternate history short story about The Beatles, "It's Real Life," was made into a radio play, was a finalist for the Sidewise Award for Alternate History, and was expanded into a novel in 2024. His novelette, "Robinson Calculator, was published in the Robots Through the Ages anthology in July 2023. He was President of the Science Fiction Writers of America (SFWA) 1998-2001. His nonfiction books, including The Soft Edge, Digital McLuhan, Cellphone, Realspace, and New New Media, have been translated into 15 languages. He has appeared on CBS, CNN, MSNBC, the History Channel, and NPR. His 1972 album, Twice Upon A Rhyme, was re-issued in Japan and Korea in 2008, and in the U. K. in 2010. His first new album since 1972, Welcome Up: Songs of Space and Time, was released by Old Bear Records and Light in the Attic Records in 2020.

BOOKS BY THIS AUTHOR

It's Real Life: An Alternate History Of The Beatles

It's 1996, and in this alternate history novel about the Beatles, WFUV disc jockey Pete Fornatale walks in the tunnels under Fordham University, then travels downtown to Grand Central Terminal and finds the world of music that he inhabits is very different. As he struggles to understand how to get in and out of alternate realities, and make sure John Lennon is not killed in any of them, Fornatale will actually dine with John Lennon and David Bowie, consult with Leonard Cohen, attend a Beatles concert with Diana Ross in Central Park in 1996, and work with a variety of real life characters you may or may not have heard of. The short story this novel is based upon won the Mary Shelley Award for Outstanding Fiction in 2023, and was a Finalist for the Sidewise Award (short form) for Alternate History 2022.

The Plot To Save Socrates

Paul Levinson's astonishing science fiction novel is a surprise and a delight: In the year 2042, Sierra, a young graduate student in Classics, is shown a new dialog of Socrates, recently discovered, in which a time traveler tries to argue that Socrates might escape death by travel to the future! Thomas, the elderly scholar who has shown her the document, disappears, and Sierra immediately begins to track down the provenance of the manuscript with the help of her classical scholar boyfriend, Max.

The trail leads her to time machines in gentlemen's clubs in London and in New York, and into the past--and to a time traveler from the future, posing as Heron of Alexandria in 150 AD. Complications, mysteries, travels, and time loops proliferate as Sierra tries to discern who is planning to save the greatest philosopher in human history. Fascinating historical characters from Alcibiades to William Henry Appleton, the great nineteenth-century American publisher, to Hypatia and Socrates himself appear. With surprises in every chapter, Paul Levinson has outdone himself in The Plot to Save Socrates.

Unburning Alexandria

Mid-twenty-first century time traveler Sierra Waters, fresh from her mission to save Socrates from the hemlock, is determined to alter history yet again, by saving the ancient Library of Alexandria - where as many as 750,000 one-of-a-kind texts were lost, an event described by many as "one of the greatest intellectual catastrophes in history."

Along the way she will encounter old friends such as William Henry Appleton the great 19th century American publisher and enemies like the enigmatic time travelling inventor Heron of Alexandria. And her quest will involve such other real historic personages as Hypatia, Cleopatra's sister Arsinoe, Ptolemy the astronomer, and St. Augustine - again placing her friends, her loved-ones, and herself in deadly jeopardy.

In this sequel to THE PLOT TO SAVE SOCRATES, award winning author Paul Levinson offers another time-traveling adventure spanning millennia, full of surprising twists and turns, all the while attempting the seemingly impossible: UNBURNING ALEXANDRIA.

Chronica

Sierra and Max arrive in 2062, and find the world has somewhat changed. Joe Biden was President from 2009-2017, and train travel is much more prominent. Was this due to the scrolls that she rescued from the Library of Alexandria? Heron's Chronica, which describes how to build a time travel device and was one of the texts Sierra saved from burning, has not yet been published, and Sierra soon realizes that Heron is doing everything in his lethal power to prevent that from happening. Her attempt to safeguard the Chronica, which she left in William Henry Appleton's keeping, takes her to the end of the 1890s, where she dines, plots, and otherwise interacts with John Jacob Astor IV, Nikola Tesla, Thomas Edison, J. P. Morgan, film pioneers William Dickson and Edwin Porter, and other denizens of The Gilded Age.

The Chronology Protection Case

When NYPD forensic detective Phil D'Amato takes a call from a lady physicist about her missing husband, he has no idea that her life, his life, and every other scientist working on a top-secret time travel project will soon be in dire jeopardy. As the number of dead begins to mount, D'Amato starts to realize that the suspect is not any one person or group but something much more sinister and dangerous. "The Chronology Protection Case" was a finalist for the Nebula Award for Best Science Fiction Novelette of 1995. The story was adapted into a low-budget movie by Jay Kensinger (now on Amazon Prime Video), and an Edgar-nominated radio play by Mark Shanahan.

The Copyright Notice Case

Can a code embedded in our DNA millennia ago kill people who violate the warning in the code? NYPD forensic detective Dr. Phil D'Amato investigates. His main source of information: a researcher with two X chromosomes and green-violet eyes.

The Silk Code

Phil D'Amato, an NYC forensic detective (also featured in several of Levinson's popular short stories and two subsequent novels), is caught in an ongoing struggle that dates all the way back to the dawn of humanity on Earth--and one of his best friends is a recent casualty. Unless Phil can unravel the genetic puzzle of the Silk Code, he'll soon be just as dead.

Winner Locus Award for Best First Science Fiction novel of 1999.

The Consciousness Plague

Dr. Phil D' Amato returns from The Silk Code, winner of the Locus Award for Best First Science Fiction Novel of 1999, with another blend of biological science fiction and hard-boiled police-procedural mystery.

Memory itself is the suspect in The Consciousness Plague - more particularly, loss of memory, in slivers of time deducted from a growing number of individuals, which plays havoc with everything from the investigation of serial stranglings to candlelight dinners. D'Amato, NYPD forensic detective, investigates a spate of unusual cases and finds evidence of a bacteria-like organism that has lived in our brains since our origin as a species and may be responsible for our very consciousness.

A new antibiotic crosses the blood-brain barrier and inadvertently kills this essential bug. Phil himself falls victim to this memory hole, and must struggle to get the proper authorities to pay attention before everyone loses so much memory that they forget that they forgot in the first place.

Winner of the Mary Shelley Award for Outstanding Fiction,

2003.

The Pixel Eye

Squirrels are spying on us in the park. Mice may have organic bombs set to go off in their brains. Holograms are taking the place of real people. Phil D'Amato investigates a case that pits civil liberties versus national security as he seeks to ward off a major terrorist attack on near-future New York City.

Ian's Ions And Eons

Ian's Ions and Eons is the name of a time-travel agency in the Riverdale neighborhood of the Bronx. This anthology contains the three "Ian" novelettes published thus far: "Ian's Ions and Eons" (2011) "Ian, Isaac, and John" (2011) and "Ian, George, and George" (2013). The time travel stories involve Presidential elections, rock music, television and movies. Real historical personages who appear include Al Gore, George W. Bush, William Rehnquist, David Bowie, John Lennon, Dick Cavett, and Orson Welles.

Borrowed Tides

August 2016 brought news - real news, in our reality - that an Earth-like planet was discovered circling Proxima Centauri, the third star in the Alpha Centauri system, just over four light years from Earth. This is exactly what happens in Borrowed Tides, first published in hardcover in 2001, re-issued in Kindle this past April. It tells the story of the first starship to the Alpha Centauri system in 2029, employing a new technology which can move it through deep space at almost half the speed of light. But it requires an enormous amount of fuel, and can only carry enough for a one-way trip. A philosopher of science and his childhood friend, an anthropologist with a specialty in Native

American culture, have a daringly bizarre plan, and talk the government into putting them in charge of the Light Through starship voyage.

In The Dybbuk's Pocket

Beware whom you take presents from ....

Slipping Time

Tripping in the rain can be very helpful.

The Other Car

James Oleson is beginning to see everything in perfect duplicate - two identical models of cars which are the same down to scuff marks and license plate, two old philosophy books with the same torn pages and inscription in old ink, and twin mail men. Is he losing his mind, or experiencing the birth of a new alternate reality via binary fission?

Peter Brown Called

Writing science fiction and songs have been two of my lifelong passions. This anthology combines them, with a selection of my science fiction and fantasy stories that has music as a theme, and my lyrics that deal with far-off suns, robots, and time travel.

Marilyn And Monet

It all started in the hot summer of 1960, when Marilyn Monroe walked off the set of The Misfits and began to hear a haunting song in her head, "Goodbye Norma Jean" ...

Robinson Calculator

The Calculators -- a secretive group of androids -- have been living off the radar for centuries or longer. Why are they now burying their dead in plain view?

Urban Corridors

an anthology of urban fantasy and science fiction stories, ranging from alternate realities to time travel to ghosts and androids and other strange things in the city

The Last Train To Margaretville

A painter desperate for money finds a way to collect what's owed him from his deadbeat clients -- via teleportation, the tunnels under Fordham University, and the train to Margaretville.

Foreseeable

Sven accidentally picks up someone else's similar glasses in a restaurant's men's room, and discovers they can give him glimpses of the future.